A DAY LIKE THIS

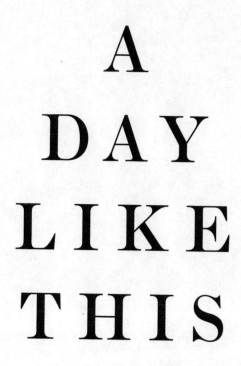

A DAY LIKE THIS

a novel

KELLEY McNEIL

LAKE UNION
PUBLISHING

Text copyright © 2021 by Kelley McNeil
All rights reserved.

No part of this book may be reproduced, or stored in a retrieval system, or transmitted in any form or by any means, electronic, mechanical, photocopying, recording, or otherwise, without express written permission of the publisher.

Published by Lake Union Publishing, Seattle

www.apub.com

Amazon, the Amazon logo, and Lake Union Publishing are trademarks of Amazon.com, Inc., or its affiliates.

ISBN-13: 9781542030441
ISBN-10: 1542030447

Cover design by Shasti O'Leary Soudant

Printed in the United States of America

For Morgan and Ella

He who loves an old house
Never loves in vain,
How can an old house,
Used to sun and rain,
To lilac and to larkspur,
And an elm above,
Ever fail to answer
The heart that gives it love?

—*Isabel Fiske Conant*

As the day is coming to a close and I'm falling asleep, sometimes I'll hear the sound of gravel beneath my feet. It comes to me like a lullaby, repetitive with each footstep, remarkable in its clarity as I long for the place I once called home.

CHAPTER ONE

I reached down to snip a couple of fat lilac blooms from the lower branches, just as a chill hit my shoulders. The sun had been high and bright in the earlier, midafternoon sky, but puffy white dots had given way to dense gray clouds that reminded me of towering medieval castles floating along an invisible river. If I looked long enough, I could almost see dark turrets in them and imagine an army gathering inside the fortress, prepared to attack. Clouds were bigger in this sky than in other places, here under the giant blue dome above my hayfield home. The breeze picked up, blowing strands from my ponytail loose so they lashed in tiny pinpricks at the corners of my eyes.

I marveled at the sight of the purple stems in my hand. The first thing I'd done after planting the lilacs seven years ago was apologize to them. It was only fair, because if anything was certain, it was that the spindly little stems were not in good hands and would never grow. If there were an opposite of a green thumb, it was mine, and they didn't stand a chance. It gave us a good laugh, and Graham had performed a comical eulogy for the poor things. I'd sprinkled water over the seedlings and wished them well.

Lilacs were kind of a thing for me. When I was a child, there had been tall lilac bushes near my house, growing wild and mostly unkempt throughout an otherwise gray city neighborhood. They hovered at the edges of cracked sidewalks, overgrown weedy things ignored by just about everyone until they created an aggravating blind spot at the end of a driveway or scratched at a window, at which point they were trimmed back, or cut down altogether, leaving an unsightly trunk of tough brown sticks poking out of the ground—too difficult to remove without considerable effort. But in the springtime, their fragrance perfumed the air with sunshine, while giant blossoms of pale purple and white dotted the bushes in the dozens, promising the arrival of long summer days.

The old neighborhood grouch at the end of the street once caught me with a pair of scissors, reaching up on tiptoes to snip off a few stolen blooms. When she yelled at me to get out of her yard, I wondered why she cared. After all, there was a grimy plastic grocery bag stuck in the branches and shards of broken bottle glass on the ground beneath it. But people were funny about their yards. I'd clutched the flowers tighter and taken off running. Once home, I hoisted myself up onto the counter to retrieve a glass, filled it with water, closed my eyes to breathe in the scent, and placed the treasured flowers in a makeshift vase as a gift for my mother. The flowers had forever reminded me of clean sheets and fresh air and hope.

When Graham and I bought this place, we nicknamed it the Yellow House after the color of the wooden siding, and then spent a considerable amount of time standing on all sides of it, heads cocked to one side, imagining where on earth to start. There was no landscaping to speak of, and when a house sits on ten acres in the middle of an endless field, you really tend to notice such a thing. A white porch spanned the entire front of the house, and from its perch atop a hill, one could enjoy the kind of view that photographers dream of. Like a number of thirty-somethings at the time, we'd left city life in Manhattan to try our hand at life in the country in Upstate New York. Not a hobby farm, exactly, but perhaps inspired by the romantic notion of one. Trouble was, we didn't know a single thing about old houses or big land. But our timing was good, it seemed—the house had been vacant for a number of years, and the grown children of the previous owners had been eager to get it off their hands. Plus, it was 2007 and they were doling out mortgages like free candy. So, after handing over the majority of our savings and signing the closing papers, we were the proud owners of a house that looked like it had been drawn from childhood dreams with a box of crayons—a little bit crooked, but perfectly so. The day we signed the closing papers, the first things we'd purchased were items we'd spotted at a roadside stand that sold vegetables, used furniture, and odds and ends. We bought two wooden rocking chairs for the porch, which we painted white, and two three-dollar Styrofoam cups of tiny seedlings marked Lilac.

"It's a sign," I'd said to Graham, after spotting the little plants. "My favorite flower!" He'd merely raised a skeptical eyebrow.

"What? You never know," I remember saying with an optimistic shrug. I imagined the scent of lilacs, wafting dreamily over the edges of the porch, while Graham and I passed evenings in the rocking chairs, looking out over the silos at the farm below. "How long does it take for them to bloom?" I inquired.

The old man who managed the stand wiped a tanned, grease-stained hand across his chin. "Eh, should be 'bout three, four years maybe." *Four years?* I grimaced, but then Graham chuckled as he handed me the cup, which I held like a new baby. He surprised me with a kiss, smiled, then grabbed a second cup of baby lilacs before echoing my previous comment: "Hey, you never know."

Optimism is infectious, after all.

Lilacs aren't hard to grow. In fact, most people would put them in the weed category. They're that easy. But my previous experiences with plants of any kind—houseplants, potted plants, vegetables—had all ended in grim death. Once when I was little, my parents had taken us on a rare weekend outing to a farm that grew acres of corn, tomatoes, and a dozen other fruits and vegetables. The farmer wore full denim overalls and let kids help with shucking corn, the scent of corn silk and tomato vines on our fingers in a place that I decided was heaven on earth. So, I felt especially bitter about the absence of the green-thumb gene in my DNA. When it came to plants, Graham told me I either loved them to death or abandoned them. Neither was good. I couldn't even manage to grow those cheap little cactus flowers they sell at the checkout counter in discount stores. As I'd stood that first day beside my porch, holding the kitchen spoon I'd used to dig the two miniature holes, looking down at the sorry little stems, I had to genuinely feel bad. They sat no taller than two inches amid a stretch of clay soil, already blowing sideways in the unforgiving hilltop wind. I figured they'd never in a million years survive.

But somehow, they did.

Throughout that first summer, I watched with a suspicious eye as they grew a little stronger, and then stood in jaw-dropped bewilderment when I realized they'd somehow lived through a tough Catskills winter. Two years later, I was rewarded with my first, very own lilac—a small little miraculous flower. And later, in the spring after Hannah was born, I'd rocked her on the front porch for hours next to a dozen purple and white blooms. Now my home was filled with vases of miraculous springtime blossoms and the fragrance wafting in on the breeze through raised windows.

When I think back on the day that Hannah left my world, recalling the details in order, one by one, it's always the lilacs I see first.

~

After I had selected a final stem, my phone chimed in my back pocket, and my shoulders dropped as I read the text message that popped up from Graham:

Flight delayed. Weather. Call you soon. xo.

As if illustrating the point in divine fashion, a raindrop plopped onto the screen, fat and splotchy. I swiped it away with my thumb just as another hit the back of my neck, surprisingly cold. I collected the blooms in my hand, along with the kitchen shears.

The front steps of the porch needed repainting. I'd noticed this every time I'd climbed them since spring had arrived, seeing the ragged chips at the edges, evidence of this year's harsh winter's snow and ice. We used abrasive kitty litter to prevent slipping, wincing over the paint damage each time. This was one of my jobs in the domestic-chore chart of family life—painting the porch. Graham hated the task, but I found something soothing about it. The long smooth strokes of taupe gray down the length of each wooden slat. The clean precision of the smaller brush as I painted the spindles and banisters a crisp cotton white. In previous years, planters would be filled with purple and yellow pansies, and the cushions would be brought out of the garage and placed on the porch swing.

I went inside and walked straight through the kitchen, opening the double french doors at the back of the house.

"Hannah," I called. "Time to come in. It's about to rain, sweetie!" Swinging under the great canopy of the oak tree, she probably hadn't felt any drops yet. My daughter pumped her bare feet and swung higher with glee, flashing a wide, proud grin. She bravely let go with one hand and attempted a split-second wave, and I clapped my hands. She'd been born with a full head of dark-brown hair the same color as mine, except that hers had grown like Rapunzel's—the nickname she quickly earned from well-intentioned if not somewhat grating distant aunts and uncles, seen on holidays twice a year. Her hair was now nearly down to her waist, and as she swung, it flew through the air behind her like a magical cape of childhood innocence, a scene playing out in my mind in exaggerated slow motion. The swing had come with the house, charming me in an instant with its old-fashioned design—two thick ropes and a solid slat of wood, hanging from sturdy branches. The initials *H.B.* were carved in the middle of a lopsided heart in the center of the seat, etched by Graham the week Hannah was born. Hannah Beyers.

The clouds were darker behind the house than they had been in the front and were now moving with angry intention, the troops unleashed. "Come on, sweetie," I called again. "Snack time." She nodded and began to slow. A rumble of thunder filled the air, rolling across the field of timothy hay blowing in waves. Hannah startled, tapping her feet across the dirt and hopping off the swing with a quickness that only a good fright can inspire. She ran in clipped little steps that threatened a stumble. "Take your time, sweetie. It's not here yet."

She darted in with wide eyes, huffing a relieved giggle when she dived into my arms. "Where'd the sun go!" she chirped.

"Sure disappeared fast, huh? Ready for a snack?"

She nodded tiredly, panting as she scooted up onto the kitchen chair. She perched on a booster seat, wearing a pink tutu with a white tank top that had a spot of orange juice on it from the morning. A plastic lei dangled around her neck, and a rhinestone tiara accented with hot-pink feathers sat nestled in her hair. I tickled her bare toes where they dangled beneath the table as she dipped an apple slice into peanut butter and twirled it around. I set a plastic *Tangled* cup of milk next to her and sneaked a hand around her to snatch a carrot for a loud, crunchy bite in her ear. This ritual usually elicited a giggle, but she rested her head on her fist and pushed the carrots and apples around on her plate with a lazy finger that made my eyes narrow a bit in concern.

Keeping an eye on her, I went to the sink and ran the water, trimming the lilac stems at an angle beneath the stream. The usually bright kitchen had grown darker with the clouds, and just as I turned away from the window, I thought I saw a shadowy dark figure of a woman standing by the tree from the corner of my eye. I stopped short, the hairs raised on the back of my neck, and swallowed. I glanced over to see Hannah watching the tree, as well. After a moment I looked back, slowly peering through the dripping raindrops on the glass as I held my breath, listening to the sound of my heart pounding in my chest.

She was still there.

Or was she? It was hard to tell.

The rain dripped, making the image dance, and then it was just the tree and swing. No one there. It was just my imagination, surely brought on by the storm, I told myself. I shook my head free of the unsettling image and picked up the purple blooms with quivering hands. The ceramic pitcher that was normally beside the sink was missing, so I tossed the last grains of coffee from a can, filled it with water, and placed them inside, their calming fragrance already filling the room. I looked over at Hannah again, wilting a little in the chair.

"Not hungry? Want something else?" I asked.

She shook her head limply. I set the flowers in the center of the table, and another clap of thunder sounded, just as rain began in earnest, tapping hard now against the windows. "You feeling okay, kiddo?" I set my hand on her forehead and frowned. "Uh-oh, I think you have a fever, sweetie." I placed the back of my hand gently onto her cheek, and she peered up at me. Her blue eyes had taken a hint of downward gray into them, a telltale sign when she was sick. I smoothed her hair back from her face just before my phone rang on the table. I pressed the speaker button. "Hey, honey."

"Hey, bad news," Graham said.

"Oh no. Let me guess . . ." I'd been checking the weather in Atlanta throughout the day.

"The flight was canceled because of storms up north."

My shoulders slumped and I again looked outside. "No, you have to be joking. There's nothing?"

"Afraid not. I'm trying to get on a flight first thing in the morning, but it's chaos here."

"Hi, Daddy," Hannah chimed in with a small voice.

"Hi, pumpkin. How's my girl?"

"Good," she said weakly.

"You guys all right?" he asked.

"I think our girl's got a fever." I took the thermometer from the cabinet and placed it in her mouth. "Under your tongue," I reminded her with a wink.

"What? How's that even possible?" Hearing the stress in his voice, I switched off the speaker and picked up the phone. "She just finally got over that awful cold on Tuesday," he added.

"I know. But you know how it goes. It probably went to her ears again." I cradled the phone against my shoulder. "Sweetie, do your ears hurt?"

"A little. This one." She tugged. I made a sad face and tickled her cheek.

Graham was quiet for a few moments. "Not exactly how we planned this weekend. I'm so sorry, honey."

I sighed, my eyes welling. "No. Not at all."

"Well hey, look. We'll still have tomorrow night, right? I think the weather's supposed to clear up. We'll have dinner on the porch, and I'll take my best girls for ice cream."

I smiled a little. "Sounds perfect." An electronic beep sounded and I read the display. "Her temperature is 101.4." I glanced at the clock. "It's four o'clock on a Friday, and she's probably going to need an antibiotic. Doctor closes at five . . ." I rustled through a basket of medicines, locating the children's ibuprofen, poured the dose, checked it, then handed it to Hannah. "Here you go," I whispered, brushing a finger across her chin.

"Think they'll squeeze her in?" Graham asked.

"On a Friday afternoon? I don't know. Hopefully. If I call right this second and get lucky."

"We don't want to wait until Monday. Maybe he'll call something in without you having to go."

"Not likely."

"All right, I'm gonna let you go. Call me as soon as you leave the doctor, okay?"

"Will do, promise."

"Oh wait, real quick . . . did the roof guy come today? Did you get the estimate?" Graham asked.

I had hoped he wouldn't ask. "He did."

"And?"

"Same as before, unfortunately."

"I thought for sure this one would come in lower," Graham said solemnly.

"I know. Me too."

"Okay. It was worth a shot, I guess. Last-ditch effort."

I heard the airport announcing flight information in the background of the call. "I'm so sorry you're having a miserable travel day. I hope you have an okay night."

He groaned. "Thanks. Me too."

"Can't wait to see you," I said.

"I know. I miss you guys. I'll try to get the first flight out tomorrow, but it might not be until afternoon." He hesitated, then added, "Are you going to be all right there tonight? You could always—"

"I'll be fine." I peered out toward the tree again and locked the glass door.

"You sure?" I could hear the concern in his voice.

"Promise. Everything's fine. We're good." The thunder clapped again and I jumped. It would be a long night.

"Okay. Well, give Hannah a kiss for me. One for you too. And try to get some sleep."

Hannah leaned over toward the phone. "Bye, Daddy."

"Bye, pumpkin."

"I gotta go and see what I can get with the doctor. Love you," I said, ending the call to speed-dial the pediatrician. "Beyers, Hannah: 5-28-2009." I explained the symptoms to the nurse with the efficiency I'd learned over the past five years. No fluff. No opinion. Just the basics. And held my breath while she paused in deliberation . . .

"Can you be here in thirty minutes?" she asked. "Our last patient just canceled."

As I calculated the time, my eyes darted to the clock, then to the rain now pouring in torrents outside. It was at least a thirty-five-minute drive to town on a perfect, sunny day, with no rain and no farm tractors going ten miles an hour . . . and even that was pushing it. I glanced at Hannah, who looked more miserable by the minute.

"Mrs. Beyers?" The voice on the other end was kind, but there was no messing around with appointment nurses at the pediatrician's office.

Phone in hand, I ran to the foyer, stuffing my feet into the first pair of shoes that were handy—a muddy pair of gray clogs I normally reserved for home only. "Uh, yes! Sorry. We can be there." I winced, hoping for the fifteen minutes of forgiveness I'd beg for when I got there. "Thank you!" I hung up and tossed my phone, scooping Hannah onto my hip. I smoothed her hair back from her face and kissed her forehead. "Okay, sweetie. We've gotta go."

"Right now?" she whined.

"Yep, I'm sorry. Right now."

"But . . ." She yawned.

"You can take a nap in the car." I cradled her head into the soft nook of my shoulder as I carried her. She was getting bigger now, and I sometimes wondered, as mothers do, when the last time would be that I could pick her up in my arms. "Come on, let's get a jacket on." I hustled to the front hall and grabbed my windbreaker and Hannah's purple raincoat. It was dotted with a repeating pattern of tiny gray elephants splashing water from their trunks. I set her down and pulled the sleeves over her arms and then did a frantic hunt for my keys while shuffling a grumbling Hannah back toward the garage door. I threw a bag of Goldfish crackers and a juice box into my purse on the way and picked up her rain boots.

"No! I hate these! They feel sticky on my feet without socks!" Hannah kicked as I tried to slide a boot over her small foot.

"I'm sorry, sweetie. But we gotta go! And it's wet outside, so we need boots!" My voice was full of fake bright cheer pulled tight like a wire that might snap. She looked up at me with big round eyes. I took a deep breath and knelt down. "Okay, how about this . . ." I picked up her glittery gold ballet flats and gently handed them to her. "If you wear the boots now, you can put these on when we get there. Deal?" She smiled and nodded. "Okay. Good."

The TV was still switched on in the living room.

The lilacs sat on the table next to the browning apple slices and carrots.

My phone lay where I'd tossed it onto the sofa and forgotten it.

I'm replaying these details again, as I have a thousand times before.

Over and over, I go, in the same way a detective might pore over evidence files, hoping to notice something new. What exactly was playing on the TV? *Imagination Movers* on the kids' channel. How many lilac stems were on the table? Five, I think. Was it apples *and* carrots? Or just apples? Definitely both. We always did both when we did peanut butter. What color toenail polish was Hannah wearing? Chipped cotton-candy pink.

Do you want more details? Because I can go on.

What song was playing while the Imagination Movers danced around in their blue and red jumpsuits as we walked out the door? "Nina's Song." Were there really hot-pink feathers dotting Hannah's tiara, or was it the plain one? Feathers. Definitely. A tiny one fell off and floated to the floor just as I took it off her head.

Her hair smelled of baby powder and grass.

Is that enough?

The breakfast dishes were still in the sink.

How many details does a person have to recall in order to prove they were real?

Every time the scene ends the same: with me wishing I'd let her put her gold shoes on right then, the perfumed scent of lilacs wafting in the air, and a clap of thunder just as I slammed the garage door closed.

CHAPTER TWO

The rain came down in sheets along the winding stretch into town, twisting left and right around dairy farms and cornfields, up one hill and down another. I knew the road by muscle memory, my hands steering the wheel and my foot aware of when to let up on the gas and when to add pressure, anticipating on their own what would come next as if performing a practiced routine. Country roads were like that, and I found comfort in the predictability of it. I preferred them over the lottery of speeding drivers and circumstances one found on highways and business routes. Still, I could feel the unnerving slickness of the rain-soaked roads testing the grip of the tires.

As I drove, Hannah stared out the window in the back seat with the languid, glass-eyed look of a simmering fever. The windshield wipers tapped and screeched, complaining and doing a crappy job of removing the rain. They needed replacing, and I reminded myself of this for the umpteenth time. Our route headed west while the storm continued its march east, and thankfully the rain began to let up. To the left, I saw the dark clouds giving way to hints of sunlight. In their wake, a pale-gray mist of fog hovered over the valleys below, and we drove in and out of it as the car went up and down the hills. Had I not been focused on my destination, I'd have slowed down to take in the sight of the landscape, the almost magical quality of the shimmering shades of blues and grays whispering through the trees and between the blades of grass in the meadows. Cows stood in small groups, chewing patiently beneath large trees like old men sitting on a bench, watching the world go by. I balanced the ticking clock and my respect for the weather, taking the turns with caution and speeding up a bit on the straightaways.

Four seventeen p.m. In thirteen minutes, I'd be late. I was less than halfway there, but more than halfway toward four thirty. If I was being honest, this was somewhat the norm—my lateness. I always insisted this drive was thirty minutes away when in fact it was more like forty minutes. It drove Graham bonkers, the way I constantly rounded down when it came to time. I would take the drive home slowly on the way back, though, letting Hannah sleep while I enjoyed the view that never seemed to get old. I would be in no hurry then.

There was a single stop sign on the route, and as I approached it, I gingerly placed my foot on the brake. It shuddered on a puddle for a split second before taking hold. I turned left and began the steady descent down the road that would eventually take me into town. I'd made good time and relaxed a little with relief, knowing our lateness wouldn't be too much of a problem.

Signs dotted the road for things like fresh eggs, a used John Deere for sale, and the Country Realty office converted from a small Victorian. Spare tires fashioned into flowerpots marked driveways, and farther down the road, horses grazed next to a small pond with a red barn in a scene straight out of a folk art painting. I glanced in the rearview mirror to see Hannah dozing, her mouth dropped open in childlike sleep, with her gold shoes tucked in her hands. A fleck of glitter caught the light. I wonder, had I not glanced in the mirror at that moment, if I might have seen the sign just a split second earlier, or the pickup truck turning onto the road from a foggy gravel drive, hidden behind a drooping, water-heavy maple tree branch. Instead, the last thing I remember before everything changed was the peaceful look on my daughter's face, a flash of construction orange marked with the words FRESHLY OILED, and the monstrous boom that I thought at first was thunder, but was not.

And then nothing.

CHAPTER THREE

They tell me I spent the next five hours drifting in and out of consciousness, murmuring Hannah's name, before I finally blinked against the harsh, unnatural white light and heard the grating sound of a steady beep. Bed. Machines. Hospital. When I swallowed it felt like my mouth had been filled with sand and then emptied again. And then, like another boom, it hit me, terror coursing through my body. I tried to sit up, grasping for some sort of call button that I knew must be there.

"Hannah!" I shrieked. A searing pain gripped the left side of my chest, knocking the wind from me.

"Take it easy, sweetie." Blue scrubs. Nurse. Young. "Shhh, sit back," she said. "It's good to see you awake! You've been out for a good few hours. Do you know where you are?"

The room spun as I tried to orient myself. Striped wallpaper border. Salmon-and-blue pattern on the chairs. I'd been here before. It was the community hospital, just a mile or so beyond Hannah's pediatrician. I nodded. The nurse smiled as she placed two hands on my shoulders, nudging me back toward the pillows, and then checked an IV bag of fluids, pressing a button that silenced the beeping. She adjusted a padded sling I realized I was wearing on my left arm. "Do you remember what happened?" she asked.

"Where's my daughter?" I struggled to sit up again, and she frowned, taking my good arm and adjusting my pillow. An oxygen tube tickled my nostrils, and I swatted it away. "Is she okay?" The words sounded thick and crackled.

"I'm sure she's fine. Everything's fine. Don't worry."

I exhaled. "Is she here? Is she okay?" My thoughts flashed, calculating: the truck had hit from the passenger side. Front. She had been seated behind me on the opposite side. Back. This was good.

"You had quite an accident." She picked up a chart and made a few notes. "We had a few come in with that nasty storm."

"Please," I begged, while my breath hitched again. "Where is she? I need to see her." She'd be frightened, and I needed to get to her.

The smile returned with faint curiosity, and she patted my hand, replacing the tube below my nostrils. "It's a lot to deal with, waking up in a strange place. I'll let the doctor know you're awake."

"Wait . . . I don't understand . . . why won't you tell me . . ." I swallowed against the grit in my throat, and she handed me a plastic cup of water. "Would you please tell me if she's okay?" I spoke just above a whisper, growing more frightened of the answer with each taut second. She hesitated, as if about to speak, and then stopped herself.

She patted my hand once more. "We'll be right back. I promise."

When she disappeared into the hallway, I gripped the sheet. *Think.* I knew this hospital. It was good, but small. Patients with more serious and life-threatening injuries, especially children, would've been sent somewhere bigger. Westchester Medical maybe.

She might have gone there.

This could explain the nurse's hesitation. Maybe she didn't know for sure and didn't want to give me wrong information. I waited.

A fresh wave of adrenaline pumped into my bloodstream just as the nurse returned, along with a doctor. Words were about to pour from my mouth but then: friendly, dark eyes and a jaunty smile. Hannah must be okay; otherwise they would look far more serious.

I took a shallow breath.

"Hi there, Mrs. Beyers. Just going to check a few things." The doctor pulled a penlight from her breast pocket, holding it to my eyes. "Look up. Good."

"Please, I just want to know . . ."

"Down. Good. Side . . . pupils look good."

"Is she here? Did she go somewhere else?" The tears were hot on my cheeks.

"It's not unusual to feel a little off after an accident. It's a shock to the body!" She had a gentle South Asian accent, Indian perhaps, her words lilting. Around my age, late thirties. "We have you on a light pain medication. I hear you were lucky. The impact was on the passenger side. Might have been much worse otherwise. You got a bit of a bump to the head, but nothing too serious at all."

What were they waiting for? Why weren't they telling me anything?

"I think it was the shock that put you out more than anything. It's the body's way of resetting after a nasty surprise. But you have fractured a rib, and your left lung was punctured. As bad as that sounds, it's not too bad, all things considered." She patted my hand. "Can you take a breath for me?"

"Is she here at the hospital? We don't have family nearby . . . ," I croaked.

She placed a stethoscope in her ears and leaned over. "Is Hannah someone special to you? Someone we can call? The nurses tell me you've been asking for her."

I startled. "What do you mean? She's my daughter! She was in the car with me!"

Her brow furrowed, and a look of concern passed between her and the nurse.

She shook her head slowly. "No, nobody else. You were brought in alone, dear. How many fingers?" Her hand moved to my peripheral vision.

My heart tripped, blood pounding to a roar in my ears . . . "Well, then where is she? Did they take her to another hospital?"

"No, I don't think you understand. What I mean is, there was no one else in the car with you. Give it a little time; you're just a little disor—"

My stomach went hollow. "No. No. That's absurd! We were on our way to her pediatrician!"

As they stared at me, I looked behind them at the window and noticed, for the first time, the night sky, and then another thought hit me with even more horror. *She was thrown from the car. It's dark. They didn't see her. She's still out there.* "They have to go back!" I threw off the blanket and started to yank at the clear tape securing the IV into my arm. I winced as hot pain shot through my chest, stealing my breath once again. In a flash, they were at my side, pushing me back into the bed.

"Okay, okay. Easy now. We've got to watch that lung and get you calm. Just give us a minute here."

"You don't understand!"

"We'll get this sorted out."

I didn't believe them. "She was in the car seat. I need to talk to the paramedics. How could they not see her? How is that possible!"

At the doctor's instruction, the nurse was at my side, a syringe in her hand near the winding length of IV tube.

"Wait, what are you doing?" I cried.

"This will help you settle just a little."

"No!" But in seconds my eyes started growing heavy. I tried to fight it. "You have to find her. You have to . . ."

CHAPTER FOUR

A knock broke the suffocating silence.

The neurologist was a squat man with a tuft of gray hair. He flipped through a clipboard of papers while he introduced himself with a name that had more syllables than I cared to learn. I'd awoken with a start earlier, horrified to see the morning sunlight, and after frantic presses on the nurse's call button and numerous efforts by the staff to placate me, I finally forced myself to appear calm. I couldn't risk them sedating me again. A while later, Dr. Syllables had appeared in my doorway.

"Would you at least tell me if they've found her?" I asked in sharp, succinct words.

"You're talking about Hannah?" Again with the damn penlight.

I complied, following it with my eyes. Left, right, up, down. He moved to the bottom of my bed, lifting the blanket. He poked the bottom of each toe with the tip of a pen, asking if I felt it. "They won't tell me anything. Is my husband on the way? Why won't anybody tell me anything?"

He replaced the blanket and stopped, pushing the glasses up his nose. "I'll tell you what. Can you answer some questions for me first?"

"But—"

"I promise we'll talk about Hannah in a moment." He set a hand on my foot.

"They found her. Didn't they?" I whispered with a tight jaw and a strangled sob. "That's what everyone is so afraid to tell me. Are you waiting for my husband?"

He moved to my side. "How are you feeling? How does your chest feel?"

I blinked as he awaited my response. *Think.* I measured my breathing. I needed to cooperate. "Fine. Better," I said finally, through clenched teeth.

"Any headache?"

"No." Not entirely true.

"Tell me, what's your full name?"

"Annie. Annie Marie Beyers."

"When's your birthday, Annie?"

"August 30, '77," I said, sharply.

"Okay, good. And do you know today's date?"

"I don't know," I snapped. "June something?"

The papery skin around his eyes crinkled with a slight smile. "Best guess."

"Friday. June 15? No, wait . . ." Graham was supposed to be back on the fifteenth, so . . . "Saturday. June 16, 2014."

"Bingo. Where were you headed yesterday?"

"The city, Manhattan."

Wait. No. *That's not right.*

Where did that come from?

My head felt fuzzy. I closed my eyes. Tried to focus. When I opened them, I noticed there was paint on my fingers, stains of deep green and indigo. *Had I been painting?* I blinked, images flickering in my head from nowhere. I shook them clear.

"Home. I was at home. On my way into town. To Hannah's doctor. Dr. Renner," I said, finally.

He made a note. "Where were you born?"

"What does this have to do with anything!"

"Just a few more, I promise. Humor me," he said.

"Scranton." The clock on the wall was ticking, as if shouting each precious moment of wasted time.

He nodded. "And you're married?"

Tick. Tock.

He continued to stare down at me until I replied. "Yes. Graham David Beyers. We were married on August 20, 2005. This is absurd. Have they talked to him? I don't have my phone."

"Yes. I believe they left a message with his office yesterday when you were brought in. We've all been working hard to get this sorted out."

My face crumpled again with a fresh wave of tears. "Please."

"Do you remember anything else?" he asked.

"I need to see Hannah. Right now. I'm not answering anymore questions. *Please.*" My voice broke.

He watched me for a few moments, then set my file on the bed and pulled up a chair. "Mrs. Beyers, here's the situation. Other than the injuries to your ribs and lung, and the scratches you see on your arms from the shattered glass, there's nothing remarkable here. There was no major trauma to the head. Nothing unusual at all, and that's great news. We can do an MRI just to be sure, and I suspect we may go that route, but . . ."

"I told you. My head feels fine. What—"

"However . . . ," he interrupted. "You've got us a little stumped." He scratched at his chin, and it made a sound like a boar's-hair brush. Whatever I'd thought he was going to tell me, nothing prepared me for what he eventually said: "See, we don't have any record of a daughter."

"They must've taken her to . . ."

"On *any* daughter."

My body went rigid.

"Mrs. Beyers? Did you hear me?"

"I . . . what do you mean? She stays home with me! Where else would she have been? She wasn't with a sitter. We were on our way to the goddamn pediatrician! Look at my car—it's full of her things, her car seat, and . . . everything! She was *with* me!" I swallowed, ignoring the pain growing in my lungs. "Just . . . talk to my husband."

"Is Mr. Beyers Hannah's father?"

"What? Yes."

"Okay." He spoke with careful, measured pacing, reminding me of the way I spoke to Hannah before I cleaned a scraped knee that I knew would sting. "When they called his office, trying to reach him, evidently they didn't know anything about him having a daughter."

I blinked.

Tick. Tock . . . Tick . . .

"That's insane." The words caught in my throat. "He has pictures of her in his office. She's been to office picnics." They all knew her. Why would they lie?

"Just try to calm down. Can you do that for me?" I took shallow, halting breaths. "Okay, good girl. Try to listen to me for a minute. Sometimes when the body experiences something traumatic, a shock like an accident, just like this, your memory gets a little jostled. Now . . . like I said, I don't believe there's anything seriously wrong. No injury to the brain. Do you have any history of mental illness?"

I drew back and my eyes laser-focused on him. "Mental illness? Is that what you think—no! I mean . . . ," I waffled, terrified of where this was headed. I knew what happened when a person's sanity was questioned. "I am *not* crazy."

He raised his hands. "Okay, I wasn't implying 'crazy.' I promise. But it's important to know. You understand?"

"I don't understand any of this! Look . . ." My thoughts again went into overdrive. "Hannah was born here—in this hospital. You'll find her records. Just look them up."

"Well, we did that, actually. Not for her specifically. But *your* records. We understand you had a miscarriage here a few years ago?"

Images flashed, blinking one after another in my head. Graham. Me. I shook my head and the room tilted. "No. Something's mixed up. I had a healthy baby girl. Her name is Hannah. And she's . . ." My eyes stung with a fresh wave of tears, the dam breaking. "Please. She's out there. All alone. Scared or . . . worse. Because of a paperwork mix-up? *Please.* Tell me you're looking for her. I'm begging you." My white-knuckled fists gripped the sides of the bed.

"You have my word that we're doing everything we can. After you woke up last night, we sent the paramedics immediately back out to the scene, just to be safe. They even went to the impound and checked the car again. They didn't find anything. Is there anyone we can call for you? Parents? Siblings?"

I shook my head again and melted into the bed, helpless. I needed to get out of there. I couldn't help her this way. I wanted to scream.

"Get a little more rest, and things will start to clear up. You'll see. I understand that Mr. Beyers is on his way in from the city, and we'll get this all sorted out."

"You spoke to him?" I sat up again, abruptly.

"Not personally, no." He stood, sliding the chair back into the corner with a screeching sound. "He'll be here soon."

When he left, there was nothing but disbelief and terror with me in the empty room. She'd somehow been missed in the car, thrown to the side of the road, and I imagined her small body, alone. The fever. She needed medicine for the ear infection, my sweet girl. She needed help. A paperwork error. Mixed up Social Security numbers in a hospital records system. A miscommunication. And my daughter could be dead because of it. If she wasn't already. I began to shiver. Not the kind of shiver you get from cold, but a primal shiver, as if the air were trembling with me. Words echoing.

We have no record of a daughter.

CHAPTER FIVE

In the hours that followed, I felt each moment like sharp little pricks. Doctors and nurses came and went. I needed to convince them I was fine so I could get out. So I could find her. And so I kept things as succinct as possible. I cooperated. I gave the answers they wanted. I watched as they checked boxes on paper in files. And I waited, powerless.

It was four hours later when Graham finally arrived, his presence bringing the first bit of relief and hope I'd felt since my arrival at the hospital eighteen hours earlier. But instead of rushing into the room, frantic with worry, he paused. "Hey, Ann."

"Graham," I cried. "Did you get this sorted out? Did they find her?"

He hesitated, then walked toward the bed. I reached out to him, eager to lean into the safe softness of my husband. He looked at me strangely before leaning down for a wooden hug that resembled a half-armed pat on the back. He cocked his head and bit the inside of his cheek, a gesture I knew well when he was thinking of what to say next.

"They filled me in on the phone. I'm so sorry about this. Are you doing all right?" he asked, flatly.

It was then that I noticed his eyes—not filled with frantic worry, or with the light that usually came my way, but instead with something else. They were languid and dull and filled with the look of someone a little bit broken.

I swallowed, reaching for his hand, but he turned. "Graham—"

"It took them a while to get ahold of me. I'm still your emergency contact, but I was out of reception for a while. Piper called my office and they got in touch."

Who's Piper?

I shook my head. "I told them you were in Atlanta."

"Atlanta?"

"That your flight was canceled because of the storm. They called your cell?" The way he moved was foreign and unfamiliar, standing back away from me.

"Uh, no. No Atlanta for me." He laughed, but without a trace of humor. "Just the Upper West Side and Connecticut."

Connecticut?

He looked over his shoulder, clearly uncomfortable, and just then a woman entered the room. She wore a long, crocheted cardigan that trailed behind her. Silver hair that once may have been blonde rested on her shoulders beneath heavy bangs. Her smile seemed out of place, and yet I noted Graham's obvious relief upon seeing her.

"Good morning, Annie. I'm Nina. I'm with the hospital."

Oh God, this was the person they sent to deliver horrible news to patients who they're afraid might not be able to handle it. The thought must have registered on my face.

"Oh, don't worry, dear. I promise I'm not that bad! In cases like this, sometimes it's helpful for a patient to have someone to ease them through the details."

"You're a therapist?"

She bobbled her head, left to right. "Technically I'm a social worker. But I wear a few different hats here. I'm sorry I interrupted, Mr. Beyers. I meant to be here earlier but got held up a bit."

"I don't need a therapist. What I need is someone to please explain to me what is going on." I turned to Graham. "I don't understand; why were you in the city? And why aren't you . . . I feel like I'm in the twilight zone here. They . . . they can't find Hannah. They can't find her at all! They think she . . . that she's some ridiculous figment of my imagination . . . you have to tell them!"

He shifted and looked toward Nina.

She nodded at him, and I realized they had already spoken privately.

He took a tentative step toward me, clearly perplexed. "Annie . . . I don't know what's happened here. And I'm so sorry. But there is no daughter. You know that, right?"

I felt the blow low in the chest, and I reeled. "Why are you lying?"

"I'm not lying. I'm trying to—"

"You're saying I'm making this up too?"

"Honestly? Look, I don't know. I'm just saying . . ."

"No." I shook my head. "NO! I have five years of memories. She's five years old! You just talked to her on the phone yesterday! You were on your way home from Atlanta. She had a fever and it was storming and your plane was canceled. How do you explain all of that?"

He shook his head, patience wearing thin. He looked tired. "I told you, Ann, I wasn't in Atlanta. I was in the city."

"Stop it! Why are you doing this? She's our Hannah!" I shouted. "Did something happen to her? Are you lying to protect me in some kind of convoluted way?"

Exasperated, he turned back to Nina. "I'm sorry. I don't know what I'm supposed to say."

"You're doing fine, Graham," she replied. "Just be patient."

I looked to both of them, coconspirators in this bizarre tactic to keep me separated from the truth. Until this point, I had been frantically trying to get them to look for my daughter, to find her. But as I watched them talking quietly together, I realized it would be futile. It was in that moment that I knew I was totally alone.

Graham's shoulders softened a little, and then he turned back to me. "I think you just need some help, Annie. You're going to be fine.

The doctors, they said things like this can happen sometimes." He gave a pleading look to Nina, and she stepped in.

"Annie, all the tests they ran this morning have come in. There's been no obvious damage to the brain. However, sometimes there can be microscopic bruising that doctors can't see. It's so minute that there's nothing to be done, and it'll heal on its own. But temporarily, it can wreak a bit of havoc and leave you quite disoriented. Paramnesia is one of the more common words for it, but there are several terms. It can lead to memory impairments and problems with self-awareness. Or it may simply be the shock, or the trauma of the accident. It can be quite jarring."

"I do not have some ridiculous amnesia. This isn't a soap opera. Look, can we just go home? Can we please do that? Her room, her things, they're all at the house." I needed to get out of here. Immediately.

"Which house?" Graham's question lay flat, more a statement than a question.

I stared at him blankly. "What do you mean? *Our* house."

"The Yellow House?"

"We don't have any other house!"

Again, he turned to Nina for guidance.

She nodded, causing her dangling earrings to bob heavily. "It's okay. I think what's best is for her to hear the truth, and to hear it from someone she trusts. Go on."

"Uh, we don't live there anymore, Ann," Graham said. "We haven't lived there for a couple of years. You live in the city now."

"What do you mean *I* live in the city?"

Hearing my meaning, he clarified. "Well, we both live in the city, but . . . you do know we're not together anymore, right? We're separated?"

I inhaled sharply, feeling a pull at my side, reeling. "Are you telling me that I have no daughter, no home, and no marriage?"

He raised his shoulders. "I don't know what else to say, Annie."

"Would you please stop saying my name like that. It's weird." The clock ticked on, marking silence. I noticed his clothes then. Slim cut, as if he'd lost weight. Dark trousers and a gray button-down shirt I didn't recognize. Fine quality. Expensive and custom fit. The kind of thing he would've worn at one time, but nothing like the more affordable jeans and chambray shirts he wore these days. I looked down, realizing for the first time that my wedding rings weren't on my finger.

CHAPTER SIX

A knot in my chest crept into my throat as I looked up at Graham. "Yesterday morning, I woke up with a husband and a daughter and a home. And now here I am in this hospital, and you're telling me everything I love most in life has just what . . . disappeared? This is madness. I remember my child! I remember feeling her growing in my belly. I remember giving birth to her! I re—"

"We did have a baby, Ann." He pinched the bridge of his nose and clenched his eyes tight with a heavy sigh. He pulled a chair over toward the bed and sat, resting his elbows on his knees. His tone had turned gentle, more like the man I knew. He smiled sadly. "It took us three tries to get pregnant."

"I remember."

He nodded. Finally, something we both agreed on.

"You were five months pregnant when you miscarried," he continued. "Here in this hospital, actually. We were still living up here then. She was a little girl." His eyes welled, and he cleared his throat and smiled slightly. "Hannah was one of the names on our list."

I remembered the list. I could see it clearly, posted on the refrigerator in the kitchen back then.

Graham continued, "It was winter. There had been a big storm and eighteen inches of snow. Finally, it had started to slow. We left to take a walk in town. We didn't see the ice on the front porch stairs, and when you fell . . ."

"No. See, you're wrong!" I said, desperately. "I remember that storm! We lost power and kept warm in blankets by the fireplace." We'd made love on the floor.

He smiled a little, looking down. "Right."

"We'd gotten all bundled up to go out. We were going to take a walk, get lunch at the café. They still had power. But just as we were leaving, the power came back on, and we decided to stay in after all," I said, taking his hand, imploring him to agree. "Remember?"

He knitted his brow and shook his head. "The power didn't come back on for another day. You were still in the hospital when it did. I'd run home to feed Charlie when the lights flickered back on." A jolt ran through me as just then an image flashed in my mind, of me clutching my stomach on the cold ground, and then it vanished. I shuddered. Confusion rippled through me.

"I don't understand. This doesn't make any sense. That's not what happened. There was no miscarriage. We never went for that walk. We had a perfectly beautiful healthy baby girl." I said this to myself as much as I said it to them.

Nina had been keeping watch from the corner and once again stepped forward. "It can be very real, Annie. Everything you're feeling, everything you're remembering. Your brain is filling in the blanks, creating memories of events. It's not intentional; everyone here knows that. Little by little, the false memories will fade away, and the real ones will return. Sometimes it's gradual, and sometimes it happens all at once."

What they were saying couldn't possibly be true.

Could it?

I took a shallow breath, the world tipping on its axis as if the sea were now the sky. "No," I whimpered. I'd seen things like this happen with my own eyes, in my own family: breaks with reality. My biggest fear come to fruition. "No."

"Just give it some time, Ann." Graham placed his hand on mine, and I interlaced my fingers in his, gripping. Pleading. He looked down at them and stroked his thumb against mine. "You'll remember everything soon." But then, as if realizing what he was doing, he suddenly pulled his hand away, his jaw tightening. I wanted him to crawl into the bed, to lie beside me and curl around me, but instead he stood. "Look, I'd better get back."

"Wait, you're leaving?" I asked. "Already?"

"I'll be back in the morning to pick you up, but I couldn't find anyone on short notice to walk Charlie, so I really have to get back." He looked at his watch again. "He'll be happy to see you. He's been moping around and pacing," he added, with forced lightness.

I stared at him, stunned. "Charlie?"

Noticing the look on my face, Graham turned to Nina. "I'm confused. I thought it was just the past few years that were mixed up for her. Charlie, our dog, is ten. She should know who he is."

"I know who he is," I whispered. I blinked back tears. I'd have explained, but what was the point of telling them that our dog had died eight months earlier and was buried beneath the oak tree, or that his leash still hung in the hallway because I hadn't had the heart to say goodbye. "He's our dog," I said.

"Oh, okay. Good. Well, anyway, Marcie is on her way, but she won't be here until tomorrow night, so I'll be back in the morning to pick you up."

Just like that, another piece of information dropped like a grenade. "Marcie? What's she doing here?"

"As odd as all of this sounds, they say you can get out of here tomorrow," he said, ignoring my question.

"Medically, you're fine now," Nina said. "You'll have to take it easy and follow up with your doctor in Manhattan while your ribs heal. And you'll want to begin therapy immediately with a psychiatrist. I'll give you a few names. It'll help a great deal."

"But what am I supposed to do?" I panicked, shocked at the thought of Graham leaving.

"You'll be fine. We'll watch you here tonight, but you'll be ready to go in the morning," Nina said.

I wanted to run. To scream. To thrash about shouting at everyone to stop. But I'd seen where that kind of behavior got someone. I knew better. None of this made sense, but it wasn't going to get any better if I were strapped to a bed. So I stayed silent, seeing Hannah's face every time I closed my eyes.

Hesitating a moment, Graham pointed to his side, to where I was bandaged. "Does it hurt a lot?" He paused, then added, "What were you doing up here again, anyway?"

I just stared at him, imploring him to stay.

"All right, then. Call, I guess, if you need anything," he said finally.

When he walked out, all the air in the room seemed to go with him, and I began to cry.

"It's going to take some time. Don't rush it." Nina walked over to stand beside the bed.

I looked up at her. "I don't . . . I don't understand any of this," I whispered. "I want to go home."

"Dr. Debodowski will come in one more time to go over everything with you, and we can start your discharge paperwork."

That wasn't at all what I'd meant. I wanted my house, my bedroom. I wanted my husband, my daughter.

"Did anything Graham mentioned ring any bells?" she asked, gently. "Even the faintest hint of familiarity?"

I shook my head. "I haven't spoken to my sister, Marcie, in years. I don't want to see her. And anyway, she lives in Tokyo."

"You had a falling-out?"

"You could say that."

"I got the impression—and I could be wrong here—but I got the impression that you and Marcie are quite close. She's been calling often. I believe your husband said she lives on Long Island."

I laughed bitterly, staring out the window at the gray blanket of clouds in the sky. "Well, now I know this is all ridiculous." I fumbled with the sheet, balling it in my hand, wiping at the unnerving paint stains I saw there.

"I called the pediatrician this morning, where we were heading yesterday," I said, quietly. It was one of the few phone numbers I knew by heart, and I'd used the bedside phone.

"And?"

"They didn't have any record of her. Hannah."

She nodded and came closer. I caught a wave of her perfume—a cloying scent that reminded me of my high school English teacher. "Do you mind if I show you something?" She walked to a table behind me and picked up a purse that I hadn't noticed before. She placed it in my lap. "Why don't you take a look."

"That's not mine."

"Go ahead." She smiled, warmly.

I didn't want to. But as she waited, I touched the deep-brown leather, struck by the luxury and smoothness beneath my fingertips. Feeling the contents of another woman's purse was no less intrusive and intimate than it might be to put your hand up a stranger's shirt, and I used my fingertips to carefully unzip it.

"Why don't you open the wallet," she said.

I knew then where she was going with this, and I shuddered. No. No, I didn't want this. I just wanted to go home. Yet, slowly, as if peering around a corner to where a monster might lie in wait, I opened the delicate black folio. Inside was the driver's license of a person with my name and my grainy photo and the address of a Manhattan street. Upon seeing the photo, I reached up to touch my hair, pulling it loose from a tie and finding it was a couple of inches shorter than it had been just yesterday. Felt the bangs that hadn't been there before. I let the items drop to my lap and laid my head back into the pillow as my stomach turned.

"Be patient with yourself, Annie. It's going to be okay soon. I know it doesn't seem that way now. But it will be."

Nina left the room a few minutes later, leaving a stranger's purse in a heap beside me. I shoved it off the bed and listened to the contents scatter across the cold white floor as I began to cry for her in muttered sobs. "Hannah."

CHAPTER SEVEN

The next morning, Graham arrived just after eleven, and the two of us walked side by side as strangers as we left the hospital. I followed him to an unfamiliar black Lexus and took a seat in the passenger side with my one personal item—the purse that felt like another woman's. I wanted to reach out to hold his hand as he placed it on the gearshift, to set my hand on the back of his neck as he drove, a habit of mine. But I sensed the invisible wall between us and stayed within the new confines of my own space.

"I need to go to where the accident was," I said, as he began to pull out of the parking lot.

"I'm not going that direction. I'm taking the thruway."

"I have to see it, Graham. I need to see it with my own eyes. And I need to see the car."

He sighed, exasperated. "It's a Sunday, Annie. The car was towed to a garage, and it's locked up."

"Then at least take me up to where it happened."

He wavered at first, but when the light turned green, he reluctantly took the left turn that would lead us up the mountain toward the county line. The day was clear and bright, and as we drove, we passed the pediatrician's office. *Just a little farther*, I thought. *Just a little farther and I would have made it to the office. Hannah would have been checked. We'd have gone home. And everything would've been fine.* I looked away, and we continued upward, the road beginning to wind. As we climbed higher, the trees grew thicker and greener. Small-town life gave way to pastures and farms on the drive I knew so well. Ten minutes later we rounded a bend, and Graham slowed. "It was somewhere around here, I think," he said.

"Just up there." I saw the orange construction sign. "Pull over."

I'd expected more, I supposed. Cones and the kind of investigation tape the police would use to mark a major crime scene, or a place where a child may have disappeared. But there was nothing there. Just a faint black skid mark and the dented area of a guardrail, where my car had landed. I opened the car door and stepped out, holding my breath, searching, every cell in my body longing for her. "Hannah," I whispered, a silent call that wanted to be a scream, bringing her to me. I gripped the rough metal guardrail and looked deep into the thick wooded brush that lined the road, scanning the ground for something. Something small. Something pink or purple or glittery or childlike. But I just found small bits of gravel, long, prickly weeds, and the stems of wild tiger lilies about to bloom.

"Annie? You okay?"

Nothing. Nothing to say that we had been there. I turned, looking farther up the road, at the narrow drive where the truck had emerged unseen at just the wrong moment, turning my life upside down. I closed my eyes. *Please. Just let me go back. I'll watch closer. I swear.*

"Annie, c'mon. We have to get back to the city by two."

I wanted to keep looking, but I knew there was nothing to be found. Graham was half standing out of the car, and I returned to the passenger seat. We continued driving, retracing the route I knew so well. *Moo moo.* I smiled through tears at the cows whom Hannah always greeted with a fond hello, hearing her tiny voice in my head.

"I want to drive past the house," I said.

"No," he said, firmly. "That's not a good idea."

"I don't care!"

35

Graham tensed immediately. I sighed. I hadn't meant to be short. "The house isn't going anywhere. Come back up if you have to," he said.

"It's less than two minutes off the main road." And I desperately wanted to go home. *Please just let me go home.*

"What is it with you and that damn house?" he muttered under his breath. "It never stops."

I didn't understand his meaning and was about to ask, but as we approached the turn, he slowed and eventually turned the car right. "This is ridiculous." He was a stranger, this man, and I turned away, swiping at a tear.

Seeing the gesture, he sighed. "Look. I'm sorry. I just . . . I don't know how to handle all this. I know it must be hard for you."

"Well, you don't seem to be making it any easier," I said. There wasn't a hint of the warmth that lit up his eyes even when things were difficult.

"What do you want me to do, Annie? What am I supposed to say?"

"I don't know this version of you. I've never seen you like this. What happened to you?"

"Oh, I'm disappointing you again, shocking. I'm doing the best I can here too. What—am I supposed to just pretend to be something I'm not because you've suddenly lost your m—"

He stopped suddenly. I spun around, glaring. "Go ahead. Say it. Lost my mind."

"I'm sorry. I didn't mean . . ."

"Right."

"No. I'm so sorry." He slowed the car and pulled to the side of the road, at the end of the long gravel driveway that led to our house. In the distance, the house loomed high in a lush field of green, reflecting the morning sun. I imagined myself on the porch, never believing that someday I'd find myself once again looking longingly up from the road.

"Wait!" Graham scoops me into his arms. "What are you doing?" I laugh. "I'll carry you over the threshold!" he says, kissing me. Together, we go

up the steps, near where the lilacs would someday be planted, and through the front door.

"Drive up," I said, pointing.

"Annie, we can't. We don't live here anymore. We can't just drive up someone's driveway."

The desperation made my stomach twist. "Please. Please just take me home." But I didn't know to whom I was begging. I broke down. It was right there in front of me, but I couldn't go in. "This is our home, Graham." Hannah lived here. She needed me. She was up there right now waiting for me to come home. Sitting on her bed, playing with Lil' Llama, or sitting amid piles of white paper, coloring.

"*Was*, Annie. It *was* our home. I told you. We moved two years ago."

"We would never sell this house. Never."

"But we did," he said.

"What happened? Can you please just tell me what happened?" I stared up at the black front door, where there should have been a eucalyptus wreath that I'd hung a week earlier but instead was bare.

"The doctors said it's better if you remember the rest of it on your own. You heard them. I'm not supposed to fill in the blanks for you."

"I know what they said," I cried. "Please, Graham. I need to have something. Some shred of anything to go on. This is impossible. I just want to go home." I placed my hand against the glass as the image blurred with tears. "This is our home."

A car drove past us as we sat in the gravel beneath the silos, the engine idling. I gripped the door handle, wanting to burst from the car and run up the driveway.

Graham exhaled heavily. "It was a lot of things," he said quietly. "It was too big for two people. You were depressed. I was unhappy. We moved back to the city. And that was that."

That was that. Like leaving the home we'd loved was so simple. "And us? What happened to us?"

He opened his mouth as if to answer but then stopped and shook his head. "It just didn't work."

In a shadowy part of my brain, I began to imagine the way things might have gone, according to what Graham said. How our fate could have been different here at this house. I craned my neck, straining to focus on the porch.

"Where are the lilacs?"

"I don't know. I think they cut them down. They were growing too high, anyway. Covered up the porch."

"No." I looked at him and our eyes met. For a moment, I thought he might reach out, but he didn't.

"We need to get back," he said a moment later, heading out onto the main road. I watched the house until the last moment, pulling me toward it like a rubber band extended until I nearly snapped, and watched as the top of the oak tree disappeared around the bend.

CHAPTER EIGHT

The drive down the Palisades Parkway into the city was a quiet one. It had been two days since the accident, but time felt like it had been twisted and bent somehow, malleable. All I could think of was Hannah. It was the longest I'd ever gone without seeing her, and each time I realized I would never see her again, nausea filled me. Twice I had to ask Graham to pull the car over to the side of the road.

In my head I heard her voice, clear and present. The delicate details of her life numbered in the thousands, millions. Was it possible that the human mind could generate such a realistic and punishing illusion? Surely not. And yet this was what they had told me.

There was little traffic on a Sunday, and after an uneventful drive down the Henry Hudson, we wove our way through the West Village into SoHo—a sharp contrast from the rural green fields we'd left behind not two hours earlier. As we turned off Spring Street, Graham pulled into a parking garage, and we walked onto a narrow cobbled street—a rare gem found in this part of town. I followed him up three wide steps that led to a glass door. I looked upward at the bright-white restored building with its tidy, photogenic fire escapes. "Anything seem familiar?" Graham asked.

"I guess." I pointed down the road. "My hair stylist is over on Broome. And there's that great cupcake place we go to sometimes." But that wasn't anything unusual. SoHo was my favorite neighborhood in the city, and we were there often. A playground a couple of blocks over was a favorite of Hannah's. In the summertime, she giggled at the sprays of water shot from colorful fountains.

"I mean anything about this building?" he asked.

"No. Not that I'd—" I stopped short as I watched him enter the six-digit code into the security pad, realizing I somehow knew the numbers before he pressed them. He looked over at me.

"What?"

"Nothing," I lied.

We walked to the second floor, and Graham opened a door to an expansive two-story loft. It had been beautifully renovated, with one wall of original restored windows. Bright afternoon light flooded into a living room tastefully decorated in shades of beige and gray. Two sofas sat over an enormous woven rug that looked like it would cost three months' mortgage, at the least. Two wide, pale-blue velvet sitting chairs sat beside a table made of stone and wood. A long industrial table accented with slightly wilted flowers bridged an area that led into a tall, open kitchen. I stood still at the entry, unsure of where to go or what to do next.

"Go ahead and get settled in," he said, dropping his keys into a pottery bowl that sat on a long console table beside the door. The table was dotted with a combination of items that I both recognized and didn't. The bowl had been on the entry table at home. A silver elephant with its trunk reaching into the air sat atop a stack of my favorite books. A framed photo of my parents taken on my sixth birthday sat nearby. Other items were less familiar—uninvited guests among my treasures. I had begun to pick up a small stack of mail with my name on it when I froze.

Hearing the familiar, soft click-clack of paws on a bare floor, I stood wide eyed as Charlie trotted slowly toward me, barreling into my calves. With some effort, he jumped up and placed his front two paws on my side, looking up at me with wide, happy brown eyes. I dropped to the floor and threw my arms around him. A hound mix, he was too big to be a lap dog but too small to know this, and he plopped heavily onto my lap and licked the salty tears from my cheeks. "Charlie," I whispered. "Look at you."

"He missed you." Graham chuckled.

"I have missed him," I replied, and then added more softly into the dog's ear, "more than you know."

"There's food in the pantry if you're hungry. And I picked up some milk and eggs and things this morning," Graham said, shuffling about in the kitchen.

I sat cross-legged, pulling Charlie into me as his tail wagged in soft taps. *How often had this dog comforted me?* I wondered. And now here he was like an angel.

"How does it feel to be here? Even a little familiar?" Graham asked in a voice shaped by a combination of frustration and hope.

"It's just strange. Nothing else." This wasn't entirely true, but I didn't want to admit it out loud. It felt oddly familiar, but at the same time not at all. It was like stepping into a decorator's vision board of a space I might *like* to live in. It felt like mine, was in many ways my taste, but at the same time foreign. "It's so beautiful," I said, looking up at the tall ceilings and the lofted walkway.

"Really? Because you hate it here," he muttered under his breath. Then added, "You hate it everywhere."

This surprised me. "I do? Why?"

He shook his head. "Never mind. I'm fixing a drink. Do you want one?" He pulled a bottle of scotch from the cupboard and followed my gaze to a large painting that hung over the dining table. It was an abstract piece in a combination of layered blues and whites. I had been staring at it since we walked in. "It's yours," he said, gesturing toward it.

I looked at him in disbelief. "Mine? What do you mean?"

"I mean you painted it. It's one from your first exhibition."

One of the few things I'd come to learn was that, apparently, I was back to being a professional artist. I was quickly learning to keep my thoughts to myself about the things I discovered in this new life. It seemed only to frustrate Graham to hear what was going on in my head. For instance, the fact that I couldn't paint something like that in a million years. Well, no, that wasn't true. I was being hard on myself. I couldn't paint something like that in maybe five years. It had been that long since I'd stopped painting in earnest. It hadn't really been a conscious decision to stop, more like a slow fade that started around the time Hannah was born.

When we'd moved into the Yellow House, we'd turned an unfinished space above the garage into a makeshift studio with windows overlooking the fields. I painted almost nonstop during the first year, inspired by the colors of the seasons. I loved it, but after Hannah was born, I loved my time with her more, and eventually the room grew quiet. I was too in my head when I was painting. Absorbed in my own world. Obsessive. It wasn't uncommon for me to stay up all night, or forget to eat until Graham tapped me on the shoulder and handed me a sandwich with a kiss. But that kind of schedule and dedication—the lack of balance—wasn't conducive to parenting a baby. And I was so enamored with the beautiful little miracle of her that after many years of painting being my first love, it began to pale in comparison to the wonder of the perfect little child's face. The studio became more of an artsy playroom for rainy afternoons, where the two of us doodled for hours.

I looked at the painting curiously. It reminded me of the melancholy blue hues of freshly falling snow at dusk in the deep winter. In truth, I thought it was lovely. A sense of pride and accomplishment arose in me, and I smiled a little.

"Graham?" I asked, turning, and again taking in the surroundings. "How can we possibly afford all of this? Who pays for it?"

"Well, we do, Ann. I do. You do."

"But how?" I couldn't even fathom it.

"Do you remember about five years ago, when Kevin Strobel offered me that job heading up the design team on the Hudson at Berkeley Residences project?"

"Yeah, I do. I was pregnant. You didn't take it because we were worried it would require too much time in the city. You'd have to commute or spend half the week away."

He nodded. "Right, well, the project ended up being delayed, and he offered it to me again a year later." I shook my head. He'd lost me. "Anyway, I took it. We ended up winning an award for it, and Kevin and I opened up our own firm. And you're a pretty huge deal in your own right." He extended his arms out to the side. "Now here we are, I guess. Or *were*, anyway." He took a drink from a lowball tumbler. "I guess it's okay to tell you about me?" He scratched his head, then added a quiet, "I don't know."

"But you don't live here?" I asked, wondering how I'd ever survived such heartbreak. "You said in the hospital you're leaving?"

"I already left, actually. I moved out last month." He gestured to the moving boxes that lined the far wall. "I just have a few more boxes to get." He looked away. "I guess I keep putting it off."

I swallowed back tears. I was desperate to go to him. To crawl into his arms and have him sort this whole mess out. To tell me it was going to be okay. At the same time, I felt a strange heaviness between us, like a lurking shadow that threatened to fray my edges whenever he spoke. "So are you leaving tonight? Or . . . now?" I asked, nervously.

His face softened a little. "No. The doctors thought it would be better if you weren't alone." He bit the inside of his cheek, as if he weren't sold on the idea. "I can stay here for a little while. Until you're feeling better and back to yourself. Marcie would stay, but Tim's out of town, and Hunter is still in school. But she'll be around too."

Charlie walked up to me, and I crouched down, leaning into his neck, inhaling the musky scent of his fur. *Then it'll just be you and me, boy.* Which sounded unimaginable.

"Marcie," I repeated the name. "I still don't get that part." Just then, the door next to me jostled with a key in the lock, and I jumped, looking to Graham.

"It's okay; it's just—"

"Oh my God, sweetie. I am *so* sorry I'm just getting here now. I meant to be here when you got home. How are you?" My sister, Marcie, walked through the door and straight to me. I stiffened as she pulled me into a deep hug, my arms lying limply at my sides. I hadn't seen or spoken to her in over five years. I took a step back.

Her eyes grew wide. "Oh God. You do know who I am, don't you?" she asked.

I nodded. "Uh, I do, but . . . what are you doing here?" I asked, and her expression transitioned from relieved to hurt. Her shoulders dropped a little. "Well, I . . ." She looked at Graham, who offered nothing in the way of support.

"Sweetie . . ." She reached out to take my hand, but I drew it back.

She cocked her head to the side and her eyes began to fill. "You said she was having trouble with her memory," she said to Graham, "but this feels more like time travel," she added with a sad smile.

Graham walked over to where we stood and put a leash on Charlie. "Come on, buddy."

Charlie remained stubbornly by my side, refusing to follow Graham.

"Charlie always did have good taste," Marcie said.

Graham rolled his eyes, but the corners of his mouth turned upward at the joke as he patted his leg. "Come on, boy." This time the dog followed.

As the door closed behind them, Marcie stood there awkwardly until finally I spoke. "Look, I'd invite you in, but . . ." I trailed off, looking around the strange home. "And I'm not really sure I know what you're doing here. I don't understand any of this. But you can go. I'm fine."

Part of me was comforted by the sight of my big sister—the girl who had shared my childhood and once been my greatest ally. But wounds from more recent years hadn't healed, and the chasm between us felt impassable. The last time I'd seen her, harsh words had been hurled like cannonballs between us, as my father lay beneath a fresh pile of cemetery dirt. Since then, we'd barely spoken.

Marcie paused, watching me, and then put her shoulders back, standing taller. Exactly three-quarters of an inch taller than me, if I remembered correctly from our teen years. "Well, too bad," she said, finally. "Because you're stuck with me. At least during the day. Tim's gone for two weeks. And you get Mr. Sunshine at night for now, I'm afraid." She pointed a thumb toward the door. "Now, you look like death, and what did Graham bring you to wear, anyway?" She looked me up and down and shook her head, fanning the summer heat from her neck. "Go upstairs. Run a bath. I'll make lunch. You need to get on the couch and rest." She went to the kitchen and immediately set to getting dishes out. Since when was she the nurturing type? I stared at her and she looked up. "We'll sort it all out, sweetie. You're going to be fine; I promise. Okay?" I nodded, unwillingly grateful. "This will all be behind you soon, and things will go back to normal." But I could hear the uncertainty in her voice. She shooed me. "Now go."

It went unmentioned—the fact that I had no idea what was upstairs or where anything was, and that it would feel like I was making my unescorted way around a stranger's home. None of it felt right. But I didn't know what else to do. Reluctantly, I started toward the stairs and took a step up, exhausted. I didn't want any of this. I wanted *my* normal. I wanted *my* bedroom in *my* home. And I wanted my family.

CHAPTER NINE

I disliked leather sofas intensely. I couldn't get comfortable because I was constantly sliding around. Not to mention that it had once been part of a living animal. I crossed my legs again, sinking back into the corner.

"I can tell you more," I said. "Want to hear about the time Graham accidentally used the wrong detergent and she got a rash on her back that lasted for two days? He felt awful. And she has a stuffed llama holding a pink blanket sitting on her bed. We call her Lil' Llama."

Dr. Higgins, my new psychiatrist, smiled. "My daughter likes llamas too. It's cute."

I stared out the window at the buildings beyond and the tips of the treetops from the sidewalk below. His office was on the third floor of a prewar building in Midtown Manhattan, and I'd seen him three times over the two weeks since the accident. "We've been over it again and again. Are we going to do this every time? It's never going to change," I said.

"Sometimes it's helpful to think through the details again, to sift through your memory and sort things out. You never know when something new might rise to the surface. Memory is ephemeral; it shifts."

"You mean like I might invent something new?"

"I didn't say that."

His voice was gentle and patient. Books lined the shelves behind him, with titles like *Psychology of the Unconscious, The Paradox of Choice,* and *Applied Clinical Psychology: Roots and Recesses of Memory.* The hospital had provided a list of psychiatrists for me to try, but it was Marcie who had ultimately found him. He was an expert in the field of memory, and his accolades lined the wall. *He's the best of the best,* she'd said.

"The tape on the IV at the hospital was a new detail this time. You haven't mentioned it before." He straightened the stylish brown glasses on his nose.

"Well, that's groundbreaking. What's that have to do with anything?"

"Nothing maybe. I'm just bringing it to light."

"It's not a big deal. There are loads of details in memories. You don't always mention all of them. The tape was too tight, and it pinched the inside of my arm. There's one more for you. Happy?" I hadn't slept and wasn't in the mood for this, the process of rehashing details wearing on my frayed nerves.

"I know it's frustrating."

This was another new and unfamiliar thing, this new version of me—it was as if a dark river of resentment and anger now flowed beneath the surface, bursting through at the tiniest scratch. Like all the softness had left me. I saw it in my hardened eyes sometimes when I looked in the mirror at the new woman staring back.

"I'm sorry. I don't mean to take it out on you. I know you're trying to help," I said. "I just don't know what it is I'm trying to accomplish, what the goal is. To forget? Or to remember?" Tears pricked my eyes, and I clenched my jaw against them. He held out a box of tissues, and I took one, curling it into a tight ball in my fist.

"I was in a drug store the other day and came across the brand of bath products we'd used for her when she was a baby. I was so particular about it. Everything had to be natural. Everything had to be perfect." I smiled, picturing the bottles neatly lined up on her dresser. "I picked up a bottle of the lotion, and she was right there. I could smell her hair. Feel the soft cushiony pads of her bare feet." I clenched the tissue tighter into a shredded ball. "We liked it so much we kept using it, even when she got older. It's such a delicate, pure scent." The mixture of Hannah's skin and the baby lotion I'd lovingly spread on her so many times was in my nose, in my sensory memory as clear as if it had been that morning.

"Did you buy it?"

"Are you following me now?" I asked, jokingly.

He laughed. "Just a guess."

I'd purchased one small, guilty bottle, which I'd hidden in the nightstand drawer beside my bed at the apartment. I couldn't bring myself to call it "home" yet. Earlier in the morning, I'd been tempted to rub some onto my hands so that I could smell her all day. But I stopped just short, keeping the magic bottled inside, afraid of diluting the memory by overuse. I wanted to keep it crystalized, perfectly intact. I'd allowed myself one scant pass of my nose over the scent and then closed it. The sight of it, the presence in my world, was in itself comforting. Placed as one might set a portrait—which, of course, I did not have. My daughter—reduced to my imagination and a bottle of baby lotion.

"What are you thinking right now?" he asked.

I swiped a tear away, whispering through a tight throat. "I just miss her so much I can't breathe. Every day, I wake up, expecting her to run into the room. And then I open my eyes, and this hell begins again. I'm mourning the loss of a child, and I'm doing it completely on my own, and on top of it, apparently she's imaginary. I have to pretend like I'm fine. I can't even mention her. Otherwise everyone looks at me like I'm crazy."

That was the one good thing about these appointments. I could talk about Hannah.

"While the situation is unusual, the feelings *are* real," he'd said. "You need to work through them just the same as if it were a real child." Dr. Higgins had given me a book to help parents through the grief of losing a child. But every time I opened it, I felt like a fraud, and all I wanted to do was throw it against the wall. The five stages of grief didn't mean crap to me. There had been no funeral. No eulogy celebrating the personality of a sweet young girl, spoken from a microphone with a large picture of my girl smiling. No grave site to visit. The book talked about the sustaining power of friends and family, but, of course, the mere mention of Hannah's name set their skin crawling, and excuses were made to change the subject.

Everyone kept talking about "getting back to normal," but what does normal look like in a life that has been forever changed? I needed time to sit with my little girl. To breathe in her presence. To care for her if she was hurt. To mourn her, if mourning was what was called for. But I could do none of those things. I could simply exist in this new life, powerless, ineffective, and alone.

I drew breath in short, painful bursts that had nothing to do with the cracked ribs that had begun to heal, but instead the vise grip around my heart. Dr. Higgins watched me closely but allowed me space.

The silence stretched on, and I could hear the muffled voices of other patients visiting other doctors as they walked down the corridor outside. Dr. Higgins waited patiently. He wore a tan corduroy jacket over a chambray shirt and slacks—a pen in one hand, poised and ready for me to speak. His hair was cropped close, neat and tidy. One foot in a brown laced loafer rested patiently on his knee. He'd encouraged me to let these waves of emotion and pain pass through my body instead of forcing them away. Finally, I managed a deep breath and swallowed the hurt back down as it began to fade a little again.

"And I miss Graham. I miss my husband," I said, eventually.

"How are things going with him in the apartment?"

"He sleeps in the spare room. It's awkward and strained, and it's painfully obvious how much he hates me," I said.

"Are you sure it's not the other way around?"

"What do you mean?" I asked.

"I just mean that you should leave room for the possibility that maybe it's *you* who is so angry with *him*. Or that both of you have had a role in getting to this place. And that he's simply hurting."

"What could I possibly be so angry with him about to cause this much damage?"

"Maybe nothing. I just want you to be open to possibilities. Are you sleeping any better? Getting comfortable?" he asked.

"A little, I guess. As much as I hate admitting it, it is a nice place. Graham says I don't like it, but it looks like me. Like what I would do to an apartment in the city if I had money."

"That's good. It's a good sign."

"Is it?" I would never admit it out loud, but there were other things about the apartment that were odd. Like the way I'd reached for my toothbrush in the exact drawer where it was on the first night. I'd found my favorite coffee mug—one I'd had since college—sitting on the drying rack beside the kitchen sink. Pictures and knickknacks I'd collected throughout the years, displayed on shelves next to books—some I'd remembered reading and others I hadn't. In my bedroom, sitting above a small desk, sat a photo of my lilac bush in a delicate frame. I'd wept, cradling it in my arms, until no tears were left, the simplicity of it representing volumes.

It were as if there were two of me—one who had dwelled here in this place, and another in the home that I'd made with Hannah.

"You mentioned the luxury of it all, and how unaccustomed you are to it," he said.

The guilt sat heavy with me every time I touched the Frette sheets, or walked into my closet, filled with beautiful pairs of black pencil slacks and buttery ivories, rows of pricey white cotton, vintage designer jeans layered with paint stains. "Money was hard for us. We were struggling at home. Graham was having trouble with work. We budgeted constantly, trying to get bills paid. But hey, apparently here we were, living large the whole time. Who knew?" I had a bitter taste in my mouth.

"And how are things going with your sister?"

"Oh, I don't know. Marcie's Marcie. And she won't go away. So, I'm trying, I guess, but I just don't understand how we got past everything that happened. She keeps acting like we're the best of friends, and for a moment, I'll enjoy it, but then it feels like I'm faking it. It would be helpful if she or Graham or anyone could tell me anything at all."

"It all must feel so strange, Annie. But you are making progress. Little by little the memories you've created will fade, and you'll be settled in reality. But it needs to happen on your own. If they fill in the blanks, you won't have any way of knowing what's true and what's not. When your mind is ready, you'll get there."

"I don't want to get there."

"Why is that?"

"I'm afraid. Because if I try—if I finally realize that all of this has been in my head, then I'll have to say goodbye. I'll have to let go," I said. "It'll be like I'm giving up on her. And I can't do that. I don't want to forget her."

My mind flashed to one of a thousand memories that passed through my mind throughout the days.

"Don't let go!" Hannah calls out, as Graham and I take turns holding the back of her bicycle seat, jogging behind her. The air is frosty with the first days of March, but the sun is bright. We've gone to the nearby high school parking lot to practice. She's smiling beneath a glittery rainbow bicycle helmet, her eyes focused hard in front of her. Her knuckles are white, gripping the handles. "You can do it, sweetie! You're ready!" I tell her, cheering her on. And then, reluctantly, I let go.

CHAPTER TEN

Confabulation. That was the clinical diagnosis they'd given me. The word itself sounded absurd to me, but apparently it was a real thing. During my first visit with Dr. Higgins, he'd explained it in detail.

"What you have, at its core, is a memory disorder. It can occur in patients who have sustained damage, however microscopic it may be, to the basal forebrain and frontal lobes. Its hallmark is that it results in the spontaneous production of false memories. These memories may be elaborate and detailed, such as in your case. Or it can be something as small as what you had for breakfast."

"But this doesn't apply to me. I didn't have any brain damage. None whatsoever," I'd argued.

"It could have been something minute that didn't show up on any tests. I also think that it could have been sparked by repressed trauma causing what we might call a kind of dissociative fugue."

"What do you mean?"

"Your childhood and mother's death, the miscarriages, a looming divorce, the loss of your house, and now the accident—it's a lot for anyone. Your mind may have, let's say, taken a detour in order to help you cope."

After he'd put it that way, I'd seen his point.

~

Sensing my current frustration, he once again tried to explain the mess going on inside my head. "See, Annie, when you think of a memory, it's not like watching a perfectly preserved videotape. It's more like puzzle pieces that the brain must put together every single time we recall it to create a picture and tell a story. Sometimes pieces go missing and the brain compensates. It starts to draw from your imagination." Dr. Higgins gestured with his hands, illustrating the process of moving the puzzle pieces around. "We sort of fill in the blanks without realizing it. If a lot of pieces go missing, you can have problems because too much information has to be filled in. Sometimes it reverses spontaneously on its own. But especially in your case, given the history—"

"My history? Right. Back to the elephant in the room."

"Would you like to talk about it? Your mother?"

"It was years ago. It has nothing to do with any of this."

"Okay."

I bit the side of my cheek in indignation. "Look, I understand that everyone's treading lightly, worried that the same thing has happened to me. But it's not. Or at least . . ." I began to cry in frustration. "At least *it wasn't*! At home with Graham and Hannah, everything was perfect! I was perfectly healthy and perfectly sane. I had a perfect daughter and we had a wonderful life and the house was great and I put meals on the table and I wasn't some kind of unhinged artist and everything was perfect and I did not run myself into a tree on purpose. Everything was fine! I'm not like her. I'm not." But everything in my current circumstances was proof of just the opposite. With shallow breaths, I tried to stop crying. I suddenly realized how *not* fine I sounded, and slumped, defeated.

"You said the word *perfect* a lot. That's a lot of pressure to put on yourself," he responded calmly, after I'd finished my outburst.

"I just wanted everything to be okay, you know? To have a normal life," I said quietly.

"That's understandable."

"I guess I'm wrong, though, huh? I guess I'm like my mom after all."

"Hey, we don't know that." He raised his hands gently. "I just think it's a relevant part of your life, and I think it's helpful for you to talk about it."

And so I'd been in therapy.

And so far, it wasn't helping.

Because all I wanted was Hannah.

When I closed my eyes, I saw her on her swing, her bare feet kicking. The newborn silken feel of her starfish hands patting at my breast as I nursed her. I felt her hair, entwined in my fingers as I braided it down her back. I saw a spray of pasta sauce and noodles stuck on the wall and heard Graham's infectious laughter as we tried and failed to feed her spaghetti for the first time. The warmth of her curling into me in bed when she'd had a bad dream.

"No one could misremember this much. Five years of my life. The existence of an entire other human being," I said.

"You'd be surprised. I've seen some pretty wild things."

"But it's more than just memories. I *feel* her. I feel her existence out there," I said, pleading for answers.

"It's very real. There are even instances of *multiple* people believing the same imagined things at the same time. A kind of collective misremembering."

I found this hard to believe, and it clearly registered on my face, because he smiled.

"It's true. On a less detailed level, of course, but it goes to show just how malleable memory can be. Entire groups of people who swear they remember something happening this way or that. There are stories of it happening throughout history, but the internet even made a fad of it a few years back. Strangers comparing notes, all swearing they remember the same exact things from politics, pop culture, even geography differently than they actually are or were."

"How do you explain that?" I asked.

He shrugged and chuckled. "Can't! We know memory is highly suggestible, though, so it's likely as simple as that. Or it's just one of the mysteries of the brain that we haven't quite figured out yet."

"Like a mother who remembers having raised a beautiful little girl. Who remembers being married to her husband and living their life outside a small town in Upstate New York."

"I'm afraid so. I'm just telling you all of this because I want you to know that you're not alone. You're not 'crazy,' as you so like to put it. And look at what you have remembered correctly: You *did* live in that house. You *were* married to Graham. These things all happened. In fact, from everything he's told me—"

"You've been talking to Graham?"

"Don't worry. I don't share anything we discuss here. I just asked him questions ahead of time. It's helpful for me to get a baseline, a point of origin. And from what I can tell, your memories seem to be perfectly intact, just until the birth of Hannah."

"Which happens to be the most important event of my life."

"Let's go back to something you mentioned earlier for a minute. I'm curious . . . the day of the accident, when you and Hannah were in the kitchen talking to Graham about the missed flight, why did he ask you if you'd be okay that night, while he was away?"

"He was just being thoughtful, I guess."

His eyes crinkled at the corners, and he cocked his head. "Eh, I don't know. It feels like there's maybe more there."

"Are you asking me or telling me?" I paused, but he didn't answer, and I continued. "It's not a big deal. Just something silly." I didn't want him picking up this thread, wasting time leading to nowhere significant. But he waited, and I could tell he wasn't going to let it go. "All right, it's nothing." I rolled my eyes, trying to make light of it. "We joke sometimes that the house is haunted."

He raised his brow. "Really? Some people would be pretty freaked out by that. But you guys joked about it? Weren't bothered?"

"It wasn't anything major. Trust me, the house was fine," I said. The last thing I needed was for him to add one more thing to the list of crazy.

"Well, tell me about it. What were some of the things that made you think it was haunted?"

"Okay, I should never have said 'haunted.' That's a strong word. It was nothing. Hearing bumps in the night, that kind of thing."

"Did Graham hear them too?"

"Yes," I said, drawing out the word. "It was not just me, if that's what you're thinking."

He smiled. "Again, just a question. So, if it was nothing, why do you think he asked if you'd be okay? Seems like you think they're related."

I thought back, considering it more carefully. "Honestly, I don't know."

The last weeks before the accident were mostly blank, and I'd been having trouble remembering them clearly. We'd been working on it, but with no success.

"Take a guess," he pushed.

"It first came up one day when we were all sitting at the dinner table a couple years ago, and Hannah mentioned, completely out of nowhere, that she'd seen a woman walking into the studio above the garage. The entrance is outside the window in her room. She didn't say anything else, just that she'd seen a woman. It was so weird, and we dismissed it as her imagination. But it freaked us out, because we'd had a similar experience years earlier in the house for a little while."

"When was that?"

I thought back. "Around the wintertime, the year I was pregnant with Hannah. I was seeing things. I joked that it was pregnancy brain. One time, Graham said he heard footsteps on the front porch, but when he went to the front door, no one was there. Things like that."

"But then you started to see her too?"

"What made you say that?"

"You mentioned seeing a figure of a woman by the tree when it was raining. Before you and Hannah left the house."

My skin prickled and I shifted on the sofa. "Oh. Right." I waved it off, ignoring the chill that had run through me at the memory. "It's not a big deal. Just old house stuff. I'm not sure what I thought about that. It was just a little creepy, I guess."

I wasn't giving him the entire story, but most of it. It was a feeling, more than anything. Glimpses from the corner of my eye out in the field. The feeling of someone standing behind me. Hannah often mentioning seeing a woman. The house had taken on a strange feel. Not ominous, but definitely off.

"Did your mom ever talk about seeing things like that when you were growing up? Figures? Noises?"

"We're back to my mother." I shook my head and looked away.

"You try to change the subject every time she comes up. Have you ever talked with anyone about her suicide? It can't have been easy growing up—"

"No. She didn't talk about seeing things," I lied.

"There's my Annie girl." She smiles and pats the cushion next to her. I take a few hesitant steps, watching her closely at first. Then I drop onto the soft, worn sofa and snuggle into my mother, smelling the familiar hint of linseed oil on the fabric of her T-shirt. A book is open on her lap, and she sets it aside, wrapping her arm around me and pulling me inward. She kisses the top of my head. I look up, and her eyes are clear and bright, and I smile widely as relief melts into my small frame. She's having one of her good days.

Dr. Higgins was still and quiet. The clock on the shelf ticked softly while he watched me in that tense, awkward space that opens up when a therapist is giving room for words to bubble up to the surface. "It was nothing. Forget I mentioned anything. It was just Graham being thoughtful. It was probably about the storm, now that I think about it." The clock showed that time was nearly up.

"So, what are you going to do with the rest of your day?" he asked, changing the subject to round out the hour. I'd barely left the apartment in a week, and he knew it. Getting out of bed was an accomplishment. My goal was functioning, not living.

"I'm not sure what I'm supposed to do. I don't know what it is I do with my day. At home, my days are filled with the schedule of life and raising a child. But here? I don't know what to do. I don't know where it is that I go. There's nothing but almond milk in the fridge. I don't drink almond milk. And I'm sick of SoHo. I just want to get in a car and head back upstate, but there's nowhere to go there."

"Have you thought about working? You're an artist, after all. It might help. Art therapy can be pretty powerful. It brings light to the subconscious. If nothing else, it might be soothing."

I'd learned from Graham that I leased a private art studio space in the West Village, where he said I spent most of my days. "I'd been thinking of going but haven't gotten to it yet."

"It might be good for you to go. No pressure. You don't even have to do anything there. Check it out. I think you need to start getting out of the apartment more. Talking, existing outside. I know you feel like you're in a bubble right now, but the world is still turning."

Was it? Because it felt to me like the world had stopped.

CHAPTER ELEVEN

I plugged the address into the GPS on my new phone and traveled two subway stops away into the West Village. Leaving Washington Square station, I walked the tree-lined streets past Federal-style town houses, playgrounds, and vintage shops with a European feel, all while listening to the navigation voice chirp in my headphones in the early summer heat. *Turn left now. Turn right.* But I did so easily and was no longer surprised by my unexplainable ability to navigate to previously unknown places by memory. Somewhere in my brain, this version of me still existed and knew exactly where I kept the toilet paper, which pair of jeans were my favorite, and the location of an art studio that belonged to a supposedly successful artist named Annie Beyers.

I reached a five-story, redbrick building and stopped, fanning the sweat from my face. Upon entering, I took a freight elevator up to the third floor and navigated a warren of hallways with wary curiosity until I reached a white door with a black-script logo on the front, fashioned from my signature: *A. Beyers.* Taking a set of keys from my bag, I instinctively selected the correct one, and the door opened with a loud creak.

The space was larger than I'd imagined, with polished concrete floors and white walls. The windows were wide and tall, some frosted, others not, allowing afternoon light to filter in like gossamer. Exposed beams and metal air ducts ran the length of the tall ceilings, and numbered wooden racks lined one side, holding dozens of canvases. Along the other side of the room, paintings leaned against the wall. Abstract mostly, though some more impressionistic. I ran my hands along the tops of them, some tagged with notes like SOLD: F. KAUFMANN, my jaw dropping in awe at the astronomical prices as well as the common item at the bottom corner of each painting: my initials in chicken scratch scrawl. Empty canvases perched on steel easels over drop cloths as if waiting for . . . waiting for me, I guessed. A laptop with paint smears sat on an industrial table beside an oversize coffee mug and scatterings of paper that looked like my kind of organized chaos. A fluffy, well-worn linen dog bed sat beside it, and I smiled, immediately wishing I'd brought Charlie with me. There were enough supplies to stock a shop, sitting atop splotched pine shelves near a slop sink where clean brushes sat in metal cans.

"So this is where I spend my time," I said to the room, half expecting it to answer. I picked up a brush from the drying rack and walked over to the empty canvas. The brush felt heavy and comfortable in my hand, fitting to the curves of my fingers and palm as naturally as my skin. I dragged the bristles across the empty white space in ghost strokes, as if color might appear. The brush twirled in my hand on the rough, stark surface.

In my mind, I heard Hannah giggling.

"Plop!" I drop a dab of blue onto the tip of her nose. She dips her finger in a circle of magenta and—"plop!"—dabs one onto mine in return. Clearly thinking this is one of the funniest things she's ever seen, she picks up a brush and drags it across the paints again, this time over green, and draws a line onto each of my cheeks. I blow air into my cheeks like a puffer fish, and she erupts into hysterical belly laughs. "Again!" she says. Her loose lavender cotton dress hangs over bare feet on a splattered wooden floor. "Okay, what shall we paint?" I ask. "Flowers!" she chirps, and then twists her mouth, squinting her eyes in thought. "Annnd, a mermaid!"

"A mermaid, in a field of flowers?" I ask. She nods vigorously. "Hmm, a creative mind! I love it. Okay, you start!" She runs to the big pad of paper that sits on the table and dips her paintbrush into the children's watercolor set, filling the page with purple dots and circles and . . .

The lock jostled, startling me as I turned to see a young woman come through the door. She held a brown paper sack in one hand and juggled her phone and papers in the other. "Oh my God, you're here!" she said cheerfully. She looked to be in her early twenties, with long red hair and a black shirt dress over tights.

"Piper?" I guessed. Graham had told me to expect to see my assistant.

"Yes!" She nodded. "I didn't know you'd be here today! I'm so glad to see you!" She set her things down and walked over to where I stood. I wondered if she always had so much energy. "Is it okay if I give you a hug?" she asked, blinking her round green eyes beneath razor-sharp bangs.

"Um, sure. I guess."

"Ugh, sorry I'm all sticky—I definitely did *not* dress for the weather today." She hugged me gently, with waiflike delicate arms, and smiled sympathetically at the fading abrasions along the side of my arm. "Welcome back. Did you have a look around?"

"Sort of. Starting to, anyway."

"This must be pretty weird for you. I can't imagine," she said.

"Graham said he talked to you?" I asked, unsure of how I was to interact with her.

Piper nodded. "He did." She continued to move about the space while I watched. I fidgeted with the brush in my hands. She emptied the bag, which contained my favorite flavor medley of jelly beans in a plastic sack, plus several rolls of masking tape and two large bottles of polymer medium.

"I'm really sorry I don't remember you," I said, awkwardly. "I want to, but . . ."

She waved a hand in the air. "Oh God, that's the last thing you should worry about. It's totally okay. You know, when I was growing up, my neighbor, an older guy, had this car that he called the 'blue car.' Which was kind of a joke because the car was bright red. But he'd tell this story about how one day he woke up and suddenly he had a different car in his driveway. That he'd remembered the day he purchased the blue car. Remembered the first time he took his wife out on a date in the car, thinking as she got in that the blue matched the color of her eyes."

I blinked, trying to keep up.

She continued, "He said he remembered having to buy *blue* paint to cover a scratch from when one of the kids in the neighborhood dinged it with a baseball. But suddenly, one day, it was red, and no one, not even his wife, could remember ever having a blue car. He wasn't a wacko, either; he was an intelligent, perfectly normal person. But he was positive his car used to be a different color."

I wasn't sure what to say. "Uh-huh."

She stopped moving, her cheeks flushed crimson. "Oh my God, I haven't any idea why I just told that story. It's nothing like what you're going through. Just a dumb story. This is totally . . . just . . . ignore me. I'm sorry."

"It's okay," I said, chuckling a little.

"No, it's not, seriously. I had too much coffee." The energy in the room was lighter, I noticed. It was easier being around her than it was Graham and Marcie.

"It's fine. Kind of a funny story, actually. Your neighbor and I would probably get along well," I joked.

Piper seemed to relax a little. "It must be awful. Not remembering. Or . . . remembering something that no one else does."

I looked around the room and at the papers on the desk, with gallery names on them. For the first time, it occurred to me to ask: "Does everybody know? About my accident?" I paused. "Not that I really know who 'everybody' might be, but . . ."

"We've kept it pretty quiet. The schedule is fairly slow right now because you're supposed to be working on a new exhibit starting in the fall. So no one expects to hear from you, anyway. You're pretty reclusive when you're painting. The timing was good."

"I see. Well, there's a silver lining, I guess. The whole art world doesn't think I'm nuts."

"Not in a bad way, anyway," she said with a wink.

I liked Piper right away, warming to her more with each minute. She felt safe, somehow. Maybe because I didn't know her before this or maybe because she wasn't in my face pressuring me to "wake up" or whatever it was that Marcie and Graham expected me to do. She disappeared behind a half wall partitioned into an office area in the corner and switched on a lamp and her computer.

"Are you here every day?" I asked, listening to her shuffle some things on her desk.

"Not every day, but mostly. I give you your space to work, especially in the mornings and at night. But most of the time, yeah." She peeked her head around the wall, smiling. "Sometimes I still pinch myself that I get to work for you."

"Really? You do?" I found this hard to believe.

"Yes! You're pretty amazing, you know."

"No. Not really," I mumbled.

I looked through some of the papers on the desk, noting that many of them were bills of sale, or letters typed on letterhead from Mitchel Morris Fine Art—two capital *M*'s intertwined at the top of linen paper. I'd go through them eventually, maybe. But it was as if every touch of the paper burned the tips of my fingers just a little, anchoring me further into this strange world away from the safety of home, where I might be playing a game on the front porch and singing to Hannah. "What do you do, exactly, if you don't mind my asking?" I said, turning once again toward Piper.

"A little bit of everything, I guess. The usual stuff. Hopefully well!"

"The usual stuff . . ." I chewed on the inside of my cheek. Whatever that might be.

She narrowed her eyes. "Oh, I'm sorry. I thought . . ." She walked over to where I stood. "Okay, let's see . . . I manage your schedule—appointments, openings, meetings, sometimes personal things. I field your emails and your calls, filtering what's needed to you. I coordinate interviews and such, though the PR people mostly do that." She was ticking off her fingers, one by one. "I coordinate with vendors?" She said it like a question. "Arrange for shipping, deal with contracts, images, tear sheets. Oh, and all your travel arrangements." She waved her arms a bit. "And I keep the studio ready and waiting for you," she chirped, clearly proud.

"And you do this . . . all for me?"

"Mm-hmm!"

"Wow." How different two worlds could be. "And are you an artist yourself?" I asked.

She shook her head and laughed. "Noo, you don't want to see me with a brush. I mean, I love art. Just not actually doing it. I went to Bard and interned at Sotheby's in London. After I graduated, I was back here in the city. I was trying to get a job at a gallery, but that was like swimming with sharks. And not the hip, swimming-off-the-coast-of-Mallorca, Instagram kind of sharks. More like snarling sharks with chomping teeth and no cage." I laughed genuinely for the first time in a long while. As she continued, she explained how we'd met. A chance encounter when she'd been working part-time at a café down the street and I'd sat down at her table. "I recognized you and we got to talking. It was fate, I guess."

"Am I a good boss?"

"Most of the time." She smiled, wincing slightly. "I'm kidding. We get along very well, if that's what you mean. I love my job, and you've treated me very well. You stick to yourself a lot. And you can be, um . . ." She chewed on her lip, and I got the sense she might be being generous with her review of my supervisory skills. "I think you're just going through a lot. And you are an artist and all. But it works." Then suddenly a look crossed her face, as something occurred to her. "You're not thinking of letting me go, are you? I mean, I would understand if . . ."

"Uh, I highly doubt that." I looked about the bewildering room. "At this point, I'm not quite sure what I would do without you."

Her shoulders relaxed. "Phew. Okay, good. You had me worried there for a moment."

"You don't by chance happen to know what I was doing upstate that day, do you?" I asked. "The day of the accident. I can't remember, and no one seems to know."

She looked away. "I can't really say for sure. But . . . you had started going up there a lot."

How odd. "And you don't know why?"

She turned her back to me, refolding a towel by the sink. She hesitated, as if about to continue, but seemed to change her mind and shook her head. "No. Not really." She glanced at me quickly, and I got the feeling that she might know more than she was saying. "Sorry."

"Hmm. It's okay. Just thought it was worth a shot." Not only could I not remember the weeks preceding my accident in my *other* life, but they seemed to remain a frustrating mystery in this one as well.

She returned to where I stood. "Annie, I can't imagine what you're going through. But if there is anything I can do to help—I mean anything. Even if it's three in the morning. Just let me know. Okay?"

I nodded, grateful for this new person who had suddenly appeared in my world. "So, did I really sell all of these?"

"Yes, you did. And quite a few more. These are just the ones that are left from the last show. I'm waiting on the shipper to come and pick them up."

"What's in there?" I asked, pointing to a door.

She spun around, returning to her desk space. "Oh, just cleaning supplies and random things. Junk mostly." The phone rang. "I'd better get this. There's fresh tea." She smiled and pointed to a small electric kettle and an assortment of fancy loose tea cans near the sink. She picked up the phone, sitting at her desk. "Annie Beyers, this is Piper."

As she talked, I wasn't sure what to do with myself. I noticed the computer sitting at the table, and after making a cup of Earl Grey, I took a seat. It occurred to me that Piper had mentioned a website, which she updated regularly. It opened immediately as the home screen in my browser. After clicking around a bit, I went to the biography section, which was annoyingly sparse. The whole thing seemed a little pretentious, but whatever. A Wikipedia search yielded far more.

> Annie Beyers (b. 1977) is an American painter. She specializes in large oil paintings that document the connection between people and the spaces they occupy. She frequently chooses abandoned places and open landscape spaces as her subject matter, merging background and foreground layers of figures, melding them into abstract forms that seem to change depending on the perspective of the eye. In discussing her work, Beyers has said: "My intention is to capture on a painted surface the unbridled, personal longing of lost spaces and the energy left behind."

> Born in Scranton, Pennsylvania, Beyers is the younger of two siblings. Her mother was a photographer and artist, and her father an auto mechanic. Raised in a low-income neighborhood, Beyers credits her mother with cultivating her love of the arts. By nine years old, under the initial tutelage of her mother, Beyers was gaining local attention with her paintings. She

went on to attend the New School before leaving the United States to study at École Nationale Supérieure des Beaux-Arts, Paris, on a full scholarship, and then returned to New York. Following the suicide of her mother, Beyers took a lengthy hiatus from painting, going on to a successful career in the field of creative design and branding. Beyers later moved with her husband, architect Graham Beyers, to the Catskills region of rural Upstate New York and, after several years, returned to Manhattan and to painting.

Beyers has had numerous exhibitions at galleries throughout the world, including the Kunst museum in Ahlen, Germany, the Forum Gallery in New York, and the National Academy Museum, as well as notable private collections. Leading British art collector Oliver Hurst purchased one entire show, along with a contract for his London gallery. Her work has been featured in *New York* magazine, *Smithsonian* magazine, and others.

It wasn't possible this was me. It was as if I were reading about a stranger—my life passing by in words on a page. Painting had been a love, yes, but one that I had left behind years ago. They made it all sound so neat and tidy. It was entirely accurate, until the end bit about returning to painting. But there was so much unsaid. So much missing.

CHAPTER TWELVE

I had been working in the art department for a home design magazine when a coworker introduced me to Graham, who made every cell in my body flutter, cradling me into his life and helping to mend my wings until I could fly on my own again after my mother's death. A year later, we signed the lease on a third-story walk-up in Park Slope, spending our days working and our nights drinking cocktails and beer beneath twinkling rooftop lights with friends. A year after that, we were married. On the weekends, I'd lie with my head in his lap, listening to the cars on the streets below as if time were an endless buffet spread out before us. Graham had dreams of opening his own firm one day but spent late nights working brutal hours for a boss he hated. The hours got longer and the city got more claustrophobic. We started talking about kids. We began with a dog, and soon Charlie came into our lives, a bundle of shivering brown and beige from a shelter. Brooklyn's charm began to wear thin. The high-paced life had grown all consuming. Then there were the miscarriages. We needed a change. I needed air.

For Graham's birthday one summer, we were invited by friends to stay at their country house in Hendricksville, New York. During the week, the little town slept, but on the weekends it came alive with Manhattanites looking to escape. There was a tiny grocery store and two stoplights. The town library and the Hendricksville Bank were fashioned out of old Victorians on a main street with just one diner and one pizza shop. Alongside it ran a stream, where families came out in droves every spring to celebrate the annual duck race, watching the crystal-clear water wind through the trees in lazy little turns until it met the Delaware River. It was only two hours from Manhattan—close enough to run in for your favorite sushi fix and a day at the museum—but it might as well have been on the other side of the planet, with all its green air and fresh eggs. Like many others, we craved spaces where starry skies would glisten like jewels and bow down to meet the hayfields silhouetted against the setting sun. For all my dreams of chasing the cosmopolitan life in the big world, nothing compared to this utopia, which spoke to something I'd dreamt of much more deeply than art, since sitting on the cracked concrete of my childhood home. We began saving every penny we had. We collected Catskills real estate magazines and flipped through them like porn. Until one cold, rainy weekend when we rounded a bend and saw the Yellow House. It felt like it had been sitting there waiting for us. Until finally we quit our jobs and began setting up the freelance work we hoped would sustain us along with our savings.

WELCOME TO OUR PLACE IN THE COUNTRY. The hopeful wooden sign had been hung over the kitchen door on the day we'd moved in. The back of the sign bore our names and the date, etched in pencil along with a heart.

The place needed a lot of work, but it felt good to bring beauty to an aging home. We brought life to the house, eating dinners alongside hanging tarps, paint buckets, and worktables. For the first year, we dropped every cent into the house, spending our days learning about the differences between split-rail fence and four-board fence, agricultural zoning tax breaks, and when the proper time was to plant lettuce in the spring. And of course we planted lilacs.

In the evenings, we made love with the windows open to the fields beyond and, alongside everything else, learned about ovulation calendars. "Maybe we'll get horses for the kids one day," we mused.

There were others like us—Jim and Sarah, lawyers who had left city life behind to open an antiques shop, where they hosted farm-to-table dinners with friends on the front porch on Saturdays. Robert and Cecille made and sold handmade chairs at festivals on the weekends and worked in advertising when the weather wasn't suitable for barn work. Amy and Sam were novelists who also made fresh goat-milk soap and had once been commodities traders. All of us dreaming of a life where the kids we would one day have could run free in meadows instead of learning the ins and outs of clubbing in the meatpacking district by the age of sixteen. We stood side by side in line at the fire hall pancake breakfasts next to locals who had lived there for generations, who were both resentful and grateful for the new customers in their pretty little corner of the world; everyone dressed in jeans and flannels purchased at Agway next to the bins of chirping spring chicks. The only noticeable difference between us and them being the Hunter boots. North Face versus Carhartt.

But as the years went on, one by one, each couple we knew retreated back to the city, worn down by the harsh winters, the cost of propane, the crash of the housing market, and the lost novelty of woodstoves. The simple grocery store, once thought charming, was criticized for its lack of organic tamari. The schools where boys went fishing after the 3:00 p.m. bell didn't offer enough language classes. Bank accounts drained into broken wells and worn-out furnaces. Marriages disintegrated under the weight of all the snow, breaking at the seams beneath the farmhouse walls they'd tried so hard to mend on their empty fields of dreams. They took their babies and left.

We had been the ones to remain, our hearts captured by the scent of grass on the breeze and the way the light turned coral over a field at dusk. The sound of Hannah giggling as she swung in long arcs beneath an oak tree that glowed golden in the fall. Graham and I had stayed.

Or so I'd thought.

Beyers was twice awarded the Greenshields Foundation Grant for painting. She is represented by Mitchel Morris Fine Art. She resides in the SoHo neighborhood of New York City.

How could two lives, occupied by the same person, in the same mind, be so heartbreakingly different? I was there. *I was there.* I knew it. I remembered it.

And yet it was gone.

I went over to the tall warehouse windows and stood, looking at the traffic below.

"You okay?" Piper stood next to me, and when I turned, she handed me a tissue.

I nodded, taking it from her. "I'm fine. Thank you." But I wasn't. Not at all.

"Well, I'm going to run out for a bit," Piper said, a moment later. "Do you need anything?" She collected her keys and purse.

"Hey, Piper," I asked, as she was stepping out. "Can I ask you a strange question?"

"Sure, what's up?"

"Did I . . . ever mention someone named Hannah?"

"Uh, okay. Random. Hmm. Doesn't ring a bell. Trying to check your memory?" she asked, twisting her hair up into a knot.

"No. It's nothing. Never mind." Rain began to fall in little sprinkles, tapping at the glass. I watched a woman covering her stroller in plastic, trying to push it through the intersection as the blinking hand commanded her to hurry, and remembered doing the same thing myself with Hannah.

"But it's funny," she said a moment later.

"What is?"

"Graham asked me that same thing one time."

I spun around. "What?"

"Yeah. It was a couple months ago."

"He actually said the name, 'Hannah'?" My eyes grew wide. "You're sure?"

"Yeah."

My stomach dropped to the floor. "But . . . why would he ask you that?"

She shrugged. "I don't know, really. He stopped in one day, which he never does, so that's why I remembered it, I guess. And while he was here, he asked if you had ever mentioned the name Hannah. It was kind of weird, actually. He seemed sort of distracted by something."

My heart pounded in my chest.

"Is everything all right? You've gone a little pale."

"Fine," I muttered, as a thousand questions went through my mind.

She seemed to hesitate. "Okay, well . . . I'm sorry I have to run to an appointment." She retrieved her phone from her desk. "Text me if you need anything at all. Doesn't matter what time. Okay?"

A moment later she was gone in a flurry. While I was once again left alone, reeling in the dark, feeling like everyone knew something but me.

What was my husband hiding?

CHAPTER THIRTEEN

I had been calling Graham the whole way back to the apartment, with the call going straight to voice mail each frustrating time. The smell of browning butter wafted through the door as soon as I opened it, and I expected to see him, but my shoulders slumped when I realized it was Marcie in my kitchen. The resentment I still felt toward her sat in my stomach, hanging on to my solar plexus like an anchor. "Oh. Hey," I said.

"Hello to you too. Sorry to disappoint."

"I thought you were Graham. What are you doing here? And why are you cooking?" I tossed my keys into the bowl on the side table. "How did you get in?" Charlie ran up to me, and I immediately sat on the floor, scooping him into my lap, appreciating his easy warmth.

"I have a key."

"Oh, right." Would the strangeness ever stop?

"Do you know how I can reach Graham? I need to talk to him." I had no idea why I was asking Marcie, but she seemed to know more about our lives than I did. I began to wonder, then, if she knew more than she was saying too.

"Sorry, can't help. But don't worry. I'm sure he'll check in later. Anyway, the doctors said we were supposed to go on with normal life, right?" she said. "So, like it or not, I'm here," she quipped with a smile. "I'm making croque monsieur, and I picked up tomato soup." She gracefully flipped a sandwich with a metal spatula and stirred white sauce in a small saucepan. "Would you like one?" She sounded tentative, hopeful. "I know they used to be your favorite."

"When I was twelve and we called it grilled ham and cheese, sure." Marcie's face fell and she turned. "I just thought you might like something homey."

I bit my tongue. "I'm sorry . . . thank you."

"I was going to make omelets, but I'm trying not to eat eggs." She wrinkled her nose. "Baby chickens and all."

I kicked my sandals off and chuckled. "You do know that eggs don't have baby chickens in them, right?"

She looked at me as if I had two heads. "Of course they do. That's what they are. That's what the yellow is. The baby chicken."

I rolled my eyes. "Nope. A baby chicken comes from a fertilized egg. *Fertilized.* A regular egg is just an egg. No daddy. No baby."

Her eyes grew wider, spatula frozen in midair. "But then where does the egg come from?"

"Seriously?"

"Don't look at me like that. How the hell do *you* know anything about eggs? What, are you a farmer now?"

"Well, maybe if you would've ever bothered to visit . . ."

She shot me a look. "Anyway," I continued, "chickens create eggs regularly, just like women create eggs regularly. It only becomes a chick if she meets a special someone and they fall in love and go to bed together before she has a chance to lay it. Hens just lay eggs on their own. Those are the ones they sell in stores. So now you can eat your omelets and sleep at night."

She was staring at me, slack-jawed. "You just blew my mind. Seriously, like, changed my life. Am I the only one who didn't know this?"

I shrugged. "It's a common misconception." Seeming slightly relieved to hear this, and still excited by this new culinary development,

Marcie removed a long bread knife from a magnetic strip on the wall and sliced into a loaf of french bread. The kitchen counters were white quartz with sleek cabinets and perfect clean lines, nothing like the countertop at home, where rows of spices sat alongside jars of honey and olive oil beneath the farmhouse window over creaking wooden floors. A fresh wave of homesickness gripped my chest. I turned and closed my eyes, now welling with tears, recalling with perfect clarity the softness of silken feathers and the sound of contented hens.

The year we decided to start raising chickens, I was surprised to learn that you could just order them up from a website that offered every breed you could want and then have them delivered through the mail. Click "Submit," and a few days later a small chirping box of newly hatched chicks arrived at your post office. Two little Barred Plymouth Rock Bantams with dainty black-and-white stripes we named Noodle and Pot-Pie. One Frizzle Cochin that looked like her feathers had been blown out and crimped at a salon had started out Easter-chick yellow but had grown up to be the purest white. We named her Marsala. One fancy white Silkie was chosen as Hannah's favorite for two reasons: (1) because she looked like she was wearing a big winter coat, and (2) because she was a chicken who thought she was a lap cat. Dumpling. And, finally, one pain-in-the-ass American Game rooster who earned his keep in song and cocky, rock star beauty. General Tso, because he strutted around like he was in charge. He looked like he belonged on a box of Corn Flakes. "So rude," Graham had said, shaking his head when we both erupted in fits of laughter after coming up with their names. "I know . . . but it feels like we've saved them from a dark culinary fate!" I'd replied, and the names, originally a joke, had stuck.

I learned everything I could about raising pet chickens. They cheeped in their new home under a warmer in our living room for a few weeks, cuddling with a teddy bear Hannah had given them, next to a plastic Fisher-Price barn set, before moving into their real house—a gently used Victorian chicken condo complete with a flowery window box. The kind made for hobby farmers and city transplants who got the idea from Martha Stewart and hipster co-ops. We fell into neither of these categories, exactly, but building a henhouse wasn't in our repertoire of talents. Colorful paint choices were, however, and together the three of us spent a summer's day painting it with long strokes of matching butter yellow with decorative trim in grape purple. Before we knew it, it looked good as new.

With the loving care of a mother, I kept the chickens warm, fed, and happy throughout the seasons. I ventured into the ominous dark on countless nights to keep their water from freezing, to keep them safe. Dumpling curled into my arms in the evenings as I stroked the silken feathers along her neck. The General woke us in the mornings with a perfectly charming cock-a-doodle-doo from the front porch, which made him well worth the added trouble of keeping a grouchy rooster among the flock. They roamed in the yard, a chicken family, and came to me whenever I called, making their contented clucking sounds and seeking scratch treats. Charlie happily lazed beside them, tail wagging in the sun as they pecked at the grass around him. In return, we were gifted with fresh eggs of varying browns, cracked into the pan while still warm from the nest.

The coop was once badly damaged, during a particularly vicious storm, when it was toppled onto its side, leaving one of the doors permanently crooked on its hinges. We meant to fix it but kept putting it off. Noodle died soon after, the result of underestimated predators, the broken door, and her decision to take leave from the nest first on a cold morning. New and naive to it all, we hadn't realized how adept a fox could be. After a funeral, complete with flowers and scattered corn, we resolved to never let harm come to another one of the birds again.

My heart seized, missing my beloved pets. Wondering what had become of them in this new life.

"Hey, sweetie, it's okay." Marcie reached over to place a hand on mine. "Are you feeling all right?"

I swallowed hard against the lump in my throat and nodded.

I turned toward the door and leaned down to kiss Charlie on the head. "At least I've still got you, sweet boy," I whispered into his fur and stood, picking my wet umbrella up off the expensive wood floors and depositing it into a stand by the door. There were splotches of rain on the sides of my jeans, and I picked up a nearby cardigan to wear over my tank top, rubbing the goose bumps that had formed on my arms.

"How did you know I would be here?" I pulled a hair tie from my wrist, twisted my hair up into a bun, and fluffed the water droplets from my bangs. The bangs were part of this new life. I hadn't gotten used to them yet and constantly touched them, tugging them this way and that as I looked at the stranger in the mirror each morning. I took a seat at a metal stool at the quartz counter.

"I called the studio. Piper told me you'd just left. Anyway, I had to run some errands in the city, and Hunter is going over to a friend's house after school, so I thought I'd make a day of it and stop by."

"Ah. Of course, it was convenient for you," I mumbled.

I saw her wince slightly as she turned away, ignoring the barb. "So you went back to the studio? That's great! Did it feel good to be there?" She tucked her dark hair behind her ears, where it sat tidily on her shoulders. A pair of stylish brogues were tossed aside, and she padded around the kitchen in bare feet with manicured toes, opening cupboards with familiar ease.

"I guess so. I figured it was time."

"Anything click?" she asked, retrieving two plates.

"I really wish everyone would stop asking me that. But no," I said, answering her question. "Nothing seemed familiar." I paused. "But . . ."

Marcie turned. "But?"

"Just thinking of something weird that Piper said. It's just been on my mind, that's all." I considered it for a moment. "Never mind. It's nothing."

"Isn't she adorable?" Marcie said with genuine affection. "I swear that girl was sent from heaven. She's your right hand."

"I liked her a lot." I meant it, but my knees still wobbled as I thought of what she'd told me. I needed to talk to Graham.

"That's really great. I knew you would." She seemed relieved to hear me say something positive.

"So you're in the real estate business now?" I asked.

She brightened. "Yes, I am! Sort of, anyway. I stage homes. Mostly on Long Island and here in the city."

Despite our upbringing, or maybe in spite of it, Marcie had always had impeccable style. "Seems a weird change. Especially for someone living in Tokyo."

"Well, I haven't lived there for a few years," she said with a wink.

"And your degree in public policy?" I asked, pointedly.

"Oh, I don't know. I never did get around to doing much with that." Marcie was getting her master's when she met her husband, Tim. He worked for a large accounting firm, specializing in international corporate mergers. His job took him all over the world, and from their early twenties, the two had moved to a new far-flung city every few years.

"That's too bad, especially considering Dad worked three jobs to try to put you through college," I mumbled.

Marcie set the spatula down heavily on the counter. "Well, again, so sorry to disappoint. It's not like everyone gets full scholarships just by waking up in the morning and waving a paintbrush. Some of us have to actually try." She closed her eyes and took a deep breath. "Look. Let's not do this, okay? Let's just have a nice lunch, eat our sandwiches. Talk about the day. What do you want to drink?" Her words were clipped.

"Why do you always do that? Gloss over everything that might be slightly uncomfortable. Paste on a cheerleader smile."

"Well, it's better than spending every minute of the day miserable and complaining," she said, the smile gone.

"Uh, I think I have a right, all things considered. Excuse me for not wanting to spend the day giggling and braiding hair."

"Yeah, because we ever did that."

"We *did* do that. Once upon a time." I softened, recalling our childhood room, picturing us amid a pile of ribbons and brushes on our bed, playing "hair salon." And later, each helping do our hair for school in our mother's absence. "But that was a long time ago, wasn't it?"

"Yes. I guess it was." She set a sandwich on a square white plate, slicing it on the diagonal with more force than necessary. She pushed it toward me. "Eat."

"I'm not—"

"Would you just eat the damn sandwich!" Her eyes were filling with tears, and she tucked her hair again, absently. Neither of us spoke as I pushed the sandwich around the plate, and she turned to make another.

I started to take a bite but set the sandwich back down. I couldn't let it go any longer. I couldn't stand all this pretending. "What are you doing here, Marcie? Shouldn't you be off in Argentina with Tim? Or snapping selfies in Paris or pictures of your avocado toast?"

She huffed. "Even if you do hate me again, I'm not going to just leave you here like this," she said, keeping her back to me.

"Like what? Losing my mind? Mourning the loss of the daughter I made up? Missing my home? Missing my husband, who suddenly can't stand to be in the same room with me? Which part of that are you referring to? Or am I supposed to just smile and eat my sandwich?"

She turned and her face softened. "Annie—"

"Not like you would care, anyway. You didn't come to a single birthday party or the day she was born or . . . any of it. You didn't even know her."

"Know *who*, Ann?" she asked, delicately.

"And now she's gone." The tears came again, and I angrily swiped them away.

Marcie took a seat beside me, willing me to look her in the eyes. "Annie, sweetie, look at me. There is no Hannah. You do know that, right?" She placed her hand gently on my leg.

I gritted my teeth and nodded. "But I feel her," I whispered, both hating my sister and suddenly, oddly, wanting to rest my head on her shoulder. My emotions, like my muscle memories, had begun surfacing in new ways.

"I'm sure you do." She rested her chin on her fist. "That name . . . Hannah. You and Graham were so set on it."

I startled. "We were?"

She smiled. "I don't know what it was about it. But both of you loved it. Every time the talk of babies came up, one of you would say it."

It dawned on me then. Graham's mention of the word to Piper had probably been innocent. *Right?* My heart fell. I'd grown more and more paranoid over the past few days, and I realized I'd probably made something out of nothing. Everyone had been told to let me find my own memories, so I supposed it was only natural that I'd have moments of feeling off about it. I felt like a fool for grasping at something . . . anything to give me hope. The idea that a grand conspiracy was somehow keeping me from Hannah had been more comforting than the truth.

I wanted to curl up, retreat into a little shell where I could hurt and cry and exist without the world watching. "You think I'm sick, don't you? You think I'm like Mom."

"I didn't say that, sweetie."

"But it's what you all are thinking."

"We're going to get through this. We'll do it together." She leaned in, and I placed my forehead against hers. For a moment, I was comforted, but then it disappeared.

Push and pull.

"But I barely know you anymore." I stood, walking away from her.

"Yes! You do! For God's sake, listen to me. I know you don't remember, but we've been through all of this. This . . ." She waved her hands between us. "This . . . us. We got past it."

"Oh, I doubt that very much. Especially since you live six thousand miles away."

"*Lived*, Annie. Past tense. We moved back four years ago. Hunter is in school right now just down the street from our house. Do you want me to take you there this instant to prove it? Because I will."

"No." I shook my head, staring up at the painting on the wall. Resigned. "I believe you." The blues and whites, the chaos of a winter storm, felt like a reflection as I desperately tried to sort the details in my jumbled mind. "Remind me: How old is Hunter now?" I asked, a moment later.

"He's seven." Marcie smiled a little. "The two of you are very close. He can't wait to see you. He's been worried." I recalled having met Hunter only once, as a baby.

"I barely know him." And like a tide, the resentment built into another wave until finally it crashed. "You left him, Marcie."

"Who? Hunter?"

"No. Dad. And me. You left us," I said, quietly, still feeling the abandonment. The anger. "I don't know how to get past it."

She dropped her head and took a deep breath. "I did the best I could at the time. I wasn't a fortune teller, Ann. I didn't know."

"You took it all for granted. Everything was so easy for you and so perfect and pretty and . . ."

"Easy?!" she balked. "Okay, Ann. You want to do this now? Fine. Let's just get it over with and do it. I mean, we've already been down this road, but hey, whatever you need. Just say it, okay? Because obviously this isn't going to work until we hash it out." Her polished exterior had cracked, and the scrappy girl I knew from childhood was in front of me, spitting mad.

"Okay, you want to know what I'm thinking? Why it's completely bizarre to see you standing there like Mary freaking Poppins making your fancy sandwiches in my house?"

"Oh, don't worry. I know exactly why. Trust me. But please, go ahead." She held her arm out.

"Graham and I were struggling so hard, desperate to have a baby. Do you know how heartbreaking and excruciating infertility treatments are, Marcie? We were scraping together everything we had. And you just pop out a baby like it's nothing! Travel the world in all your expensive cities, like it's nothing! Easy breezy! Dad was so sick, Marcie. Mom was gone. And there I was driving back and forth to Scranton every damn week in the dead of winter, trying to take care of him."

"Here we go . . ."

"And where were you? Snapping pictures of bento boxes and perfect little white onesies and wooden rattles in Japan? All he wanted was to meet his grandson. To meet Hunter. Just once, Marcie. Do you have any idea how hard he tried to hold on?"

Her eyes had filled, and a tear escaped down her cheek. She clenched her teeth. "I have regrets, too, Annie."

"Do you? Do you really?" I spat.

"Yes."

"Do you know what I would've given to have had the chance to see him hold *my* baby? To hold Hannah? And I was there helping him when he was so sick and frail he couldn't even make it to the kitchen. I needed your help! He did everything for us, Marcie. Everything! Our whole lives! And you couldn't even bother to get on a plane to come home to say goodbye?" Marcie and Tim had tickets to bring Hunter home to see our father, but he died two weeks before they got there—while they were on vacation in Malta. Which, evidently, had been more important.

"I had no idea how bad it had gotten." Her voice was thick and swollen.

"I told you! Over and over, I told you he didn't have much time. In the end, he was asking for you every single day. Did you know that?"

"Yes. I did. You have told me," she said through clenched teeth.

"On the day he died, you were at the beach. On the beach! Holding a damn mojito, wearing a fedora, bragging about your fabulous life.

Seeing how many *likes* you could get, acting all perfect. Was that really more important than getting on a plane to see your dying father? More important than helping me just one tiny little bit?"

"I'm not going to do this again. I can't do this." Marcie slid her shoes on, trembling, and went to get her purse. She laughed humorlessly, swiping her eyes. "This is the worst case of déjà vu ever, I swear to God." She shook her head. "I know I made mistakes. I have to live with them. He wasn't just your father, Annie. Yes, you may have been their favorite. Fucking perfect, talented Annie. But I loved him." She pointed at her chest. "He was my father too. I am sorry, Annie. I am so, sooooo sorry. Is that what you so desperately need to hear? Again?" She put on a black rain jacket and went to the door. "You sit there, judging everyone around you, blaming everyone around you for the sadness inside you. For everything that you think is wrong. And you know what? Yes, I do think it's time you at least consider the possibility that what's happening here may be the same thing as what happened to Mom. Both of you, always lost in your heads. Two peas in a pod. Dreaming of whatever it is that's not in front of you until it appears and you start talking to air . . . or about imaginary daughters . . . until one day you jump in front of a train."

If she had hurled an anvil at my chest, it would've hurt less. And by the instant look of regret that flashed on her face, I could tell she knew it. But she wasn't finished. "Look around! You have everything you ever wanted, and it's *still* not good enough. People would kill for your life. To be able to do what you can do. I have a beautiful son who I adore. I am not going to apologize for that. He's the one thing I've ever done well. I'm sorry you don't have that. I am sorry you couldn't have every single thing you wanted. Really, I am. But you know what? Even if you did, you'd still find something to wish for instead. Something more. Something else. You need to open your eyes, Annie, and look at yourself for once. And realize that maybe the problem is you." She walked halfway through the door. "No wonder your marriage went to shit."

She slammed the door and was gone, and I found myself suddenly standing alone in the middle of the room, my mouth hanging open. I would have stood frozen in place, processing the words in endless echoes if not for the burning smell that startled me free. I went to the stove and turned the knob, removing the charred sandwich from the pan and throwing it into the sink.

When Marcie and I were small, we were so attached we used to sleep in our small shared bed, curled like twins in a womb, limbs intertwined. At only eighteen months apart, we were inseparable, prancing about in our own little universe, residing in one another's heads with ease. Two waiflike girls, twirling in pajamas with dark hair, climbing up onto countertops to steal snacks from the cupboard while waiting for dinnertime that might not come until far after our bedtime, when our father arrived home exhausted and smelling of gasoline and oil, while our mother floated about in her own world.

Somewhere along the way, as adolescence turned into the makings of adulthood, we forked off in different directions and never made our way back. And yet, everything she said rang true to an infuriating and unsettling degree, as if she'd peeled back layers I didn't even know were there. I couldn't imagine how we had finally managed to bridge the gap between us, or what that day may have looked like—maybe it looked just like this—but the softness of her nature and the tentative nurturing in her approach when I'd first arrived back at the apartment told me that something had, in fact, changed. Maybe forgiveness. Maybe a unified healing of the past. Or just the appreciation that we were the only two people who would travel an entire lifetime together, from childhood to old age, sisters bonded in our DNA. Funny thing was, I understood her, maybe for the first time in a long while. And this time, I also understood her as a mother. Hunter was her crowning accomplishment, the one part of her life that made her bubble with unwavering pride. While Hannah had been mine.

CHAPTER FOURTEEN

The loft felt empty and cold, and it was nearly ten o'clock in the evening when Graham finally got home. When he walked in, I took in the sight of him, handsome in a navy shirt and slim trousers, finishing up a phone call. "Hi," I said, releasing a breath of relief at the sight of the man who brought me such calm. I'd craved his company all day, but I'd recently learned better than to show it. "How was your day?"

He ended the call. "Just a day, I guess."

I wilted at his dismissive tone, pulling my knees inward on the sofa. "That's good. Are you hungry? I made lasagna." It was his favorite—layers of spinach and cheese and the sauce I'd perfected. Cooking it had made me feel a tiny bit less homesick. I stood, going to the table that I'd set hours earlier. But the look on his face told me that perhaps I should've made something else. Or nothing at all.

"Lasagna? Seriously?"

"I thought you might like it," I said, quietly, and turned so he couldn't see the hurt cross my face. He barely seemed to have time to eat these days, I'd noticed—working twelve-hour days and grabbing food only when he could. I innately wanted to be the respite from his work, settling into something as normal as a meal shared at the end of a long day. We had always taken care of each other. Clearly, I was wrong. I didn't know anything about what he needed or didn't need anymore.

"Thanks. But I grabbed something after work." He tossed his jacket onto a stool, avoiding my eyes. "I'm going upstairs to take a shower." I had been looking forward to seeing him all day, waiting patiently, and I wondered—had he simply grabbed a sandwich on the way out of the office? Or had he sat down to a meal elsewhere, with wine and good food and company that was anyone but me. I had the stinging realization that I had become little more to him than an obligation. I turned, suddenly embarrassed by the provincial dinner I had made him, thinking of the lovely food he was probably accustomed to now in this new life he'd acquired.

Everything was flip-flopped. Marcie and I, once estranged and bitter, were now the closest of friends. Graham, the love of my life, was a distant stranger.

Two weeks ago, I would've never imagined the possibility of such coldness between us. I could feel my brain shifting, my thoughts and memories getting sorted and refiled without my bidding. The good times were beginning to feel like part of a far more distant past than should have been chronologically possible: the gentleness of his touch, as if I were made of the most priceless china; the way I'd find him sleeping next to me, shirtless and wrapped against my back in the middle of the night after he'd stayed up late working; the way he would stroke my hair when I was upset. I needed to fix this somehow. If only I knew what it was that needed fixing.

The lights were dim in the living room while I sat on the couch, hoping he would eventually join me. Maybe if we just started with talking, it would help. I poured two glasses of wine and went up the steps to take him one. His shower was running, and I could hear him on the phone again, this time more quietly. "No, nothing is changing. She's still seeing the therapist. I know it's frustrating, but we have to wait. Keep her doing her normal routine as much as we can." His tone was hushed, and I hesitated near the top of the stairs, holding my breath. "She went to the studio earlier. No, I think it's fine. She's still not right about things, but she's hardly brought her up again, though, so I think we're getting there. But whatever the case, she can't find out. Not now." His voice came closer, and I quickly turned, sloshing a drop of wine onto my pajamas. "She's downstairs. I have to go," he said. A moment later I heard the shower door close.

I was at the kitchen sink, rubbing out the red wine spot with trembling hands when he entered the room behind me. "All finished with work?" I asked, my voice cracking a little.

"Finally, yeah. I'm exhausted."

"Who was that on the phone?" I asked. *And what is it they don't want me to know?*

"Nobody. Just a work thing. Kevin." He picked up the glass, attempting a smile that didn't quite reach his eyes. "Is this one mine?"

I nodded and returned to the sink, holding a towel against the fabric.

"I'm sorry about dinner," he said. "You don't usually cook, so it didn't occur to me to call." The sudden change in his tone led me to wonder if he suspected I might have heard him. It felt like he was handing me a bouquet of flowers while smelling like someone else's perfume.

"It's okay." I had wrapped the dinner in foil and placed it in the refrigerator.

He took a seat on the sofa, stretching his long legs out in front of him. It was such a natural position for Graham, and if I put my hands on the sides of my eyes, tunneling my vision, I could almost believe he was on our *real* couch. This was the first time he'd sat still, taking a break from his seemingly nonstop flurry of movement in my presence since the accident. I could smell the soap on his skin from his shower, and I wanted to bury my head into the crook of his shoulder and rest. I took my glass to the other end of the sofa, where he might have propped his feet up on my lap at one time. Instead, Charlie hopped up and spun around twice before plopping into a doughnut shape between us. *You know something's up, don't you, boy?* I thought, as he set his chin on my leg and sighed contentedly.

"What's going on between you two?" Graham asked, seeming both amused and curious. "I'm not sure which one of you is more attached to the other these days."

I smiled warmly, running my hand in long strokes along the dog's back. "It's a long story. I doubt you'd want to hear it."

He tapped the top of his glass absently, gazing into it, before eventually looking up at me. "I'm sorry I've been so impatient." And there he was, a glimpse of the caring man I knew.

"Thanks. It's okay. I understand it's been hard on you too," I replied.

"How are things going with Dr. Higgins?"

"Fine, I guess. I had a follow-up with the neurologist, and he gave me a clean bill of health. My ribs are still a little sore, but not too bad. Everyone's just telling me it'll take some time. To be patient. But it's hard."

"I can't imagine. But for what it's worth, I think you're doing better than you realize."

I looked up, a little surprised. "Really?"

"Yeah. Little things. Like did you notice how on your first night here, you went straight to the cabinet with the glasses when you wanted a drink of water? And you knew which sink in the bathroom was yours. Little things like that, here and there."

"I guess so." I was pleasantly surprised he'd been paying such close attention. He'd been so aloof.

"Baby steps, they said."

I nodded. "Yeah."

"So? Tell me your story. About Charlie." He seemed genuinely curious.

"Really?" I hesitated, afraid to add one more block to the wobbling tower.

"Really." He gave me an encouraging nod.

"Remember Dr. Pete?" I asked.

"The vet? Sure."

"Well, the way I remember things, about a year ago, Charlie started acting strangely, sleeping all the time. He stopped eating. So we took him in to the vet. He did some tests and found a clump of tumors on his liver. He said they were inoperable. There wasn't anything he could do." I cleared my throat, swallowing against the lump forming there. "We took him home. Did some research, which all said about the same thing. There were some trials showing promise, but there weren't really any guarantees at all, and it would only have bought a little time, without a cure. The clinics were far away, and he was just . . . it was too much. And Han—" I stopped, catching myself.

"It's okay. Go ahead."

I wavered. "Hannah had gotten sick a couple months earlier, and we'd had to make a trip to the emergency room. And the furnace broke, all at the same time."

"Of course it did." He rolled his eyes. It was always breaking at the worst time.

"Our credit cards were maxed out. It was all so expensive, and we just didn't have the money to drive to Cleveland and spend thousands of dollars for something that probably wouldn't have helped much in the end. It was hard." I stopped, listening to the rain patter on the dark windows. I forced a smile. "He was nine years old and had a really wonderful life. He was happy. We woke up one morning a few weeks later, and he was gone. We buried him out by the oak tree." I smiled sadly. "We planted flowers. But I took it really hard." I exhaled deeply. I didn't tell him that Charlie's bowls still sat in the kitchen a year later, and that his leash still hung by the front door.

I suddenly felt embarrassed, knowing how ridiculous I must have sounded to Graham, and sat up straighter. "Anyway, that's the story. For what it's worth. But he's here now, obviously. Perfectly fine," I chirped. Charlie was one of the only things that gave me peace here in this strange place. Graham turned the wineglass in his hand, back and forth. He always had nice hands. Long fingers and smooth, fair skin. I could feel those fingers on my skin, tracing the lines of me. Exploring. I felt heat hit my cheeks as a ripple coursed through me, and I looked up at him, willing him to look into my eyes, to see the love that was still there. But instead . . .

"Hemangiosarcoma," he said. He was staring at Charlie first, then glanced at me. "Right?"

"Yes. It was." It came out half in surprise and half in question. "But wait . . . how did you know that?"

As if sensing we were talking about him, Charlie whined a lazy yawn and shifted. "Part of what you're remembering isn't off. It just wasn't back at the house—it happened here." Graham went on to explain that the dog had been diagnosed with the exact same type of tumors, a specific type of untreatable cancer that affected only a handful of breeds. "We researched it, like you said. Got second opinions here in the city. Everything came back the same, giving him a month, maybe two to live. But we ran across the trials you mentioned." He looked up at me, eyebrows raised. "They worked," he said happily. And then added, "Sort of. I guess. We've managed to buy him a little bit more time, anyway. A year, so far. Hopefully a little more with the special diet and the supplements we're giving him. We keep a close eye on him."

"I wondered about those. I saw them in the kitchen."

"And yes"—he chuckled—"it cost us a fortune. But it's worth it."

"They said it might only give us an extra few months, though? That was it." I was still trying to process the turn of events.

"Yeah, but they don't know our guy," he said, winking. "Do they, buddy?" He sat up, ruffling Charlie's fur. He shifted his feet up to the table, relaxing back with his head against the sofa. I looked down at the dog between us, realizing then how deeply he had been sleeping during the day. How sluggish. As I had before, I'd just assumed it was old age. I rested my hand on him.

"You know that's the first time you've mentioned anything even slightly negative about your other life," Graham said. "The utopia in the Yellow House, painting flower fields, sunshine and roses."

"It wasn't utopia. But we were happy." An uncomfortable silence hung in the air but eventually passed. "What did we do with everything? Our things, the furniture. And I've been wondering, what happened to the chickens?"

"We sold most of the furniture with the house. When we first moved back to the city, we just had a small one-bedroom walk-up and didn't have the room to bring much."

I had an intense attachment to things—objects, furniture—and it surprised me that we had done this. "I must have hated that."

"Yeah. You did. I think it was pretty hard on you. But you did it." Inside, I felt myself harden, as if another personality were taking over. Without fully understanding it, I could feel the physical shadows of pain and bitterness.

There were a few items from home, but most of the furniture and decor in the apartment was new. I wondered what had become of all our things—some sentimental, passed down from parents or collected as we made a life together over the years. Where were they now? It was as if we'd left everything behind, abandoned. The absence of them hurt daily, as they took turns coming to mind, more things to grieve.

"An older couple, snowbirds, bought the house, though I have no idea what they'll do with all that space. And it wouldn't be cheap to close down for the winter. But whatever. Not my problem. We gave the chickens to Jennifer Michaelson."

"That's what Robert and Cecille did with theirs too," I said with a faraway voice, just above a whisper, for fear I might break in a jagged line down the center of my body. "Her place was nice."

Without thinking, I leaned my head onto his shoulder, cradling it into the soft spot it belonged. He allowed it, but only for a few moments, before he tensed. "I can't do this, Annie. I'm sorry." He swiftly moved away, and my heart sank.

"But I don't understand why. Could you please just tell me why?" I pleaded.

He seemed to struggle with what to say. "You don't love me anymore," he said, finally, the words bursting from him in a puff of relief. "Look, I know you think you do. But you don't. You haven't for a long time. And you're going to wake up from this whole mess and remember."

"It won't change anything. Graham, you're the love of my life." I took his hand and held it firmly.

He pulled it back. "No, I'm not. Trust me." I could hear the pain in his voice.

"I'm so sorry. For whatever I've done, or whatever we've done to get to this place. But can't we just forget it and start over?"

"It's not that easy."

"Why? Tell me what happened."

He sighed, running a hand through his hair. I knew he was frustrated and exhausted, and I hated that I was making things worse for him. "It didn't work. Nothing we did worked," he said. "The strain of it all, after we lost the baby, it was like a cloud descended upon the whole house. It was our last shot. We couldn't afford any more treatments. You were miserable. All of our friends had moved back to the city. I was working, trying to keep us afloat. And failing spectacularly, I might add. You were trying to take odd freelance jobs, but hated commuting. You started locking yourself up in the studio and painting nonstop. You wanted to get back to the art world. But you flat out refused to consider leaving. But we had to go. I had to sell the house."

"What do you mean, *you* sold the house?" I asked.

"I mean I sold the damn house! I had no choice!" He stood, running a frustrated hand through his dark hair.

"I didn't want to? We didn't agree?"

"You didn't have a choice! The damn place was a money pit, and every empty corner of it reminded us of what we'd lost. It was never meant for two people. Every corner of it was haunted by the family that we would never have, down to the half-painted walls in the nursery and the swing in the back. There was nothing left for us. We didn't talk. We just . . . existed, floating around one another, surviving. So I made the best decision I could—for both of us. Our life was here. Our friends were here. But you never got over it. And everything . . . *everything* was my fault." The anger poured off him in waves. "You finally got your career, but all you talk about is going backward. What you've lost. What you've missed out on. Things moved on, but you were miserable here too. Going on about your life without kids. Wanting to be back upstate. It was like the mere sight of me reminded you of everything you'd lost. I just . . . I couldn't do it anymore."

"I heard you on the phone. What are you hiding from me?" I blurted out.

"What? Nothing," he said, looking away.

"What do you know that you aren't telling me? What are you so afraid I'll find out?"

He held his hands up. "Look, Annie. I'm sorry. I wish I could be here for you. I thought I could do this, but I can't." He stood suddenly, heading up the stairs. When he returned, he wore a light jacket and carried a bag.

"Please don't go."

"Here." He dropped a book on my lap, and I recognized it as the journal I'd kept for years. "Read it. I don't give a shit about what the doctor said. This has to stop. I can't sit here and listen to you talk about a daughter I never had. It hurts me, too, Annie. I wanted kids too."

"Why did you ask Piper about the name Hannah," I said pointedly, realizing then how much I needed to know.

"What?" He looked confused.

I stood, walking toward him. "She told me that a few months ago you asked if I'd ever mentioned the name Hannah."

"Oh," he said, eventually. "That. It was nothing. I just . . ." He exhaled heavily, his eyes slowly closing and then opening again. "We were thinking of giving it one last go." His voice was softer now.

"A baby?" I asked.

"No. Us. And . . . it was just one of those silly, hopeful moments, I guess. Asking what someone thought of a name. Nothing more than that." He gave me a sad smile. His cheeks had reddened a little, as if he'd been embarrassed by the admission.

"But it didn't work out?"

"Nothing ever did—did it?"

"Maybe it could now?" I pleaded, taking his hand in mine.

"No." He stepped back, holding his hands up. "It can't. I wanted the life we planned, too, Annie. But it didn't work out that way, and I won't do this again." His eyes filled with tears. "You were enough for me, but I was never going to be enough for you. *You're* the one who gave up on us. Not me. So, I've moved on. And when you wake up from this mess, you'll be glad I'm not here." He went to the door.

"Please don't go, Graham. We can figure this out."

But the look on his face told me that I was wrong. I could feel it. Deep down, from the mysterious place where my memories of this life lived, I understood that so much damage had been done, nothing could heal it. My heart was breaking because I stood there in love with this man, knowing I'd lost him.

Some things, like fences and furnaces, old houses and marriages, were too broken to fix.

CHAPTER FIFTEEN

All around the mulberry tree
The monkey chased the weasel
The monkey thought 'twas all in fun
Pop! goes the weasel
A penny for a spool of thread
A penny for a needle
That's the way the money goes
Pop! goes the weasel

Hannah hums along in a little tinny voice, echoing like an image in a hall of mirrors. Pop! Graham pops Lil' Llama's head over the chair in the corner of her room, sending Hannah into a fit of laughter, darting away and then returning quickly as the second verse begins. Children's music is playing through a small speaker in soft, musical tones while early-morning sunlight casts bright rectangles of light onto the floor. I smile, recalling the way my mother had often sung that same song to me, and now it was a favorite of my daughter's.

In a corner sits a rocking chair next to a window, where in the glow of a night-light, I'd sat with the baby nursing in my arms, staring out at the moonlit fields while listening to the coyotes sing their eerie songs on countless nights. The room was adorned in pale sage and powdery lavender during the last few weeks of my pregnancy.

I smile from the doorway as I watch my two favorite people in the world flitting about the room, and then laugh as I realize how Graham would hate the idea of being described as "flitting." The song continues to play, and Hannah has picked up two more stuffed animals to join their morning party. I tiptoe in behind Graham and take a seat in the rocking chair, and as I do, Hannah stops the parade. Her eyes light up, and she tentatively walks toward me as I open my arms, inviting her to barrel into my lap, which she doesn't. The chair lets out a creak, and Graham turns his head, looking over his shoulder to where I sit, rocking back and forth in the tiniest arcs. Hannah holds Llama up to show me. But as he watches his daughter, I see the smile leave Graham's face as he pales, and I wonder what's wrong.

"Snack time, little bug," he says, barely glancing at me, as if I weren't even there, and quickly scoops her up as she begins to cry.

"Mommy," she says, reaching out for me. "I miss her."

Graham hugs her tighter, and I see his eyes welling. "I know. Me too."

What are they talking about? "I'm right here, guys!" I say, standing.

"Why don't we pick a few lilacs to bring to her. Sound good?" Graham says.

Bring to me where?

They turn the corner to leave the room. Over Graham's shoulder, Hannah waves a tiny goodbye.

All around the mulberry tree, the monkey chased the weasel.

CHAPTER SIXTEEN

I woke in the morning to the melody of the children's song singing through my head, and the scent of lilacs as the scene began drifting off with the night. For a precious moment, I forgot where I was, certain I was in my own bed, in my own house, back where I belonged. But it was just a dream. I tried to lasso it for a little longer. *Please stay,* I begged it. I clenched my eyes tight, the feeling of Hannah's sweet presence, about to jump into my arms; willing Graham to tell me what was wrong. But like morning fog, it retreated, leaving only the tiniest sparkle behind on the tips of my thoughts. Hoping to find it again, I pulled the covers over my head.

~

"So you cheated," Dr. Higgins said with a chuckle later that afternoon.

"What?" I asked, startled. My thoughts had drifted to the waking dreams I'd been having, more real than dreamlike.

He smiled wryly, an eyebrow raised. "You were talking about the journal Graham gave you."

"Oh. Right. Yes, I cheated and looked at it. I had to know. I can't do this anymore. I tried it your way, but it isn't working. If I'm going to live this life, I need to know what this life is."

"Hey, look, you're the captain of this ship, not me. If you felt like you needed to read it, then I'm glad you did. What did it feel like?"

I thought about this for a moment. "Good, I think. And bad. It was a mix, for sure. At least I don't feel stupid anymore. I felt like I've been walking around with a blindfold on, bumping into walls while everyone around me watched. I feel more in control this way. But you were right. It's complicated. Now I have two versions of everything in my head and am starting to have a hard time distinguishing between what I'm actually remembering versus what I'm supposed to be remembering."

"Did it help to put any pieces together?" His legs were crossed as he sat in a leather armchair, a pad and pen on his lap. A small clock ticked in the corner.

I had never been very good at consistent journaling. I would write in it every night for months and then forget about it for a year as it collected dust on my nightstand. After Graham had left the night before, I'd opened it eagerly, expecting all the answers to be on the pages. Instead, I saw that the entries only went up to the time when we'd left the house and moved back to the city, when it seemed I stopped writing. Still, there were details that filled in the outlines drawn by Marcie and Graham, pictures that came to life with the proof of my own handwriting. Dozens of entries, some short and some that were pages long.

October 13, 2008—I heard the baby's heartbeat today! She's a strong one, I can tell! Graham has a way of falling asleep with his hand resting gently on my belly now. I did something that I didn't tell him about—I picked out a little pink llama from a store today. I couldn't help it and I know I shouldn't have, but I did. He has started emptying the room to get it ready. (I can't even dare say the word, but it makes me smile to think about. Nursery.) I returned from Dad's last night and will head back this weekend to finish packing up. Found some old things of Mom's. I wish they could be here to meet this beautiful little person growing inside me . . .

February 17, 2009—I've had enough of this weather. I swear, it seems the winters get more brutal every year. Graham had to shovel a tunnel for Charlie to get out to pee, and it's hilarious watching him walk between walls of snow that are three feet tall on every side. Little Eskimo dog. We've been cooped up for a day without power, keeping cozy by the fireplace. Graham used the time to start painting the nursery. Six months! Three to go! I've been reading . . .

May 29, 2009—I tried to go into the room today. The hallowed room at the end of the hall with the half-lavender paint job. It looks like a ghost in this big fucking house. I talked to Marcie briefly today. She says she's coming to see us this summer, but who knows. I won't hold my breath. (Though between me and these pages, I miss her so very much.) I should be changing diapers and singing lullabies right now, this week. This day. Instead, I'm going to paste a smile on and put together some kind of dinner. For just the two of us. Two. Two. Two . . .

March 5, 2010—Kevin called Graham about the Hudson at Berkeley Residences project again. It's a good job. Maybe it's what we need, right? But then I think about selling this house, with all its ghostlike dreams haunting the empty rooms, and I think—no. In my mind, I know it's probably the best thing to do—to leave. It's too big for us, the walls feeling like they're expanding and contracting at the same time. With the garden and its invading weeds and broken gate, reminding us of our failures every time we look outside. But in my heart it's like it's part of me, and leaving it feels like abandoning a part of myself. This house, it breathes. I've been having dreams about painting. And other dreams I don't talk about. Last night, I woke to the sound of a baby crying and found myself standing in my nightgown in the lavender room. She'd be here now. I wish I'd painted it blush pink instead. Painting. Painting. Maybe I'll start . . .

April 20, 2012—I walked the gravel on the driveway for the last time today, feeling the crunch beneath the leather soles of my shoes. This house, with all its mystery and hope, no longer belongs to me, and we're back to prepare it for the new owners. I've fought Graham every step of the way, but I lost. Because deep down, I've accepted he's right. Though right now I hate him too much to tell him. Everything inside me twists at the thought of leaving. This house was the kind of place where people land for good. A final destination home where roots are planted, beloved pets are buried, picnics are held, and grandchildren visit. Most people don't leave yellow houses. And most people don't leave things behind. But sometimes, they do.

As I write, I'm sitting on the porch swing, where I've sat countless nights watching dusk turn into countless stars. My arm is being tickled by the green leaves of the lilacs. Every year, I've trimmed the blooms, adding them to vases and filling the rooms with their powdery scent. This year, I won't be here to snip them, and the branches will be filled with crusted brown remnants of the blooms that will go unseen. It'll be the grandest year for them yet. The branches tower a good eight or nine feet. But lilac bushes don't belong next to a porch, I've learned. They're a wild and unruly breed, and they'd begun to block the views. The new owners had commented on this. They are planning to cut the lilac bushes to the ground when they arrive later this summer. Pull up the roots. Replace them with something tidier. "You did a good job," I whisper to them. "Thank you." Lilacs don't grow where we were going. And the city is no place for a porch swing.

Graham is calling me now in his hardened voice. He's irritated. It's time to leave. My skin prickles with anger as he insists on ruining even this, my last goodbye. I look out onto the silos. When the breeze picked up a moment ago, I swore I heard the sounds of a child's laughter in the rolling waves of uncut timothy hay, and then, from the corner of my eye, a woman who vanished the instant I turned my head, becoming only a small tree. I'll even miss the ghosts . . .

After reading the journal, a new reality began to take shape in my mind alongside the "other" life. Graham began to take on new form, and suddenly, I no longer craved the feeling of his arms. In the pages I read, I saw a new side to him, and a new side to myself—hardened and angry—and I now understood where this part of me had come from. He was wrong—I didn't blame him for losing the house or for all the sadness and lost dreams. What I blamed him for was the way he'd handled it. The lack of compassion and the condescending way he'd gone about forcing the decisions before I'd been ready. He thought I blamed him for the broken house, but I equally felt like he blamed me for not having a baby. For my inability to conceive a baby or carry a baby or, as it seemed, for the bad clumsy luck of slipping on a piece of black ice and losing our daughter and our last chances at carrying a child of our own. He blamed me for dreaming of the house in the first place. I had hardened too. But in fairness, it seemed as if I'd failed to acknowledge that he may have been hurting too. His losses had sharpened his softness. He had buried himself in his work and in the fast pace of the city, while I'd hidden away in a studio. There was a permanent divide between us.

But I learned that in those times I had also been given the gift of my sister. A month after I'd lost the baby, Marcie showed up at my door, and was a surprising comfort to both Graham and me. Slowly, acceptance had turned into forgiveness, and forgiveness had turned into friendship. She'd moved back to the States to be closer to me. I discovered we'd become inseparable once again; two sisters, allies, intertwined.

"I was getting a little worried about you. You missed your appointments last week," Dr. Higgins continued.

"Sorry about that. I've been working through some things. I found something else. I was going through some boxes in the closet and found a couple baby things I must've kept. Remember when I told you about Lil' Llama, Hannah's toy? I almost jumped out of my skin when I spotted her."

"I can imagine."

"Until I saw how pristine and new she was. Still with the tag. Last time I saw her, in Hannah's arms, she was faded from a hundred washings. Hannah never left her out of her sight. But it was brand-new. Never used. Something about seeing it that way . . ." My arms were tightly crossed, and I curled inward against the tight knot forming in my sternum, shifting on the leather sofa. "Maybe I need to start letting go. Maybe in some weird way, I did . . ." I took a deep, heavy breath, willing the words to form. "Maybe I did make it all up."

"Do you really believe that?"

"I'm trying to. Intellectually, I know it's the way things are. But here, in my gut, I miss her every second. I *feel* her every single second. But then later, I don't. I can sense her fading sometimes, like fog slowly retreating. And I feel guilty for it, but at the same time, I know what I'm supposed to be doing to get past all of this, so I try to keep it at bay. It's this constant back-and-forth." I cleared my throat, sitting up straighter, willing tears away. Anger and frustration were fortifying, I had found. "Anyway, I threw away the baby lotions. I put Lil' Llama, or . . . whatever we would've called it . . . back into the box and sealed it up. I have to get on with things, I guess, but . . ."

"But what?" he asked.

"I've been having these weird dreams." I had hesitated to bring it up, but they were growing more unsettling each day.

He leaned forward slightly with eyebrows raised. "Oh yeah? Tell me about them."

"It's like I'm watching her. Like a fly on the wall. I can see her, sometimes with Graham, playing in her room. He can't see me, but she can. I wake up in the morning and swear I hear her voice singing a song in my ear, or hear the clock that ticks on our mantel above the fireplace. It's so real."

"The brain is capable of incredible things, isn't it? Art. Music. Stories. Piles of bedsheets turned into magical forts by a child's imagination. It's capable of creating wondrous, extraordinary things. We've only begun to scratch the surface of understanding. You're making some progress, Annie. Just be patient with yourself. One day at a time. You suffered tremendous loss and disappointment, and you eventually simply had enough, and the dam broke. But now you're past that. Now you're beginning to heal. The false memories will begin to fade. Or . . ." He seemed to waver.

"Or what?" I asked.

"Or maybe they won't. You need to accept that possibility as well and learn to live with it. You have a lot to be proud of. Things like your career. You talk a lot about the isolation you felt in your house, even with Hannah. When we discuss it, I hear all about Graham and Hannah and the house, which is wonderful, but what about outside of that? You sound lonely and unfilled in other ways. Here, today, right now, you have your sister, you have an enormously successful career and a great life in the city, and, from what Piper has told you, you have an active social life."

I rolled my eyes. "Piper says I'm reclusive. I don't think I have many friends. The social life is just work stuff."

"Still. That's a lot to go on. You can build on that. And listen, every day you have a chance to write new beginnings in your life. You're angry that you lost your house. The dream of conceiving a child. I get that. But you have the means now to buy another house in the country. One that no one can ever take away. Obviously loads of people from the city do that. Spend your weekends elsewhere. Take a trip upstate. You have a whole life ahead of you. There are other ways to be a parent. You have lots of options; you just have to be willing to open yourself up to happiness."

I couldn't think about any of that, at the moment. But I understood what he was saying.

"I guess no life is either all bad or all good," I said.

"Now we're getting somewhere," he said, smiling warmly.

"My mail is filled with get-well messages from people I've never heard of. I've been letting my phone go to voice mail because I never recognize the caller."

"You could start there," he suggested.

I shook my head. "I don't think so. Not yet, anyway. Everyone besides Graham, Marcie, and Piper just think I've been in an accident. They've kept a tight lid on the rest of it, which I think is smart. It's not the best idea for people to think an artist with an upcoming exhibition has lost her marbles. There's too much on the line, and the art world is too fickle."

"I see. That makes sense. Maybe in time, though. You'll figure out a few people you can trust and let them in. Rebuild friendships. Or, of course, make new ones."

I nodded, trying to come to terms with it, while feeling like every word I said was in some way a betrayal.

Maybe things would have been different if it hadn't been raining that day, pouring down in thick sheets over oiled concrete. If the storm hadn't rolled in at just four o'clock, in time for me to call Hannah into the house and notice that she had a fever before the doctor's office had closed. It was just a little fever. An ear infection left over from an everyday sniffle, easily treated at an urgent care on Saturday. I could have waited. Or maybe things would have been different if I'd have let her wear her gold shoes when she first asked, instead of taking the extra twenty seconds to switch to the boots, and then the truck would have pulled out twenty seconds before we turned the bend, and we'd have made it to the doctor. Maybe I would have still been a mother. *Unimaginable heartbreak.* I'd heard that said about parents who had lost children. But I could imagine it; I could feel it, even if it wasn't permitted. But unlike the loss of a real child, with each passing day it was retreating like fog. Not lessening, but rather fading imperceptibly. Motherhood, separating from my body.

CHAPTER SEVENTEEN

"I thought I was meeting Graham," Marcie said. A look of surprise had crossed her face a moment earlier when she'd spotted me at the table and a hostess brought her over to where I sat. She looked beautiful, with soft, petite curves and the barest makeup on her lovely skin. Her dark hair sat neatly on her shoulders, and she carried herself with effortless grace. She had a wary expression and I could see in her eyes that she was cautious, afraid of being hurt.

"I asked him to call you," I said, standing. "After the other day, I was worried you wouldn't come if I called."

She gave me a stern look. "Of course I would come. Don't be ridiculous. But, Ann, if you're here to—"

I wrapped her into a tight hug and held her there, cherishing the feel of her. "I love you, Marcie."

She tensed, unsure of what to say. "Oh. I love you, too, but . . ." She pulled back. "But I don't understand." Then her eyes grew wide. "Oh my God, have you gotten your memory back?" she chirped, smiling widely as she clapped her hand over her mouth.

I shook my head. "No. Graham gave me my journal, and I read about everything that happened between us. I understand a little better now."

"You do?"

"It's weird. I know it, and I believe it because I read it—in my own handwriting. It's just going to take a little time for it to sink in. But if you can bear with me, I'd really like to know this version of us. Because, honestly? I have missed you so much."

She pulled me back into a hug. "I know. Me too."

"You were there for me through it all, weren't you?"

"Well . . ." Her eyes welled with tears. "I tried to be, anyway. I tried to make up for it. For not being there for Dad. And for you before. I couldn't let you go through something so awful again without me there. I couldn't . . ." She shook her head, choking up.

I rested my hand on her arm. "It's okay. I understand. Or, at least, I do in the best way I can without remembering it in my own mind." It was more than that, though. I felt it in my gut and heart as well. Even without the specific details in my mind, I could sense the truth of our reconciliation. "I'm glad we found our way back to each other."

We took our seats at a table by the window, and a waiter approached, asking if we'd like something to drink.

"I'm sorry about last week," I said.

"Oh please, it's not the first time we've fought like two cats." She waved a hand, dismissing it, but I could tell that she'd been hurt. She swiped beneath her eyes, carefully fixing her mascara. "It's fine. I get it. Believe me, as hard as it was for you to forgive me, it was nothing compared to how hard it was to forgive myself." She looked out the window at the diners talking at small sidewalk tables. "I think I was so wrapped up in my world. So wrapped up in trying to prove how I'd gotten out, gotten away. 'Look at my amazing life, aren't I awesome? I live in Rome, or Tokyo or wherever,'" she said sarcastically and rolled her eyes. "It was like everything I'd left behind here was encapsulated in a bubble, never changing. Even though I knew it was happening, I just couldn't imagine Dad getting old or sick. He was always so strong. I just let the time pass, and then suddenly it was too late. And I left you here to deal with it all." She held my eyes. "I really am so very sorry, Ann."

"I know," I said. "It's okay. I know."

A moment later, the waiter brought drinks, and Marcie squeezed a lemon into her iced tea. "So, tell me what I've missed. You're coming around a little, I guess?" she asked. "With everything?"

"I'm working on it. I'm going to try to move forward."

A small glass containing a stem of magenta sweet peas sat between us on the table, and I leaned down to smell them, but they had no fragrance. Marcie watched the gesture and raised an eyebrow.

"I thought I smelled flowers," I explained. "Must be someone's perfume." I hesitated and looked around.

"You said something like that the other day too," she said. "At the loft. You asked if I was wearing lilac perfume."

I nodded, recalling. I'd also gone looking for some sort of fragrant candle that might be there.

"I smell them sometimes. Lilacs. It's weird." I smelled them almost every morning, as soon as I woke. At random times in the day, in the oddest places, I'd catch a scant wave of the scent. "They must be stuck in my nose," I said, attempting to laugh it off.

"You sound like Mom," Marcie said, smiling.

"I do?"

She nodded. "Remember when she tried to grow her own?" I shook my head, and Marcie continued, "You may have been too little. She tried to plant some lilac seedlings in that tiny little patch of grass between the basement windows and the driveway. Needless to say, they didn't grow."

"We used to pick them for her from the neighbors' yards."

Marcie smiled, a faraway look on her face. "They were her favorite, weren't they? They were the only thing that calmed her sometimes, remember?"

I nodded, recalling the two of us placing hopeful glasses of the blooms on her bedside table in a darkened bedroom. She would open her eyes and smile at us.

"I used to wish they would grow all year round," Marcie said.

"I grew them," I said. "At our house."

Marcie laughed, clearly finding great humor in this statement. She knew full well that I could barely keep a cactus alive. "That's funny. Sure you did."

"Honest, I did!"

She laughed again. "I find that even more difficult to believe than you having an imaginary family." I winced slightly. "Ouch," she added quickly, looking impish. "Sorry."

I waved it away. It was almost funny, even I had to admit. "I know. It's ludicrous. I can't grow anything else in the world. But I did grow lilacs." I smiled then. "Lots of them."

Marcie's eyes grew soft, watching me talk about the flowers. "Mom would have loved that," she said. "She hated it so much that we didn't have a yard. 'I need space!' she'd say. 'Green space!' She would've loved your old house."

"I think so too," I said. "I've been talking to Dr. Higgins about her a little."

"About Mom?"

"Yeah. It's hard. Sometimes I feel like, it's so obvious, right? That I've turned out just like her."

Marcie placed her hand on mine. "Ann."

"But then other times?" I exhaled heavily. "I don't know, Marcie. This just doesn't feel like the same thing. I don't feel out of touch with things the way she did. I feel . . . I don't know . . . perfectly normal. I just remember so very clearly something different. I can't prove it. But I know it. I don't know what to think . . ." I trailed off.

"And we don't know what Mom felt like, either, I suppose. What it was like in her head. Right?"

"Yeah. You're right."

"Well, whatever is going on, we'll get through it together. Okay? Just give it some time."

It felt so good to have her with me. "Okay."

We sat in silence for a few moments, and then Marcie spoke up.

"So what's going on with Graham? Still at the apartment?" she asked.

"No. He left a few days ago."

"Oh?" She looked concerned.

"No, it's okay. I'm all right with it." Perhaps if I kept telling myself that, it would become true. "Trying to get back to normal." Whatever that meant. "I think I'm going to start painting. See what happens."

"I think that's a wonderful idea. You need to get out of that apartment," she said with an encouraging smile.

"I can't imagine where I'll start. But I guess we'll see." I stirred sugar into my glass, hesitating. "But I have this weird feeling Graham is hiding something. I can't shake it." It felt like there was this wall all around him, and behind it was a hidden truth.

"Really?" She leaned down, retrieving her phone from her purse, furrowing her brow as she swiped and tapped. "What do you mean?"

"I don't know. I heard him on the phone the other night. He said something like, 'She can't find out.'"

Marcie looked up just briefly from her phone. "Oh, I'm sure it's just a work thing."

"Maybe," I said, absently.

She put her phone down, picking up the menu and changing the subject. "So, what are you hungry for? If you're interested, I'm happy to tell you that you love the crab bisque here."

While we ate, Marcie told me all about Hunter and Tim and their life on Long Island. It felt good to talk about someone else for a change, trying to let inertia carry me forward. We talked about Hunter's upcoming birthday, which Marcie was holding at a petting zoo, and I swallowed, chewing hard to keep myself from telling her all about Hannah's last birthday. Graham and I had taken her into the city, letting her ride the carousel in Central Park. She carried the balloon around like a treasure, the string tied to her wrist. Marcie must have sensed my thoughts and delicately changed the subject to her current projects. In addition to staging homes for real estate firms, she had become a lifestyle blogger over the last few years and had more than a hundred thousand followers on Instagram, where she posted photos of styled tablescapes and entertaining tips, beautifully decorated living spaces, and travel photos in airy pastels. She held out her phone, scanning through them. She proudly pointed to a picture of Hunter taken on the beach in Southampton.

"He's getting so big!" I said. The last photo I saw of him had been several years ago. "He's beautiful, Marcie."

"He is, isn't he?" Marcie's eyes sparkled. "He misses you," she said. "I told him you're still getting better and that we can get together just as soon as you're feeling up to it. I just felt like it might be hard on him, you not knowing him. He's old enough to understand a little, I think. But still . . ."

"No, you're right. We'll give it some time. I don't want to do anything to upset him."

She flipped through some more photos, holding them out for me to see.

"Look at you!" I said. "You're one of those moms that makes the rest of us feel like schlumps! These are beautiful pictures!"

She laughed, but I saw the way her cheeks brightened with pride. "Thanks." She waved her hand. "It's just silly stuff. And trust me, I push all the mess to the side before I take the picture. But it's fun." She held out an unedited photo of him in mismatched clothing, happily grinning in her arms as he held up a toy in front of a messy kitchen counter. "Normally, we look more like this."

"It's not silly at all, Marcie. There are a lot of people out there who clearly think it's pretty great."

"Thanks, Ann," she said, seeming genuinely touched. "I just started doing it for fun a couple years ago after we moved back. But it kept growing. Want to hear something wild? I was approached about a book, but I don't know . . ." She tucked her hair behind her ear.

"That's amazing! Are you going to do it?"

"We'll see. I haven't decided yet. We—"

"Annie?" A woman and her friend were walking past our table when the pair stopped. "Hi!" the woman said, looking right at me.

I had no idea who she was. "Um, hi . . . ," I began, darting a nervous glance toward Marcie. She shrugged, ever so slightly. She didn't know the woman, either, it seemed.

"Gwen," the woman said, politely finishing my sentence.

"I'm so sorry," I said. "Of course. I just blanked for a moment."

"She has the worst memory," Marcie chimed in. I threw her a look. Ha ha. So funny.

"Oh, that's okay. I'm terrible with names too," Gwen said, waving a manicured hand. She wore slim jeans with a white tucked button-down shirt and sleek sandals. Her warm brown skin was flawless and her smile genuine. "Hey, I'm so sorry I never called. I completely meant to, but you know how things are."

"Yeah, I do. No worries. Things have been hectic for me too." I struggled to fill my end of the conversation. Was she a work contact? Did she work at a gallery? One of Graham's coworkers? I hadn't the foggiest idea. Thankfully, she held a finger up to a friend waiting for her at the front door. "Okay, gotta run. But hey, let's get together before the end of summer! Do you still have my number?"

"Uhh . . . I think . . ."

"Don't worry about it. If not, I have yours." She set a hand on my shoulder.

I pasted on a smile. "Sure, absolutely. Looking forward to it." Off she went toward the exit, toting several bags.

"Smooth," Marcie said.

"Well, what was I supposed to do?" I sighed, dropping my head in my hands. "Am I going to have to deal with this forever? People popping up out of my past. What will I say? 'Oh, sorry, see my brain was scrambled, and I have no idea who you are. I remember the other world—you know, the *imaginary* one,'" I whispered and winked dramatically, and Marcie laughed, sympathizing. In that moment, joking about it, I instantly felt sickening guilt. How could I joke about something so heartbreaking? It must have registered on my face.

"Ann. It's okay to joke a little, I promise," Marcie said, taking my hand.

I swallowed the lump in my throat. "Ready to go?" I asked, changing the subject. "I want to hear more about this book thing on the way!" We collected our things and hailed a cab back to my apartment.

CHAPTER EIGHTEEN

When we arrived and opened the door, Graham was riffling through the kitchen.

"Hi," I said, surprised. I hadn't expected to see him back at the apartment so soon. "What are you doing here?" I asked. He flashed me a look, ready to get defensive.

"No, I didn't mean it like that. I just meant it's the middle of the day, and I'm surprised to see you. That's all."

He relaxed a little. "I left some papers here and had to pick them up. I'm just making a quick sandwich." He waved hello to Marcie and licked mayo off his finger. "Looks like you two made up."

Marcie plopped down on the sofa. "Do you guys mind if I hang here for a little while? I have an appointment to meet a client at a carpet store at four and have some time to kill." She picked up the remote.

From the kitchen, Graham rolled his eyes. "Of course. What else is new? Our house is your house."

She flipped him the middle finger over her shoulder. It felt curiously odd to watch them this way. Graham and Marcie had met just twice in my mind, at our wedding and at hers. I'd never seen them interact or talk, and here they were with what seemed like such a familial relationship. Like a brother-and-sister pair. A somewhat caustic one, as it may be, but then maybe this was just their way. I couldn't be sure.

Marcie had the TV remote in her hand, flipping through channels. I patted Charlie before going to talk to Graham. As I moved closer, I could smell his cologne, imagining the feel of sliding my arms around his waist and the warmth of his skin beneath the fabric of his shirt. He would lean down and kiss me hello with a smile. I would lean over and sneak a bite of his sandwich as he held it out for me. This was who we had been. I had to take a deep breath to contain the swelling hurt and longing in my chest, pushing it down.

"How are things?" I asked him, as brightly as possible. I felt like I was walking on eggshells, and any indication of sadness on my part would be a disappointment to him. I couldn't stand the idea of seeing his shoulders slump in response to my presence one more time.

His mouth curved, as if relieved. "Good, thanks. But I should probably be asking you the same thing."

"I'm good, I guess. Better maybe. I've been going to the studio. Not painting yet, but soon." We stood there awkwardly, and the pain in my chest rose again. "What kind of projects are you working on now?" I asked.

"Nothing much. Just the normal things."

I didn't know what the normal things were, but I didn't say that.

"I'll probably just pick up the rest of these boxes on the weekend, if that's okay. And take Charlie for a few days. Good?" I'd learned we had come up with a system of shared custody for the dog. I wasn't ready to part with him but didn't have much choice.

"Oh. Sure, okay. Maybe we can—" I froze and spun around. "Marcie, stop."

She looked over her shoulder to where I stood.

"Turn back," I said. "To that kids' channel."

"Um, no. I only get so much grown-up time and—"

"Please, just do it." Reluctantly, she did so, and the screen filled with flashes of primary reds and yellows with a large mouse in the center of the screen and goofy men in bright-blue jumpsuits. *Everybody shout . . .* I was singing along with the theme song in low, quiet tones, walking toward the screen with wide eyes. *Imagination Movers. Imagination Movers . . .* I sang the theme song of Hannah's favorite show, my throat tightening in a vise.

"What are you doing?" Marcie asked, looking cautiously at me, then toward Graham.

Scott in the red goggles. Dave in the orange hat. Smitty plays a guitar. Rich goes ratta-tat-tat.

"Annie, sweetie? Everything okay?" Marcie was at my side, concern knitted across her delicate features.

"Warehouse Mouse," I said, pointing at the screen. The familiar sound of the song—one I'd heard sometimes a dozen times a day—together with the images on the screen, made a hole open in the place where, in another life, Hannah should have been.

Marcie followed my gaze toward the screen. "Uh-huh. That's a mouse, all right. Hey, Graham, why don't you get us a glass of water."

"No, that's its name. Warehouse Mouse. And Nina," I said through warbled tears that made the images flicker on the screen. "See, that's Nina. Their neighbor."

Hannah twirled in a red tutu in my mind's eye . . .

"I think we should turn off the TV, don't you?" Graham said, muting the volume. I glanced at him. "Imagination Movers," I whispered. "They're Hannah's favorite."

"Oh, really?" Marcie's voice was sugary sweet, placating me as if I were a child.

"Don't you see?" I asked, looking at both of them. "Why on earth would I know all the words to those songs if none of it happened?"

"Annie, you probably just watched it one time." Graham didn't hide his exasperation. "Maybe with Hunter when he was little?"

Marcie shrugged but shook her head no.

"This is the one when Nina plans a trip to Hawaii and the guys help. They're all going to put flower leis on soon and . . ." I pointed.

"See?" The scene unfolded just as I'd said, and a moment later the four guys stood in front of a Hawaiian backdrop with bare feet and sand.

"Sweetie, why don't you sit down," said Marcie. "Graham's right. Look at me." Reluctantly, I turned and faced her. "You probably just had it on TV one time. Who knows."

"Do *you* routinely watch shows like this in the middle of the day, when there are no kids around?" I challenged.

"I don't know. Maybe?"

"And I just happened to learn every single word? You do it. You have a kid. *You* sing it."

She shook her head. "I'm sorry, sweetie. Hunter doesn't . . . we don't really watch these shows. I don't know."

"Nina's about to teach them the hula. She's always there for a helping hand. She works for her uncle. He only wears brown." I narrated along with the muted TV. "See."

"All right, we get it," Graham said, sharply, and I jumped, the tears spilling down my cheeks as I saw the hard set of his jaw and the coldness in his eyes. *Please just remember. Please,* I silently begged him. *She was yours too. How do you not know? How can you not feel her? She's right here.* I missed them. I missed both of them. My family was gone. My head felt fuzzy and began to ache.

"Do you think we should call Dr. Higgins?" Marcie asked him. As they talked in hushed tones, I leaned against the edge of the couch. When I closed my eyes, I saw Hannah hopping in front of the screen at the Yellow House. We took her to see the Imagination Movers in concert one time. She wanted to wear their T-shirt on the first day of . . .

. . . on the first day of . . .

My eyes popped open. "Oh my God," I said, standing suddenly. I spun around to Marcie. "I just remembered!"

"What?" she asked.

"Gwen. The woman at the café. I remembered who she is!"

Lights spun in a thousand directions, a starburst in my head as scenes flashed in waves.

I stared at Graham and Marcie where they stood beside one another, while in my mind I traveled back to the months before the accident. Looking away into the distance, I spoke as the pieces dropped into place. "It was at an open house for kindergarten. Registration for the following fall. *This* fall. All the parents were there with their kids, touring the rooms, meeting the teachers. The kids all went to play. They had an arts and crafts table set up." The scent of paste and paper filled my nose. "It's different. The school. Really amazing. It's on a farm that was turned into a school. There were gardens and sheep and a barn, where the kids would play at recess and grow things." I could see the wooden rafters next to rows of state-of-the-art computers. "Trails into the woods, where the teachers would give hands-on lessons about leaves and bugs, and nature." There were sleds, where the kids could play in the snow in the winter. "She was so excited to start there. We couldn't wait. We scraped together extra money to send her. Graham took on an extra project."

I looked up, but he looked at me blankly. "The parents all met in one room," I continued. "There was apple cider and small bottles of fresh maple syrup." Wind chimes hung outside the main entrance next to a wooden sign etched with children playing by trees. "That's where Gwen and I met. Her daughter was starting at the school as well. She and her husband had just purchased a second home nearby and decided to start living there year-round so they could send their daughter to the school. All of our friends had moved away, and I was so excited to meet someone new. We planned to get the kids together over the summer." I looked up at Marcie and Graham, who stared at me with unified, concerned faces mixed with something else—pity. I knew the words were tumbling out of my mouth too quickly. "How do you explain that?"

"Annie, please . . . ," Graham said.

"No!" I shouted. "How do you explain that? Marcie met her today too!"

Marcie spoke gently. "I don't know for sure. I think we really should just call Dr. Higgins, and maybe he can help sort things out."

I stood my ground, defiantly. "I can prove it."

"Annie, you have to stop," Graham said. "I'm calling Dr. Higgins. I think you need more help than you're getting."

"Remember Tabitha, Annie?" Marcie asked, walking slowly toward me. "Remember?"

I halted suddenly.

"Mom's cat," I muttered, after a moment.

"Right. Mom's cat. She called out for it for weeks. Made us look for it every day. Remember, Ann? She put a food bowl out on the kitchen floor for it. She had us staple missing-cat posters onto all the telephone poles in the neighborhood. Do you remember, she didn't have any pictures, so she asked us to draw them? We lied and said we couldn't remember the exact color of her and asked her to pick the crayons. Pictures of a gray cat?"

I shook my head hard. "No."

"Remember, Ann?"

"No. It's not like that." I trembled, remembering the unsettling hours we'd spent helping Mom search for a cat we knew we would never find.

"Look at me." Marcie took my hand in hers, speaking slowly. "Then Dad came home and made us tear them all down. He picked up the bowls and threw them out."

I shook my head again, swiping a tear with the back of my hand.

"There was no Tabitha, Ann. We never had a cat. Dad used to say he was allergic, but it was that he just didn't like cats and refused to get one. Do you understand? Mom imagined it all."

I swallowed hard. "This isn't like that," I whispered. *Please don't let this be like that.*

I looked to Graham, hoping for support. But his face was drawn, with deep, sad lines etched in long creases. He looked tired.

"Can we just do one thing, please?" I pleaded. "Just let me try something. If I'm wrong, I promise I'll listen. I'll do whatever you guys ask. But can I try something? Just let me make a phone call." Marcie was unconvinced. "Just one call," I asked again. She looked at Graham, who shrugged, wearily.

"What does it matter?" he said. "Sure."

Moving to the dining room table, I pulled my phone from my purse. I looked up the number for Hannah's school, and dialed. After four rings, a woman picked up, and I placed the call on speakerphone.

"Good afternoon, Oak Tree School." The woman's voice was older, efficient but warm.

"Yes, hi there. I was wondering if you could help me with something." I cleared my throat, attempting to sound brighter and keep it from trembling. "I was there in the spring for your open house, to register my daughter for the fall. I just wanted to double-check, to make sure she's registered. Would you mind?"

"Of course, dear. What's her name?"

I glanced nervously at Graham and Marcie. "Hannah. Hannah Beyers."

"Oh yes, hi, Mrs. Beyers. I remember we spoke on the phone." I held my breath. Graham and Marcie looked sharply at one another, shocked, while I sat bolt upright. "I'm sorry I missed you that day," she continued. "It was my day off. Let me check here . . . yes, here she is. Hannah. We were looking forward to seeing her in our kindergarten room in September, I believe."

"Were?" I asked.

"Well, she was never registered. I'm afraid we're full now, but there's a wait list if . . ."

"No, that's not right." I remembered signing all the papers. Writing the check.

"Give me just a moment. I can look again." I listened as she shuffled some papers. "Okay, here it is. We have your name on the guest list from the open house, but no registration. As I said, some parents do change their minds, and I can keep you on our list in case a place opens."

I was silent, and utterly confused.

"I . . . no, that's okay. Thank you, though."

I trembled, all my muscles tightening as I tried to make sense of it. I was about to hang up when another thought occurred to me. "Actually, could you help me with one more thing, please? While we were there, we met a really nice woman with a daughter the same age. She's new to the area, and we planned to meet for a playdate this summer. I've misplaced her number. Would you happen to have the number for Gwen? Gwen Von Button, I think?" The last name had popped into my head, and I hoped it was right. The woman placed me on hold for another moment before returning to the phone and giving me the number, confirming this new detail. I thanked her and ended the call.

Everything inside me bubbled like lava wanting to burst through to the surface. While Graham and Marcie watched closely in silence, I made another call, dialing Gwen's number. When she didn't answer, I left a voice mail with my number.

"I told you," I said. "I don't know what's happening. Or where she is. But now we have proof. I'm not crazy. Something is going on. We were there at that open house."

"Annie, it doesn't prove anything," Graham said, gravely. "Except that you went to a school and looked around."

"Why? Why on earth would I do that?" I shouted, standing, knocking the chair backward. "You heard her! She knew us!"

They exchanged a long look.

Graham walked toward me. "She never said anything about actually meeting Hannah. She said herself she wasn't there that day."

I realized he was right. She had said that. "No. This is ludicrous. You're doing this on purpose." I looked at them. "Both of you!"

Marcie shook her head, sadly, and took a step closer. "No, sweetie. We're not. Graham's right. It doesn't really prove anything."

"Graham, you remember that school. I know you do."

"Of course I do," he said softly.

"We couldn't wait to send her to that school." Half the people we knew had moved up there just to go to it. We'd spoken about it from time to time, feeling so lucky to have it nearby.

He looked away, clenching his jaw against tears that had begun to form in his eyes. Against all the dreams lost.

"This is absurd." I cradled my head in my hands.

"Why don't you let me make you some tea, and you can get some rest? We'll call Dr. Higgins. He'll probably say this is just a normal part of the process. Maybe the brain fighting back or something. I don't know?" She looked to Graham for help. Just then, my phone rang, and I startled.

"Hello?" I answered on speakerphone.

"Hi, Annie, it's Gwen. I'm so glad you called. Sorry I didn't pick up in time. I realized after I saw you today that I wasn't sure I still had your number, after all. It was so nice seeing you!"

"You too," I said, mustering some semblance of cheer. "How's Annabelle? Enjoying the summer?" I asked, looking pointedly at Marcie and Graham as I recalled the name of her daughter with ease.

"She is! We've been going back and forth from the city, setting up the house. Are you upstate all summer?" I stood, pacing back and forth across the kitchen floor.

"Uh, mostly. Hey, listen, I have the oddest question. I was telling Hannah about the kids in her class. You know, getting her excited about new friends and all that. But I couldn't remember . . . did Annabelle get a chance to actually meet Hannah? Did you . . . meet Hannah?"

She hesitated while my heart pounded in my chest, blood rushing in my ears, awaiting her answer. I knew it was a strange question, but what did I have to lose. "Well, no," she said, finally. "Remember? She wasn't there. You said she couldn't come because she had a bad cold. She was home with your husband."

My heart sank.

"Hello?" she asked.

"I'm sorry, yes. I'm here," I replied, weakly.

"Well, listen, I have to run now, but I have your number here, and maybe we'll catch up soon." She hung up quickly, ignoring any ideas of making plans. Who could blame her . . . I sounded loony.

I crumbled, throwing the phone onto the countertop, suddenly exhausted. They were right. I really had concocted a whole world inside my own head, and I reeled at the thought of how far I'd gone. At the same time, I had been so close to something resembling proof of Hannah's existence that I began to fall apart, the full weight of missing her bursting through, tearing me open. "Please . . . ," I muttered through thick tears as I sank to the floor, begging. To whom, I didn't know. The universe. "Please. Give her back. Just one more minute with her." Like an out-of-body experience I heard myself keening. "Please."

Suddenly Graham was there on the floor with me, wrapping himself around me and cradling me in his arms. "Shhh," he whispered into my ear.

I cried out into his shoulder, my shoulders racking with sobs. "I want my daughter."

Marcie pleaded. "Annie, you have to—"

"Stop, Marcie," Graham said sharply.

"But—"

"I said that's enough."

Marcie retreated, and he held me. "It's going to be okay," he said, his breath warm in my hair as he gently brushed it away from my face. "I've got you, sweetie. It's going to be all right."

It wouldn't be, though. She was gone, forever, and I feared the weeping would never stop.

I don't know how long we stayed that way, Graham and I entwined on the floor as Marcie looked on, helpless. Eventually, I supposed I began to calm, curling myself against the warmth of my husband until the sobs finally subsided and he carried me upstairs to rest.

CHAPTER NINETEEN

Graham has the kind of voice that people want to listen to, its tone both smooth and strong at the same time, with articulate, clear speech. When we first met, it was his voice that caught my attention, before I turned to see his face and never wanted to look away again. I can hear him talking in the distance now. He sounds frazzled. A man joins his conversation, the voice tinny and far away.

"It's been weeks now, and there's been no improvement."

"She's perfectly healthy by most accounts. And we are seeing some signs of improvement, however small they may be, which is hopeful." I don't recognize the voice of the person he's talking to.

All around the mulberry tree, the monkey chased the weasel.

I'm listening to the sound of Hannah humming quietly nearby.

"But you still think she may be better off at this other place?" Graham asks.

"She could improve at any time. Days, weeks, or longer. But it'll most likely be gradual. In the meantime, yes, we could try sending her somewhere that specializes in this sort of thing."

"And we can visit?" Marcie is talking now. "I feel like we're abandoning her."

"Absolutely. In fact, we encourage it. She needs to be with her family, talking to her about regular daily life. The longer she goes on this way, the less likely it is that she'll recover."

Pop! goes the weasel.

"I don't know," Graham says. "I just don't know."

"Why don't you go for a visit and see what you think? You don't have to decide now."

Lilac season is fleeting; they deliver their heavenly scent from lush blooms for just a few short weeks. Birds, butterflies, and bees are enticed by their sweet scent. A silvery mist of honey and jasmine, clean and pure, their fragrance is carried on even the barest hint of a breeze, nearly otherworldly in its beauty. The scent of them is all around me now, along with the powdery almond scent of Hannah as she leans in close.

In the dark, I feel her:

"Mommy, can you hear me?" she whispers.

CHAPTER TWENTY

I gasped for air, sitting bolt upright in bed, my heart pounding. The curtains were drawn tightly, but morning light peeked from behind them. I immediately clapped my hand over my ear, where the tickle of a child's breath and whisper had left it tingling. I could feel her there. The combined fragrance of her skin and the lilacs was still in my nose, and I looked around for the source, expecting to see big purple blooms in vases on every surface of the room. The air was filled with their essence, the spirit of these two beautiful living things that were once mine, but there wasn't a bloom in sight, and I was alone again.

I picked up the water glass from the nightstand, draining it of every remaining drop, waiting for my pulse to slow. Downstairs, I could still hear Graham talking, and I realized I must have been half-awake as I'd heard him. I lifted the thick gray duvet and padded over to the doorway. He was talking with his office, clearing his schedule for the day.

I remembered the conversation I had overheard in the margins of waking, putting the pieces together, and realized . . . *oh my God, they must be thinking of committing me.* They were giving up. But surely he wouldn't, not after the way he was last night. Would he?

I needed to get it together. Now.

Thirty minutes later, I was showered and dressed and walked downstairs. Graham was in the kitchen, pouring boiling water into a french press. Recalling the way he'd held me last night, I went to him, placing my hand on his lower back, and leaned into him. He tensed, holding still for a moment before shifting away. "Morning." His voice was as tight as a wire that might snap. The tension rolled off him in waves, pushing me away. "How'd you sleep?" he asked.

I stepped away, giving him his space, and he relaxed a bit. His coldness stung deeply, but I did my best to hide my disappointment. For a little while, I'd almost believed my husband was back. I was wrong.

"Good. I feel much better," I said, keeping my voice steady, and then looked around. "You're still here? Where's Marcie?"

"She left last night, right after you fell asleep. She had to get home to Hunter. I stayed. We didn't think you should be alone."

"But I heard her talking a little while ago."

He looked at me oddly. "No, just me." He pulled two mugs from the cupboard. "Coffee?"

I nodded. "Was anyone else here?"

He turned to the refrigerator, removing the carton of cream. "Nope. Like I said. Just me." There was a hint of bitterness in his words.

I tried to remember a single time when Graham had lied to me but couldn't think of one. He was honest nearly to a fault, even when the jeans didn't flatter or a new painting wasn't the best. I loved it about him. Graham and I didn't keep secrets. Our relationship was a bubble, and we were an impenetrable team. But I knew, watching him there in the kitchen with his shirt untucked, and his sleeves rolled, frustratingly sexy, that I could not trust him anymore. I was on my own. He wasn't telling me everything.

"I'm sorry about last night," I said, feeling embarrassed. "I decided to go to see Dr. Higgins today." I watched him carefully, hoping he would believe me. "I think you and Marcie are right. Things must still be a little more jumbled up than I wanted to admit. Yesterday was a bit of a wake-up call. But everything is a little clearer this morning, and I'm ready to put this whole thing behind me."

"I'm so glad to hear you say that, Ann. Really. You sound a lot better than you did yesterday." His face had brightened, a small amount of the burden lifted.

Tears pricked at the corners of my eyes, as the years of trust were broken, but I forced a smile. "Definitely. I think I'll head into the studio a little later. Start acquainting myself with the work again." At least that was the truth.

He hesitated. He knew me well and could tell when something was wrong, but, eventually, he let it go and moved on. "Well, great! It'll be good for you." He lowered the plunger down on the press and poured two cups of strong, dark coffee.

"Are you working today?" I asked.

He looked away. "I have to run out of town. Meeting a client up in Connecticut."

I blew on the coffee, looking down to hide the sadness. Evidently, my morning performance hadn't been enough to cancel his visit to the institution. But maybe it would buy me some time.

There was something going on—unknown puzzle pieces that I'd yet to find. I had felt it in my gut from the moment I'd first woken in the hospital after the accident. And despite the oddness of it, something about yesterday's events had only reinforced my instincts. I had been forcing myself to discount my memories, insisting even to myself that it was just a trick of the brain. Maybe it was. And maybe it wasn't. But I needed to find out more.

∼

My studio had begun to feel like a refuge—a place where I could safely explore, putting the pieces together, shifting them left and right, trying to assemble a greater picture. I sat at my computer, determined to learn something more—not only about my condition, but the validity of my memories. I tested myself. Were there more details of my *other* life that

I knew, existing and waiting to surface? How much could the brain manufacture of its own accord? And if I had snapped, broken from reality in the weeks before the accident, how far had I gone to craft my imaginary world?

I picked up my phone, and with no assistance from the internet or contacts, dialed a number by memory. My thumb tapped the numbers without hesitation. A few rings later, a receptionist answered. "Diamond Pediatrics," the woman said.

"Yes, hello, I'd like to make an appointment with Dr. Renning for my daughter for her annual checkup," I explained. "Is he still off on Mondays?"

"Yes, he is. But he has availability this . . ."

Click. I ended the call. Still off on Mondays.

I pulled up the pediatrician's website. I clicked on the gallery, as scenes of Mother Goose popped up, confirming what I knew. The rooms were decorated in murals, scenes from nursery rhymes. Baskets of children's books sat beneath the exam tables to entertain waiting children. Would I have been that detailed? Researched something as mundane as a pediatrician, simply to satisfy a grand delusion. I knew what Graham would say. What Dr. Higgins would say. But in my heart I heard Hannah's whisper.

Mommy, can you hear me?

And a shiver ran up my spine.

Furiously, I began to search for another option. Maybe there were other cases like mine. I entered the search term *Stories of False Memories*. At first, the results were as expected—clinical studies. But then I searched *Stories of False Memories in History*, and suddenly the results opened up to numerous stories, albeit many far-fetched, in which a person reported having memories of activities or details that differed from the reality in which they lived.

As I began to read, Piper walked in.

"Morning," she said, setting a bag of croissants and tea in front of me.

I smiled up at her. "Thank you. That was sweet."

"My pleasure," she chirped. She walked to her desk, arranging her belongings before bustling over to some papers, perpetually in motion. "Dare I ask," she said coyly, "are you going to be painting today?"

"Huh? Oh, I don't know. Maybe," I said, distracted. I skimmed more stories on the screen. "We'll see."

She raised her hands. "No pressure, just asking." She blew the steam on her tea. "What are you working on?"

"Research. Sort of." I sipped my tea, scrolling through results on the screen. Piper watched, waiting for me to elaborate. "Something that my therapist told me. It was just a story, but I keep thinking about it. Remember when you talked about your neighbor who swore his car changed color?"

"Sure." Her deep-red hair was in a sleek ponytail, and she moved it over one shoulder. With pale skin and a few freckles, she wore nearly no makeup, with the exception of a narrow line of perfectly drawn black eyeliner and wine-stained lips.

"Did you know there are other people with stories like that out there? Who swear they remember a whole different series of events playing out in their lives? Pop culture references that apparently never existed, or existed differently than most of us remember, that sort of thing. Normal everyday people who woke up to things being different in their world. It's weird."

"Definitely. But that must be comforting in a way, yeah? Knowing that you're not the only one who's experienced something like that?"

I laughed. "*Comforting* isn't the word I'd use. It's mostly people wearing tinfoil hats and also talking about green men."

"Ah, I see. I can make you one if you'd like. Order you a chic one from some awesome designer. Wear it to the Met Gala."

"Ha ha," I said. "I think I'll pass."

"Want some help?" she asked.

"Really?" I perked up, as I realized it was the first time anyone had asked me that.

"Of course! Two heads are better than one," she said. She went to her desk and picked up her laptop, bringing it over to the table and sitting in the chair across from me. "What?" she asked, when she saw the expression on my face. "I'm a sucker for weird conspiracy stories."

"That's not why you're helping," I said, wanting to reach over and hug her. "Thank you."

She winked sweetly. "Okay. Let's see . . ." She began tapping away as we both scanned websites. "Oh God, I see what you're saying. Lots of bizarre stuff. People are *so* weird."

"Yep." I sighed.

"But here, listen to this one. It says, 'How would things be different if you had taken that job you turned down? What would you be like if you hadn't broken up with your fiancé before the wedding? What if you hadn't missed the plane? One woman claims to have woken up in a life different than her own.'" I leaned over toward her computer, and she shifted the screen into view as she scanned the article, reading out loud. "In 2008, a woman claims to have woken up one morning, frightened when she noticed minor differences in her surroundings that became more significant as the day wore on. At first, it was her bed-sheets. Everything in her bedroom was the same, but her sheets were a different pattern, and not ones that she'd previously owned." Piper shivered. "That would be so creepy. Anyway, let's see here . . . as the day went on, she went to work, but they didn't know who she was, despite the fact that she knew countless details about the office. And she learned she was still dating her ex-boyfriend, who she hadn't seen in more than a year."

"Wow," I said, startled by the similarities. "That's bizarre."

"The woman didn't know what to do, so she reached out on the internet, I guess looking for help. There were other things about her life that were changed—clothing she didn't remember buying, emails she didn't remember typing, little things about her family members' lives being different. But the date was the same. It says at first she thought she'd had a stroke or amnesia or something and went to countless doctors, but everything checked out."

"What happened to her?"

Piper shrugged. "It doesn't say, really. There's a quote from one of her online posts. Says she knows no one will believe her. She said she believes she woke up in an alternate universe. And then it just ends. She drops off the web after around 2009."

"Huh," I said. "She's right. It's impossible to believe. People would think she's nuts for sure."

Piper offered a sympathetic smile. "Hey, the world is a strange place. You never know!"

I laughed. "All right. Let's see what else we can find."

Piper continued scrolling, while I did the same. "Here's one," I said a few moments later. "The Man from Taured—the country that never existed."

"Sounds sketchy already." She arched a manicured brow and craned her neck toward my screen. "That's creepy," she said, when I pointed at a grainy black-and-white photo of the man.

"This all sounds like alien-hunter stuff," I echoed. Nothing like what I was experiencing. It wasn't real life. It was sci-fi.

"Sort of. But there are lots of other stories. Maybe there are others out there that are a little less—"

"Weird?" I said.

"Yeah, pretty much. But hey, look, it's not all kooky. Here's a TED Talk by Brian Greene on parallel universes and the science behind them. I've seen this, actually."

My skepticism must have shown on my face.

"Honest! It's pretty cool. Did you see him on *Colbert*?" she asked.

I shook my head.

"You've never heard of him? Do you not watch *The Big Bang Theory*?" She groaned disapprovingly. "He's this rock star mathematician physicist who explains things in a way so that normal people can understand. Here . . . watch." A TED Talk started playing from YouTube. "It's all about string theory and how the calculations of it show the likelihood of multiple dimensions and whatever," she said. "Freaky stuff."

"Did you just say 'string theory'?" I stared at her.

"What—I like science." She shrugged.

I stood and walked over to the windows. "Forget it. I'm starting to sound ridiculous even to myself." It was a foolish waste of time.

"Annie, listen," Piper said. "Don't be so hard on yourself. If I were you? If I were in your shoes? I'd be wondering all the exact same things. No matter how far-out or ridiculous they seemed. Even if I woke up to something so mundane like my sheets were different, or, God forbid, I was still dating some loser from last year, it would be awful."

"It's just that I'm remembering so much. Things that I don't feel like I could have possibly made up. But I can't seem to prove any of it. Everything feels like I'm in a fun house, with hundreds of mirrors everywhere and no way to tell which reflection is real. Do you know I actually went to a bereavement group the other day? For people who have lost children? It was unspeakably awful. I didn't talk. I couldn't. I just sat there, listening, and crying. I felt like a horrible fraud."

She looked up at me with kind eyes. "I'm so sorry."

"And I have these odd sensations, images from nowhere popping into my mind, and now I'm questioning everything. Like the way—"

"Hey, come look at this." She walked over to the printer and retrieved several pages as they spit out. "Oh, sorry," she said. "I didn't mean to interrupt you." I waved off her apology. "This was in *The Guardian* last year." She pointed at the screen, leaving me with the pages as she returned to her computer and continued talking. "A journalist in London did a lot of research on this stuff, interviewed neurologists about how and why people are misremembering things and seeing them differently. Some of it's silly things, like songs or movie quotes that have changed and such, but it looks like there are some more concrete things also."

I raised an eyebrow, and Piper shrugged while I continued to scan the article.

"This guy is the real deal. Not a quack." Piper clicked away at the computer, reading aloud. "Jonathan Deveraux is a British newspaper columnist and commentator. He is a frequent contributor to *The Independent*, the *Daily Telegraph*, and several BBC News shows, prior to which he was a weekly columnist for *The Guardian*, for which he still contributes intermittently. Nominated for various awards, journalist of the year, yada yada. Looks like he covers investigative journalism, mostly political stories. Oh wow, he was the South African correspondent for *The Guardian* for two years. Ooh! And he's cute!" She popped a jelly bean into her mouth. "I think we should call him."

"And say what?" I asked.

"I don't know . . . maybe tell him you're researching . . . weird stuff or something. For your work."

I cocked my head. "Seriously?"

"Or tell him the truth. Whatever. But we have to call him. He's done all the work already! Look at this: he's talked to every single top-notch specialist from psychics to psychiatrists to Nobel Prize–winning scientists. What harm could it do to talk to him?"

"I can think of a lot."

"He's the first person we've found who seems legit and who has at least acknowledged that things like this are happening to people. Annie, he's got access to the best experts out there."

"That's true." I continued reading, considering it. "Maybe I could get some contacts from him, at the very least. Is there anything else like this from him?"

Piper squinted at the screen. "No, not really. It looks a little outside his norm. And he doesn't seem to have done much at all recently."

Piper was already dialing. She asked to speak with Jonathan Deveraux and, a moment later, left a surprisingly authoritative voice mail indicating that she was the assistant to the artist Annie Beyers and needed to speak with him, urging him to call her.

I sighed, going back to the window. "I don't know . . . this is all too bizarre. I feel like if I could just figure out what I was doing up there near my old house that day it would be a key. But there's nothing." I groaned, frustrated. Piper was silent behind me. "I'm sorry," I said. "This isn't in your job description." I chuckled, but when I turned, she had a serious look on her face. There was a thick silence in the room.

"Piper?"

She seemed unwilling to meet my eyes, taking a deep breath before she finally spoke. "I think I should show you something," she said.

"Show me what?"

She seemed unsure. "I don't know. I just don't know. But it doesn't seem right anymore to keep it from you. I can't."

"Piper? What's going on?"

"I think I know what you were doing that day. The day of the accident."

CHAPTER TWENTY-ONE

"You know why I was upstate that day? Why didn't you tell me?"

She wrung her hands together. "I'm so sorry. I felt awful not saying anything."

She went to her desk, where she reached to the back of a drawer and retrieved a key. She talked as she walked over to the locked closet. "After you got home, they said it would be better if you didn't see these. It's the project you were working on—the exhibit for this fall." She fumbled with the key nervously. Finally, she opened the door. It was larger than a closet, more like a small, adjacent room, smelling of fresh paint and dark, enclosed spaces. I stepped in gingerly as she held the door. When she switched on the light, I gasped.

On canvases lining the walls and floors, in varying forms, was a single repeated image:

Hannah.

My beautiful child, the images ghostlike. Going to one of the paintings, I ran my fingertips over the rough surface. She was smiling, running, in profile, her personality captured in its purest essence.

"What . . . why . . . where did these . . . ," I stammered, looking at Piper.

She fidgeted, her expression tense. "I'm so sorry. I wanted to show them to you right away. But everyone thought it would complicate things for you and that it wasn't a good idea. You had become sort of obsessed with this little girl . . ." She seemed lost for words. "Anyway, Graham had me move them all into storage while you recovered."

"I don't understand. How could he do this? He knew about her? Why is he hiding her from me?"

Piper cocked her head to the side, confused. "I'm not completely sure what you mean. But if I'm understanding your question right, yes, he did know about the paintings and that the subject of the exhibition featured images of a small girl. It's entitled *The Ghost*. The exhibition, I mean."

"*The Ghost*," I whispered. In each of the paintings, Hannah was the subject, but at the same time, not outwardly so. Her image was ethereal and barely apparent in its translucency, layered over scenes of storms and trees, back country roads, lush fields and snowfall. One had to look carefully in order to make out all her features, nearly an illusion. She was there, but not. A number of the paintings featured the oak tree from our backyard.

"How could he have kept this from me? He knows about her. Somehow, he knows about her." I turned to Piper, waiting for an explanation. But she had none.

She walked closer, the barest smile on her face. "The first time I walked into the studio and saw one, I was speechless. You had been up the entire night, not sleeping for days. For weeks before that, you had been intensely focused, sketching or staring at the blank canvas for hours at a time. We barely talked, and I mostly just let you be. I came in after a weekend, and suddenly this was here." She pointed to a large painting, perhaps five feet square, of a dark-green meadow of goldenrod blowing sideways in waves beneath dark clouds, over which was painted a ghostly image of Hannah running barefoot with her hair spread out behind her, blending into the blades of meadow grass, nearly indiscernible.

My mind spun with the possibilities.

Piper continued as I dragged my fingers over the images, feeling the roughness of the paint beneath my fingertips. *I've missed her so much,* I thought, tearfully. *My girl.*

"Over the past few months, you started taking frequent trips up to the Catskills. But you were . . ."

"I was what?"

She seemed to be searching for words. "You barely talked over the past few weeks. You'd disappear. Graham would call, looking for you. He was worried. Your sister was worried. We all were. I figured it was just some artist's . . . thing or something. I mean, look . . ." She waved her hand at the paintings. "They're extraordinary."

"Piper, this is her. This is our house. Our yard, where she plays. This is her."

"I don't know what to think, Annie. Everything you've told me; it's just all so strange, isn't it? I'm starting to think maybe . . . I don't know what to think. But it's strange."

I turned quickly, tearing myself away from the paintings. "I need to call Graham."

When he didn't answer on the first call, I dialed again, and again, until he finally answered.

"Hey, Ann, I'm on the road. Can I call you—"

"I saw the paintings, Graham. You knew about her?"

There was a long pause. "Annie, listen to me. We thought it would be confusing if you saw them."

"It's her, Graham! It's her! In the paintings. You've been watching me suffer. Blaming everything on the accident, when you knew about her well before that."

"Knew about who, Annie? She's a figment of your imagination. They aren't portraits of a real person. Don't you get it? *The paintings* are what you have been remembering. You created it all in your head!"

I reeled.

I knew he could be right but felt it differently in my gut. I ran through the images in my mind. "No. This isn't some artist's imagination." *Right?* "You need to explain this to me. How could you keep this from me? Is this what you've been hiding?"

He didn't answer right away. "I'm not . . . Annie, you need to listen to me very carefully." His voice was pulled tight, at the end of its length, about to snap. "You need help."

"Oh, is that what you're doing up there? In Connecticut. I heard you on the phone. Is that your idea of helping me?"

"What? No. It's not what you think." His tone had become gentle and measured.

"What else are you keeping from me?" I asked.

"We're just trying to help you. We're worried about you and can't risk another episode or accident."

"What do you mean, *another*?"

He sighed heavily. "The week of the accident. You'd been disappearing. Sometimes a day at a time. You'd been depressed for months, barely sleeping. We were barely speaking. Then a few days before the accident I got a call from the people who own the old house. They said they'd seen you walking in the fields here and there, which they didn't love, but tolerated. Said when they called out to you, you just ignored them, like you were sleepwalking or something. But one morning they found you in the rocking chair on the front porch, and that was it. They were decent enough to call me instead of the police. You snapped out of it and apologized up and down. It seemed like things were better for a few days, but you were obsessed with going up there. You had created this whole world inside your head of a life that didn't exist there. Then the accident happened. I guess you'd gone back up there. Annie, just get some help."

I shook my head. "No, it doesn't make sense."

"What doesn't?"

"The road that I had the accident on . . . it doesn't lead to the city. Why would I have been on that road? The only time we ever went that way was when we had to go to the pediatrician."

Graham was silent. I could hear him breathing.

"I don't know what to say, Annie. I'm exhausted. I don't want to do this anymore. I *can't* do this anymore." He was adamant that I needed more help than I could get in twice-weekly sessions and that something needed to be done.

As he talked, I stared at them—the paintings, her image. They were so accurate. So perfect. Then on one of the paintings, in the distance, sat the hazy view of the back of the house. I looked closer, the paint splotches getting thicker with each step. Silhouetted in the darkness of the kitchen window, I saw the outline of a figure looking out, watching my daughter play. The hairs on the back of my neck raised, and a ripple went through me.

"I've gotta go, Graham. Do me a favor: pick up Charlie tonight after you leave work."

"What? Annie, wait. I—"

I ended the call without saying goodbye and looked closer. Startled, I began walking backward, adjusting my perspective, not taking my eyes from the canvas. "Piper, when did you say I painted these?"

"Most of them were done just within the past few months."

I picked up my keys, collecting my things. "I have to go. Let me know if you hear back from *The Guardian*. I need to talk to that writer."

"I already did. He called while you were on the phone with Graham."

I stopped. "And? What did he say?"

"Uh, it wasn't good. He was all right at first. Not the most social guy. But when I started to tell him why I was calling, he got pissed. Told me never to call him again. He hung up on me."

"He refused to even talk to you?"

"Seems so, yeah."

"But you did reach him in London? He's there?"

She nodded.

Jonathan Deveraux was the only thread I had to go on. Trying to reach more experts was only going to take time that I didn't have to waste. He had everything I needed to know, right in one place. I wasn't going to give up now. A moment later, I went to the sink and opened a drawer, retrieving a razor blade.

Piper was up in a flash. "Annie? What are you doing with that?" I went to the closet and slashed into the canvas, freeing it from its frame. "Annie!" Piper cried.

I carefully rolled it into a tube and headed for the door. The phone rang in my hand. Seeing the number, I hesitated before answering it.

"Did Graham call you that fast?" I asked Dr. Higgins.

"Annie, he's worried about you, that's all. Why don't you come in. Tell me what's going on."

"Why, so you can commit me? Are you waiting there with a straitjacket?"

"Absolutely not. Tell me what's going on."

"I have proof. Or at least . . . something like proof." I told him about the paintings. About what I'd seen. About everything I'd experienced in the last twenty-four hours.

He was quiet for a moment. Then he said, "Come in. I promise you can trust me. I think I may be able to help you."

"No way. I'm sick of everyone telling me what I remember and what I don't remember. I need to find out more about what's going on. Or at least explore some option other than that I'm losing it."

"I completely agree. Listen, just come in. I promise you . . ."

I disconnected the call, then turned to Piper. "Email me everything you can find on Deveraux, could you please?"

"Of course. But where are you going?" she asked.

"I'm going to find out if I'm crazy or not."

CHAPTER
TWENTY-TWO

All around the mulberry tree, the monkey chased the weasel . . .

The phone rang, jostling me from jet-lagged sleep and interrupting the song as it drifted back into my dreams. I turned my aching body over, silencing the ring as I focused on the interior of the hotel room with its high ceilings and crown molding. The room was laden with airy blues and amber, with a combination of period furniture replicas and modern comforts. For a moment I'd forgotten I was in London.

I sank farther into the deep pillows. Piper had made the travel arrangements for me, and when I'd checked in to the hotel, the staff recognized me, greeting me by name and sending me to my "usual suite," which had made me shake my head with a sad smile of disbelief. Graham and I had last been in London many years ago, and I'd had fun introducing him to the city. We had visited the hotel where I now slept, and he'd been captivated by its history and the pedigree of its architecture, still under renovation at the time. The hotel had once been considered the most beautiful hotel in all the world, we'd learned. Sitting conveniently adjacent to Saint Pancras station, its Victorian-Gothic architecture had been a spectacular creation when it was first unveiled in London. It featured lobby windows towering more than fifty feet and finely painted ceilings.

"Look at this, Ann." I can see Graham pointing excitedly upward toward a magnificent stone staircase. *"The architect, Sir George Gilbert Scott, once said that he designed this so that it appeared to defy gravity while snaking upward toward a starry painted sky."*

I smiled, recalling the way he'd turned his head this way and that, and how much I'd loved him in that moment. And the way he'd turned toward me and taken my hand, sneaking us off into a small corridor off the main staircase, pulling me into his arms and kissing me deeply, the two of us intertwining and making out wildly.

"Someday, when this hotel is finished, I'll take you upstairs, and we'll stay in one of the suites, and I'll make love to you all night long," he whispers into my ear, his lips brushing my neck.

We hadn't been able to afford to go back, but apparently now it was no problem, and I wondered if in our new life, the two of us had ever ended up staying here together, or if I was always on my own.

I thought of the history of the suite I was now in, and the people who might have once stayed within its walls. I was sure there were other trendier or more private hotels in London, befitting the famous artist I had apparently become. But I liked that I had remained true to this one throughout the years.

"After its opening in 1873," I can hear Graham reading from a brochure, *"the hotel remained a gem in London's crown, where champagne and ball gowns flowed, until 1935, when it was forced to close. The building remained abandoned and moth-eaten for over seventy-five long years, until it was rescued from decay to be brought back to its former grandeur. Ooh, maybe it's haunted,"* he teases.

Looking about the room, I imagined the way it might have appeared during that forgotten time, inside boarded windows, and shivered. It was now restored to a contemporary version of five stars, where shadows of the past loomed large amid winding stone hallways and fine linens that transported visitors to another time.

How fitting for me to be among its ghosts.

. . . the monkey thought 'twas all in fun. Pop . . .

Hannah's whispers were still warm against my ear, from sleep, as tiny and delicate as a dandelion in the breeze, calling to me. Coupled with the memories of Graham, I ached for home from a wound deep in my center. I reached over to the empty pillow beside me and imagined the feel of curling against Graham's warm skin, feeling more alone than ever as I willed myself back into the escape of half sleep, hoping to visit them again, for a second, a minute, for anything, if only in my imagination.

Sometime later, the phone began to ring again, until finally I emerged from my slumber.

"Hey, Marcie," I mumbled, glancing at the screen as Graham and Hannah drifted off into that place where dreams live.

"What the hell are you doing in London? Annie, what is going on? I talked to Graham, and then when nobody could reach you, I called Piper. She said you're trying to meet with some journalist or something?" Her voice was shrill, and I held the phone away from my head as if hungover.

"Slow down. I'm still waking up." I sat up against the headboard, the oversize room feeling painfully empty. My eyes felt puffy and swollen where I pressed gently with my fingertips. I'd been crying in my sleep again.

"It's afternoon there," she said.

"Yeah, well . . ." I heaved the thick duvet off and shuffled toward the coffee maker in the room, pleased to find a silver kettle and a selection of teas. I was still wearing my travel clothes and needed a shower. After snagging the last flight out of New York, I'd arrived at the hotel just after ten in the morning. Even though I knew better, I'd allowed myself a fifteen-minute nap, which had turned into two hours, and now I was groggy from jet lag. Needing something stronger, I opted for the espresso instead and dropped in a pod. "Just hear me out, would you please?" I gave her the grounded, scientific short version of the story and left out the tinfoil hats. Marcie was as concrete as they came.

"Okay. Well . . . ," she said, after seeming to consider what I'd told her. "Do you want me to come over there? You shouldn't be alone right now. I can ask Tim to cancel his business trip tomorrow to stay with Hunter."

I smiled, still unaccustomed to this version of Marcie—willing to drop everything and be by my side when I needed her. I sipped the warm liquid and went to the floor-to-ceiling windows overlooking a sunny view onto Euston Road below. "Actually, with the exception of feeling like I could sleep for another twelve hours, I feel completely fine, clearer than I have been since this all started. Like I have some purpose other than waking up every day with the same problem. Maybe it's a wild-goose chase; I don't know. But if there are people who know more about these things than I do, then it's worth exploring, don't you think?"

"What more is there to know? Just give it some more time. Listen, maybe Dr. Higgins—"

"What if it were Hunter, Marcie? What if Hunter and Tim left your life? Would you take a holiday at a mental health farm and eat Jell-O and talk about your feelings?"

There was silence on the line. "No. I'd fight like hell."

"So you understand."

"I guess," she said, reluctantly. "Ann?"

"Yeah?"

"I'm so sorry I didn't tell you about the paintings from your new exhibit. The portraits of the little girl. We didn't know what to do, but please . . . know that we meant well. We're all just trying to do the right thing."

I sat on the bed, leaning back against the cushioned headboard. "I know."

"I'm worried about you," she said.

"I know. And I know why. And because of that, you have my word—let me do this my way. See what I can find out. And if I don't learn anything useful, I promise you, I'll come home and check myself into the best mental health facility in the world."

Marcie chuckled on the other end. "All right, well, good luck today. Piper says this guy's an asshole. That he keeps hanging up on her. Won't return her emails. He won't even talk to you. What are you going to do?"

"I don't know," I said, honestly. "Convince him, I guess."

~

Piper said the one call she got from Jonathan Deveraux had come from a number at *The Guardian*'s main office. He was a freelancer, so it might be tough to pin him down, but we figured it was as good a place to start as any. Conveniently, *The Guardian*'s offices were near King's Cross station and the hotel. The late-afternoon sun was still high in the sky, and it was pleasantly warm in the city. New York had begun to feel claustrophobic, and I'd always loved the long days of London in June. To my recollection, it had been ten years since I'd been in the capital on the trip with Graham, but my instincts—looking right first instead of left at the crosswalk and my knowledge of the neighborhood, not to mention the Oyster card I'd found in my wallet and my reception at the hotel—told me I was here frequently these days. This pleased me, in some way. I'd lived in London for two years in my early twenties and, at the time, had believed I would stay there for good. For the younger version of me, it was as far away as I could get—a polar opposite of the broken streets in the Scranton neighborhood called the Flats where I'd been raised. When my first collection was purchased in its entirety just after I left university, the nights were long, alcohol-fueled blurs with friends in Camden, and the days were filled with a buffet of culture and beauty that London never failed to provide.

It was a welcome respite, being back, and had I not been on a mission, I would have taken my time along a scenic route. Conveniently, however, I didn't have far to go. The short walk north was along a stretch that was decidedly not one of London's more picturesque roads, and I passed by the mishmash of shops and towering cranes quickly until I reached Kings Place, staring up at the ultramodern, undulating glass building that housed the editorial offices of the newspaper, overlooking Regent's Canal.

I entered the lobby of *The Guardian*'s offices, looking up at the smooth, stark-white walls dotted with primary blues and reds, heading straight for what seemed to be a large reception desk. I'd thought through what I would say to Deveraux when I met him. How I would best be able to persuade him to talk to me. *Give me five minutes.*

The phone jostled in my pocket. A text from Piper:

He's not there! Works from home . . . 350 Theberton Street.

The text was dotted with house and confetti emojis. I had no idea how she had managed to get his address, but I commended her resourcefulness. A guard was about to ask what I needed when I turned on my heels, plugged the address into my GPS, and walked back to King's Cross station, where the Northern Line quickly took me two stops away to my destination. I arrived at Angel station ten minutes later, the wind whipping behind me as the train left the tunnel. I hurried along through the underground warren with the rest of the crowd, watching the theatrical posters pass by on the wall and fidgeting nervously as the tallest escalator in the city took me up to street level.

Meeting the guy at his office was one thing, but stalking him outside his home was quite another, and as I made my way past the busy shops and bus stops along Upper Street, I wondered if there might be any other way. Deciding there wasn't, I turned left onto Theberton Street, where the restaurants and real estate offices gave way to residential townhomes. One by one, I checked the numbers on the row of colorful doors until I reached a town house marked with the number 350 in large black metal script, paused, and then finally rang the bell. When no one answered, I rang again. And then I did the only thing I could do—I sat down and settled in for a wait.

Some of the houses were accented with pots of flowering pink geraniums, greeting visitors in tidy, cheerful symmetry. Others were plain, with delivery boxes or recycle bins on the steps in front of doors in shades of London blue, pinks, and turquoise—rows of alternating colors all the way down the street toward leafy Gibson Square. I was leaning against the wrought iron railing, the afternoon sun on my face, when the door behind me opened suddenly, startling me. I turned as he nearly tripped over me.

"What the . . . ?"

I instantly knew it was him from his picture. He had the rare kind of face one tends to notice, and a smile that could stop a person in their tracks if he offered it, which he didn't.

"I-I'm so sorry," I stammered, jumping to my feet. "I did ring."

He pulled the door closed behind him, raising a satchel onto his shoulder. "Right. And I didn't answer. I hate to be rude, but could you please leave my steps now, or can I help you with something? If you're looking for George, he's away for the week, I think." He pointed down toward the basement flat, where I assumed a tenant lived.

"Are you Jonathan Deveraux?"

"Afraid so." He seemed only mildly affected by having found a complete stranger on his front step, so I found that somewhat promising.

"My name is Annie. I'm here because I need to talk to you about a story you wrote. About, er . . . multiple universes, memory, some weird conspiracy theories."

His whole demeanor changed as he rolled his eyes, suddenly aggravated, and brushed past me down the steps. "Right. Yeah. I'm late, got to go."

I followed behind. "No, please. Just give me five minutes," I called. It had sounded less whiny when I'd practiced it in my head.

He hastily walked down the sidewalk, crossing the street abruptly and narrowly missing a bike as it flew past him. I walked faster, struggling to keep pace with the stride of his long legs. "Listen, I'm not leaving. Just hear me out. I promise, I'm completely sane." *I think.* "I'm not some alien-chaser worried about someone going back in time and changing the lines to *Star Wars*," I said, referencing one of the minor points from his story in *The Guardian*. "I genuinely need to know some information, and you have contacts that I can't reach. I think something has happened to me, and I need your help."

He spun around, shooting daggers that stopped me short. "Did Liam put you up to this? Ha ha, joke's on me! You got me. Now tell him to piss off." He turned the corner onto Upper Street, dodging the afternoon crowds with their H&M bags, bubble tea, and headphones.

"I have a five-year-old daughter who has suddenly ceased to exist, and I'm not leaving until you talk to me." He slowed and dropped his head with a dramatic sigh, then turned.

"Look, lady, I'm sorry. For"—he waved his hand—"whatever it is you have going on in your world. Honestly, I am. But I cannot help you."

As a bus passed by, he hesitated a moment and then continued across the street, walking past a row of bike rentals beside a small park, where people lounged lazily in the grass, in contrast to my urgency as I followed on his heels past a French restaurant and bookstore. "I woke up, and my entire world had changed. I can't explain anything, except that maybe it's all in my head. But I don't think it is. I know things I shouldn't. Have memories of things that aren't there. And I have a daughter. A child. Or at least I did."

We crossed another busy street, ignoring the crosswalk and barely escaping a speeding car. "Are you following me?" he asked, spinning around.

"All I'm asking for is five minutes."

He slowed to a stop and pinched the bridge of his nose. "Five minutes? And you promise you'll leave me alone?"

"I promise."

He shook his head, appearing to consider his options. "I know I'm going to regret this," he grumbled to himself. "Fine. After you, then." He held out his hand, gesturing toward the door of a dimly lit pub tucked into a pedestrian side street.

I followed his glance toward the pub. "Really? You'll talk to me?"

"Do I have a choice? I'm going in here, anyway. You might as well follow."

CHAPTER TWENTY-THREE

I quickly entered before he changed his mind and waited awkwardly while he ordered a pint and took a seat at a dark wood table by a window. Groups of friends were chatting with drinks beneath the bar's flag bunting, and coffeehouse music played from a jukebox. Outside, a beer garden was filled with people talking and laughing beside flower boxes.

Jonathan Deveraux wasn't entirely what I expected. There was a weariness to him, a rugged exterior covering a posh gentleman, forgotten but still there. The kind of person whom I could see rolling out of bed at 5:00 p.m., splashing water on his face, and throwing on a tuxedo. He was about my age, late thirties if I remembered correctly from the bio that Piper had sent me. He wore slender black jeans and an untucked, slightly crumpled, cornflower-blue button-down shirt, the same color as his eyes, rolled at the sleeves with the top buttons undone. He looked like he hadn't slept much.

"You're not getting anything?" he asked. I shook my head, not wanting to waste any time.

"Water's fine," I said to the barman.

"Suit yourself." He took a long drink, draining a quarter of his lager in two long gulps. "Okay, five minutes. Starting now." He tapped his watch, emphatically. "Go ahead."

I hesitated, looking out the bay window, then down at the cardboard coaster advertising strawberry summer pilsner. I'd come all this way but was suddenly aware once again of how crazy I would sound.

They were probably right. Graham, Dr. Higgins. Everyone.

And sitting there, in front of this stranger, it finally sank in.

"Well?" he said. "Are you going to say anything?"

I felt my cheeks warm. "Actually . . . you know what? I'm so sorry. I think I've wasted your time." I picked up my bag, tears pricking the back of my eyes. "Sorry again."

I stood and turned to leave.

"Wait. That's it? You stalk me outside my house, follow me to the pub, and now you're leaving?" He groaned. "Look, I'm sorry, okay? I don't mean to be a prat. It just . . . comes naturally sometimes. Sit." He gestured to the seat across from him. "Honestly, I really only have a little bit of time, and then I have to meet someone, but you're here, so you might as well ask me what you need to or tell me your story or whatever it is."

Somewhat reluctantly, I sat back down, staring longingly at Jonathan's beer. It was uncharacteristically hot in London, and I was warm. "I could probably use one of those, after all," I said. He pointed toward the bar. "I'd better not, though. I have a hard enough time keeping a clear head these days."

"Oh, fantastic."

I chuckled. "Not big on conversation, are you?"

"Look, do you want to tell me why you're here? Maybe start with your name? And maybe how you found me, which is of slightly more concern, if I'm being honest."

"Oh, right. Sorry." I extended a hand. "I'm Annie. Annie Beyers. My assistant, Piper, called you."

Realization dawned on his face as he shook my hand. "Ah. She is very persistent, that one. And resourceful, it seems." He had a posh but relaxed London accent that hinted at a private school upbringing.

"Yes, she is." I chuckled. "Both of those things." He glanced at his watch. Time was running out, so I hurried. "Okay, well, I guess the main thing I want to know is, What made you write that article? I looked into your career, and I couldn't find a single other story that was even remotely like the one you wrote. And you haven't written anything like it since."

"That's because that damn story nearly wrecked my career. I wish I'd never written it."

"So . . . ," I said, when he didn't continue. "Why did you, then? Did something happen to your memory?"

"God, no." He waved a hand. "It's much simpler than that. More ridiculous, in fact." He swallowed another gulp of beer. "Pub trivia night."

"Excuse me?"

"It's true. Pop culture junkie," he said.

"I have a hard time believing that."

"Just down the street, in fact. We were in the lead, final question of the night. 'State the iconic line in the *Star Wars* trilogy that occurs when Luke Skywalker confronts Darth Vader.'"

He stared at me; then I realized he expected me to answer. "Oh, uh . . . 'Luke, I am your father,'" I said. This was absurd.

He sighed theatrically. "See? Thank you. Ask anyone to quote a line from classic *Star Wars*, and that's precisely what they'll say. But as it seems, that is *not* the correct line. And so we lost pub trivia that night."

"Yes, it is." My father used to imitate James Earl Jones's baritone voice when we were little.

"No. Trust me. It is indeed not the line. Or, at least, it's not *anymore*. He doesn't say the name 'Luke,' but for some reason, we all remember it that way."

Evidently this was an important distinction, though at the moment, I really couldn't see why. I started to get the impression that this was not his first beer of the day. "What does this have to do with anything?"

"So that night, after a few too many drinks, I googled it, convinced I'd gotten the answer correct. And lo and behold, all these stories pop up with people swearing, like me, that they clearly remembered it one way, when in fact it was another. I ended up down the rabbit hole of YouTube, as happens, watching dozens of videos showing all kinds of similar instances—music lyrics, logos, iconic movie lines that people swore had changed. 'If you build it, they will come.' Name the movie."

"Are you drunk?" I asked, annoyed.

He glanced at his watch. "Not yet." He took another drink for effect. "So?"

I sighed. "Whatever. *Field of Dreams.*"

"Bingo. But people are all remembering it incorrectly. That's not the line."

"It's not?" I had no idea what any of this had to do with me, frustration threatening to turn into disheartened tears. This guy was an idiot.

"People thought it was all proof that we were living in a parallel universe. Or had switched to one, or some such. I did a story on it. That's it."

"Really. That's it," I said, flatly.

"Yep." He drummed his fingers on the table. "So—are we done here?"

I let everything he'd said process for a few moments. This man was Oxford educated, had begun his career working in Moscow as a contributor for the *Observer* and the *Evening Standard*. He'd lived in Pakistan and Afghanistan on assignment. He had a list of accolades a mile long.

I narrowed my eyes at him and leaned in. "No."

"No?" He raised a brow.

I shook my head. "No. I don't buy it. None of that stuff matters. You wouldn't write a story based on a bunch of pop culture nonsense. There's more to this."

He set his phone down heavily. "You don't give up, do you? Look, I told you I can't help you."

"But you don't even know what it is I need help with," I challenged.

"You're asking about that story. That one, ridiculous story. Trust me, that's all I need to know."

I didn't respond, both of us sitting in silence, waiting the other out.

"Fine," I said, defeated. "If you're just going to make fun of me, I don't have it left in me." I gathered my things and stood, tears of disappointment once again pricking the back of my eyes. I'd been a fool to come all this way.

"Ugh. What does it matter why I wrote it? Why do you care?" he groaned as I started to walk away.

I turned back toward him. "Because of who you are. You're an educated, award-winning political war correspondent, and yet, out of the blue, you do an article on a subject that, in your own words, is completely ridiculous. If someone like you gave it even a shred of possibility, then I need to know why. And if it's all nothing but a bunch of nonsense, then I need to know that too. Okay?"

His phone screen lit up, and as he read the text, a shadow passed over his face, and his shoulders dropped. He ran a hand through his dark-blond hair and leaned back in his chair. His expression began to soften, as if he had decided to stop whatever act he'd been putting on moments earlier. He looked off into the distance, as if he didn't fully know the answer to my question himself, and gestured for me to sit back down. "It's a long story, okay? Like I said, it started out as something I came across one night after pub trivia."

"Yeah, I got that part."

"I know, deeply intellectual. Anyway, it doesn't really matter. But it niggled at me. I found that there was kind of a pop culture phenomenon happening—scores of people swearing things in their lives had changed. It was like a thread, and once I pulled it, more and more stories came with it."

"I know what you mean. The same thing happened to me when I started looking all this stuff up. It's how I found you, actually," I said. "But what made you give it any credit? I mean, it's pretty out-there."

"Yeah, it is. But, like you, apparently, I wanted some explanation for it. I mean, how could this happen? So, I started talking to neurologists and psychiatrists, who explained the effects of mass suggestibility and memory disorders. I talked to experts in physics who cited string theory and Newton's multiverse and Schrödinger's cat, Tesla and Einstein claiming that multiple versions of past and present might be simultaneously possible. I found incidents throughout history—really bizarre stuff, but oddly compelling. Sometimes happening to just one person, or sometimes happening to an entire group. So most people say, What's it really matter, right?" He leaned forward. "But it *does* matter. Because, you see, what does this tell us about history and our perception or retelling of it? What's truly accurate and what's not? The story was never meant to be much of anything. It was a side thing. Far from what I normally do. But I was between projects, and I needed a break from it all. Just . . . a damn break."

He sat back with his glass resting on his stomach. "So on a whim, I put everything into a story, my editor made the mistake of publishing it, and the next thing I knew, I was the patron saint of every whacko, ghostbuster, and conspiracy theorist who was sure they were living in a parallel universe or had time traveled from another dimension."

"I see."

"No offense," he added.

"Right. So you don't believe any of it, then . . . even after everyone you've spoken with, everything you've learned. Even some of the world's leading scientists."

"No. I don't," he said, emphatically. "Or, at least, not the way that it's implied. What I believe is that people have an innate need to apply meaning to things that confuse them, and humans seem to have a natural fascination with the mysterious and spooky. It excites us. And we embrace it. But that doesn't mean it's real. And, more simply, memory is just—inaccurate. It changes every day."

He was right, I knew. Dr. Higgins had often said similar things in our sessions.

"And when it comes to science," he continued, "we're just scratching the surface of what's possible, and we really don't know. But when we do figure it out? I doubt very much that it'll have anything to do with something as tiny and insignificant as a line in a space movie from the 1970s, no matter how great a movie it is."

Something as tiny and insignificant as a five-year-old little girl and a family that lives in a yellow house. I thought about all the stories just like mine that had been lost and discarded over the years as utter nonsense. "And you've talked to the world's experts on this. Everyone? Every single one?"

He waffled. "I mean, not everyone . . . but yes. If I'm guilty of anything, it's of being too thorough."

"And nothing. Not one thing anyone said gave you the slightest hint of a possibility that any of it could be real or possible."

"What . . . that we all might be living alternate lives out there somewhere? Sliding doors and all that? There are some very compelling theories out there. Especially when you talk to the astrophysicists. But no. I'm afraid not."

He'd given me a lot to think about, but nothing that really changed anything.

"By the look on your face, I feel like that's not the answer you were hoping for. Sorry." He said it somewhat sincerely.

"It's all right. I can't say that I'm shocked. Honestly, I don't believe it either."

"You don't?" He seemed surprised.

"No. Not really. I just didn't know where else to turn, and was looking for answers, I guess." Which had led me exactly nowhere.

His phone chimed again, and he frowned. "You said something about a daughter?" he asked, distractedly.

"Yeah. But . . ." He was busy typing out a few lines of text on his phone. "I think you've given me what I needed. I won't take any more of your time." What had I been thinking coming here? That I was some special, scientific breakthrough with the keys to unlocking the universe? I didn't know whether to laugh or cry.

"For what it's worth, despite your tendency to stalk perfect strangers," he said, briefly looking up, "you don't seem anything like one of those nutters to me. I've encountered my fair share."

"Thanks. I suppose you would know," I joked.

He drained the last sip from his glass, standing. "Sorry about earlier, by the way. You wouldn't believe how many strange people have approached me. It's sort of my defense mechanism to send them on their way."

"I have no doubt it works."

He laughed a little sheepishly. "Whatever it is you're going through, whatever has brought you all the way here, I hope you find what you're looking for."

I felt like the wind had been taken from my sails. There was nowhere left to go. "Thank you. Really. I'm sure I'll be fine."

He picked up his bag, a rugged brown leather satchel, and hoisted it over his shoulder diagonally. As he walked away, he took his phone from his pocket, and then stopped, turning. "You know . . ."

I looked up.

"I am curious now, though, I'll admit," he continued. "Professional hazard, I guess. I have to ask now . . . Why exactly *do* you want to know about all this?"

"It's nothing. You wouldn't believe me."

"Come on." He waved a hand, inviting more. "Out with it."

I shrugged. "Oh, you know. The usual. Just that I'm convinced I remember living a totally different life with my apparently now-former husband and that my daughter—who, by the way, never existed—is trying to reach me. You know, your average normal stuff." I was drained, and the combination of sarcasm and sadness rolled from my tongue.

He scratched at his beard, trimmed close to his skin. "Well . . . that would be intensely unnerving; I'll give you that."

I nodded.

"So is that it, then? What are you going to do now?"

"Nothing I *can* do. Go home, I guess, right?"

"Really?"

"I mean . . . I stumbled upon this one woman, Eunice Brown," I said. "She's this . . . I don't know . . . person who seems to be the expert on all this. She has probably the largest collection of stories out there—references dozens of examples in which people like me claimed they were seeing new, alternate versions of their own history happening in everyday things. I would have liked to have talked to her as well, but what's the point, I guess? I suppose it just got into my head." I was embarrassed just saying it. Hope could make one desperate.

"Yeah, I know of her."

"You do?" I looked up at him, surprised.

"Like I said—if I'm guilty of anything, it's of being too thorough. No stone left unturned and all that."

"Gotcha. I emailed her but her website looks like it was made in 1999 on Myspace. Complete with blinky stars and broken links. I never heard back."

He laughed. As he did, the corners of his eyes crinkled in a way that told me his fair skin had spent a great deal of time in the sun over the years. "Yeah. It's bad. And you're right; there is a lot there. But you won't hear back from her. I tried."

"*You* wanted to talk to her? A psychic medium? Somehow I doubt that very much. You seem more like the debunker type."

"Well, be that as it may, her name kept coming up over and over. I was actually pretty disappointed I didn't get a chance to talk to her. And ultimately started to wonder if she's a real person at all. But yes, in general, that's very much true. No magic for me. I believe in black and white, concrete facts."

"I get that."

"But you don't agree?"

I walked with him to the door. "A month ago? Yes, I would've absolutely agreed. But now I don't know what I believe. Nothing in my life makes sense anymore. Nothing is black and white or concrete, it seems." The breeze drifted warm from outside the door, and a couple walked in as we moved to the side. "You know those optical illusions—the ones that look like a picture of one thing. But you blink and suddenly the picture turns into something else entirely? That's what it feels like. I think I've been grasping at straws. But I'm sure the answer is much simpler. No magic. No mystery. Just a bit of miswiring." I tapped my forehead. "I was in a car accident."

"Ah. Sorry." Just then his phone chimed again, and he looked at the screen. "Unfortunately, I really do have to go this time," he said. "But it was lovely meeting you, Annie Beyers. I wish you much luck." He bowed his head slightly in farewell and was off. He jogged across the street north toward Highbury, while I turned in the opposite direction. The doors of the pub opened onto Camden Passage, and as I walked, I watched as couples and friends went about their normal day, meandering through the cobblestone alley of shops, cafés, and antiques vendors selling their vintage wares. I intended to take the tube from Angel station, but instead passed it by and walked all the way back to the hotel. After all, what was the hurry? The city's sidewalks were filled with the after-work crowd spilling out of pubs and restaurants, cheering on their favorite team in loud roars, and bubbling with the energy that courses through London on the rare, balmy summer night when the sun doesn't set until nearly ten. I felt a desperate longing to be part of laughter and conversation and friends—to be part of the world, as for the first time I realized how completely alone I was. With every smile I passed and every sound of laughter or the clink of a pint glass, the isolation became more silent and deafening, sitting like a heavy weight. I felt like an outsider, peering in, wondering when life would ever look that normal for me again.

CHAPTER
TWENTY-FOUR

"I'm so sorry you didn't get more out of it," Marcie said.

I sank down into the duvet in my empty hotel room, holding the phone to my ear. I pulled a thick terry-cloth robe around me. "I'm glad I talked to him. I liked talking to him, actually. Oddly, I almost feel better."

"Really? He sounds like kind of a jerk."

"He's not really. I think he's just . . . a very intelligent man who almost lost his career. If there was any shred of evidence out there that something weird could be going on, he would have found it. But he didn't. At least I don't have to wonder anymore."

"Wonder what?"

"I don't know. Whether there might be some shred of hope that the things I'd been remembering might somehow be true."

"So you're going to come home? You're done?" Marcie asked, sounding more like a mother than a sister.

"Yeah. I guess I am. I'm not sure where else there is to turn. Time to face the music. Though honestly, I'm not going to whatever place Graham has been hiding from me. Mental hospital or whatever."

Marcie laughed. "What are you talking about, mental hospital?"

"I heard you guys talking the other day. I know you think I need more help than I'm getting. First he hid the paintings from me, and now he's secretly trying to have me committed." Though, I guessed, who could blame him?

"Whoa, I have no idea what you are talking about."

"His big secret trip to Connecticut? I know, Marcie. You guys don't have to hide it," I snapped.

There was silence on the other end for several moments, until Marcie finally spoke. "Ann, I think you've misunderstood some things. Yes, Graham and I were talking the other day, and both agreed that you might need a little more help than what you're getting. But jeez, we didn't mean sending you away. Only that it might be helpful for you to start seeing Dr. Higgins more often, or consider some other options, like coming to stay with Tim and me for a little while. Something like that. You don't have to do anything you don't want. I promise, Annie. We'll get through it in whatever way works for you."

"Oh," I said, surprised. "It just felt like there was something going on. All these hush-hush conversations, and then the paintings and mentions of Connecticut."

"I see." Marcie went quiet before speaking. "I've been holding off, but . . . I feel like I should tell you; that's not what Graham's been hiding."

"What do you mean?" My heart quickened, as I realized something inside me didn't really want to hear more.

"First, I want you to know that he hasn't been *hiding* anything from you, exactly. Not really, anyway. At least, not to be cruel or conniving. He's a good guy, Ann. He would rather die than hurt you. Even after everything you've been through. You know that."

"I know."

"Which is why he felt like he shouldn't tell you. It wasn't just that he moved out—he's with someone else now, Ann."

I sat upright. "Someone else? What do you mean?"

"C'mon, Ann. Are you honestly that surprised? Given everything you've learned?"

I dropped my head in my hands, pressing my palms against my eyes. "No. I guess not," I said through choked-back tears. "Still, I can't believe he was cheating on me."

"He wasn't cheating on you at all. It was after you separated. You've known all about it. Or, at least, you *did* know. It wasn't a secret. Annie. *You're* the one who wanted out of your marriage, not Graham. You broke his heart."

This new revelation made me curl inward. "I did? But he seems so angry all the time. He can't stand to be in the same room with me."

"Can you blame him? He's been through a lot. He fought like hell for you. But eventually he had to move on. He's been trying to start over, and this is killing him."

I thought of all the time he'd been at the loft—sleeping in a separate room. Avoiding every touch. "Wow. We were much more separated than he let on, weren't we?"

"All that was left was for the papers to be signed."

"Wow."

"Naomi has been pretty pissed, from what I gather." Marcie chuckled. "Not like I give a shit. But still."

"Naomi?" I winced, the name crawling across my skin.

"Yeah. He works with her. She lives in Connecticut."

I felt like I might be sick.

"But he still came back to the loft? To stay with me those first couple nights? He went to all that trouble?"

"Yes," she said, pointedly. "He did. The doctors thought it might help ease the transition for you a little. And he was worried about you being alone, Annie. He cares about you that much."

The Graham I remembered, the kind and loving man I knew, was still there after all, I guessed. Just no longer with me.

I expected more tears to come, but, oddly, they did not. "It's weird."

"What is?"

Part of me felt like I should be collapsing into a ball, sobbing, but another layer, a more recent part of me, felt a certain level of understanding and acceptance. "The idea of this other woman is awful. But it's weird—it doesn't hurt like I feel like it should." In another life, it would've destroyed me. Why not here?

"It's because it's what you wanted. Not for him to be with someone else specifically, obviously. But for you to go your separate ways. You both had been through a lot, and it was time to let it go. *You* had moved on."

I exhaled, letting all this new information sink in. "So, please tell me that's it. No more secrets, then?" I wasn't sure I could take much more.

"I think that's about it. Promise. No more surprises."

I looked out the window at the traffic passing below and people bustling down the sidewalks. The streets of London, always in perpetual motion. "I'm going to try to get a flight home tomorrow, I guess." As lonely as London could feel at times, I wasn't especially eager to return to New York. The more I thought about it, the more New York didn't feel like home. London had been a comfortable distraction, reminding me of a haven from my younger years. It predated Graham, the house, everything, and, for this reason, somehow felt more comfortable.

"You know what?" Marcie said, as if reading my thoughts. "On second thought, why don't you stay for a few days? Relax and take a breath. Maybe it's good for you, being away. Out of New York. Someplace different. You always did love London."

I closed my eyes, tilted my head back against the cushioned headboard. "I did, didn't I?"

I was homesick. I could feel the rocking chair drifting back and forth in the cool evening air, with the silos and farm spread out before me, the mountains rolling out into the distant horizon beyond. The house was a magnet pulling me toward it, but as I sat across an ocean, four thousand miles away, I knew that it was no longer there to go home to, that someone else now sat on that porch. The hole in my heart—the one left by the loss of my husband, my daughter, and my magical home—would always be there, but perhaps it was time to start letting go of it. To start expanding to allow a new life to unfold. There was nothing left for me in New York City, and the streets there reminded me only of the illusion of what used to be, infused with a kind of longing and bitterness that would always make me want to get onto the Palisades Parkway and head upstate. But here, in London, I felt a shift toward possibility that a new life could perhaps be crafted out of the threads of loss, and a glimmer that another life could begin. In my veins, in my heart, I felt the love that existed in the dreams of raising my child, free to wander in the green grass of a beautiful farmhouse. But life had clearly placed me on a different path. The bustling energy of London, a complete opposite to country life, had an unexplainable familiarity to it that acted as a salve, somehow soothing the hurt and allowing something new to grow. Not now. Not quite yet. But perhaps someday.

CHAPTER
TWENTY-FIVE

"I caught one, Mommy! Can you see! It's blinking!"

On summer evenings, we often eat dinner at a small table on the front porch, the scene set perfectly by the setting sun on the farm and the distant green horizon. As night descends and the sky fills with stars, we run about the yard in giggles, catching fireflies in mason jars before setting them free to continue their journey into the flickering fields.

. . . blink. "Mommy, come chase me!"

I close my eyes and smile, but can't catch her. Fireflies dance before my eyes, and I can smell the cool evening grass.

. . . blink.

Morning. I can smell the pancakes Graham is making for breakfast on a Sunday morning.

. . . blink.

. . . blink.

~

I had barely slept, jumping at every sound. When I'd mentioned to Jonathan where I was staying, he had joked that the hotel was reputed to be haunted. I'd laughed at the time but found no humor in it in the early morning witching hours. The clock ticked on, and I drifted in and out of the unsettling space between sleep and awake as Hannah called out for me, out of reach. Haunted or not—ghosts of the past always wandered in places like this.

When my phone chimed on the nightstand beside me, I sat up. I scanned the text and returned Piper's call. It was 4:00 a.m. her time, but the girl never slept, it seemed. We spoke briefly, and after hesitating for a few minutes, I placed a second call and prepared to leave a voice mail.

"Hello?" His voice was soft and gravelly, as if he had been half-asleep as well.

"Jonathan. It's Annie. Annie Beyers. I wasn't expecting you to answer."

"Annie." He cleared his throat. "Hello." Fortunately, he sounded less perturbed than I would have expected. "It seems your trusty assistant managed to get my personal number. Remind me to change it." It sounded like he might have smiled when he said it.

"I'm sorry if I woke you."

"It's nine in the morning, why would I be sleeping?" I couldn't tell if he was being sarcastic.

"Well, the thing is, I wouldn't be calling—it's just that . . ." I trailed off, unsure myself if what I was about to say made any sense.

"It's no bother. Really. What's up?"

"Well, I just got off the phone with my assistant. It seems Eunice Brown—you know, the psychic expert—does in fact exist and has agreed to meet with me. I thought you might like to know."

"You're joking."

I fiddled with the tie on my robe. "Uh, no. I don't joke much these days. I'm heading up there this afternoon."

"To where, exactly?" He sounded skeptical.

"She lives west of here, somewhere near Glastonbury."

He chuckled. "Of course she does." I could almost see him rolling his eyes at the mention of the town and its associated history with all things mystical. The phone jostled on his end again, as if brushing against bedsheets, confirming my suspicions that I'd woken him. "How did you manage to get ahold of her, anyway?" he asked.

"According to Piper, it seems she's a fan of my work."

"Really?" He seemed surprised and then recovered. "Sorry. I'm not much into the modern art scene."

"No problem. Anyway, I know you couldn't care less about that article, at this point, but I guess I thought you might like to . . . I mean, I wouldn't mind the company. If you're still curious." There was silence on the other end of the line, and I chewed my lip, waiting. I had no idea why I was asking him to go. I wasn't even sure why I was going at all, myself, after all. I had only intended to offer him the information about Eunice as a sort of thank-you for his time yesterday. The invitation had left my mouth before I'd realized I'd said it. "I'm sure your schedule is packed. It's no big deal if you don't. I just figured—"

"What time's the train?"

~

I started to doubt he was coming, but just as the train began to pull out of Paddington station, Jonathan dropped into the seat across from me. He wore a lightweight gray sweater over a white T-shirt. He looked different, but it took me a moment to figure out why. "You're wearing glasses today," I said, after it dawned on me. They suited him. Made him more approachable.

"Contacts irritate the hell out of me." He dug through his bag, locating his wallet and placing the ticket into it.

"I wasn't sure you'd come," I said, before taking a sip from a to-go cup of tea. "Why *did* you come?"

He laughed. "I have no damn clue. Just couldn't pass it up, I guess."

"You were able to clear your schedule? I feel like you should be running off to some war-torn country or some such." I pictured him with a duffel bag perpetually packed at the front door.

"Ah. Well . . . my schedule these days is a little lighter than I'd like. Truth be told, I've taken some time off for a little while to regroup. Partly by choice and partly forced. Still recovering from some poor career choices, as I mentioned, and assignments are a little light these days."

"I see. Sorry."

He lifted his shoulders. "Such is life." He finished settling in and leaned back in his seat. "What about you? You don't look like you slept much." *Guess I wasn't the only one who noticed things.*

"Gee, thanks."

"No, no. I'm sorry. I didn't mean it that way at all."

I waved off his apology. "It's fine. You're right. I didn't sleep much. No thanks to you, I might add. Planting ghost stories in my head."

"I was just joking; you know that, right? That hotel is most definitely not haunted."

"Yeah, well, try living in my head for a day."

"Ah. I'll have to keep that in mind. No ghost stories," he said with a smile, pretending to jot it down on his hand. The train took off, speeding past the urban landscape of London.

I was grateful for his company, as much as I hated to admit it. I thought back to what Dr. Higgins had said: that I might find comfort in meeting new people, more than I would in fighting with the memories of people I used to know or was supposed to know.

"If I'm being honest, I'm glad you're here," I said. "It'll be comforting to know that there's someone levelheaded to keep things from getting too out-there."

He cocked his head. "Have you always been this way? Not trusting in your own judgment?"

The directness of his question took me aback. "No," I said, adamantly, while considering my answer. "Quite the opposite, actually. I've always been pretty levelheaded."

"You sure about that?"

I narrowed my eyes. "Why do you ask?"

"Well, it *is* what I do, after all. Investigate." He paused, and the corners of his mouth turned up. "I looked into your history a bit last night."

"Gotcha." I sighed. I had forgotten my whole history, including my mother's mental illness, was now online, perfectly available to anyone. I felt terribly exposed, like someone had opened up all my dresser drawers and peered inside. "So now I'm *really* wondering why you've come along. Now that you think I'm crazy and all."

He turned his head again, watching me closely. "No. I don't think that at all. But surely you must admit . . . it does give one pause. And you know what they say—usually the simplest answer is the right one. Mental illness can be quite hereditary," he said, gently. "It's nothing to be ashamed of, you know."

I stiffened. "I know that. And I'm not ashamed of her at all," I said firmly. "I'm proud of my mother—for everything. What happened to her wasn't her fault."

"And no one would fault *you* if you had inherited similar issues."

Ouch.

"Oh, sure, unless you run around asking about invisible children." I wrapped my light jacket around me tighter, a turtle retreating into a shell. I was beginning to question my decision to invite him. The last thing I needed was someone judging me.

"I'm sorry," he said. "It's none of my business."

I didn't disagree.

"Look, all I'm saying is that something going on in your brain is most likely the root of everything happening here. But if you want my

169

opinion? Given everything you've told me, I'd probably be doing the exact same thing as you."

I looked up. "You would?"

"You want answers. I applaud you for trying to get them. And gut instinct is a powerful thing. You can't ignore it. I don't."

"Thanks for saying that."

"Sure."

The dreary outskirts of London began to turn to patches of rolling green as the train made its way down the smooth track outside of the city. Passengers were listening to headphones, scrolling through their phones, jostling in unison at the occasional bump or turn. A group of young Swedish backpackers, blond and tan, laughed in a group as they continued their journey west.

"So, what can you tell me about Eunice Brown?" I asked. "You probably know more than I do, and I don't really know what to expect."

"She's not really your average psychic type, with a neon sign and all. She started out as a new age author, with a doctorate in philosophy, living in the States. In later years, she left academia and published a few books on the paranormal. Claims to have been born a natural psychic." In truth, it sounded somewhat fascinating, though I wasn't going to admit it to Jonathan. "Then she moved to England, and it seems like that's when things took an odd turn."

"Odd how?" I asked.

"A few years ago she was researching the time slips that were happening on Bond Street in Liverpool." He paused, checking to see if I was familiar with what he was referring to, which I wasn't. I shook my head, and he elaborated.

"People on this one street in Liverpool started claiming that they suddenly were being whisked back to a different time period and then returned minutes later."

"That's bizarre." I shivered at the creepy thought.

"Agreed. But the events there prompted her to explore the subject of time and space, and how she vividly recalled a different version of several world events. It went a bit viral. After that she became a bit of a recluse."

"Oh, I see. This makes sense now . . . how she caught your attention."

"Supposedly she has the most information collected on the subject. From a metaphysical point of view, anyway. The scientists were easy for me to get my head around. But this stuff, well . . . it's not really my thing. I was curious more than anything, I suppose."

"If she really has collected the most stories about people in situations like mine, then I guess I'm on the right track."

"So to speak." He nodded at the train and I laughed.

"I'm still surprised you managed to get a meeting with her," he said. "You said she's a fan of your work?"

I shrugged. "Evidently."

He cocked his head. "You seem surprised. But you're gifted. Truly. I did my homework."

I smiled, pleased that he liked my work, even if it didn't feel like mine yet. "Thank you."

He crossed his arms, leaning back farther into the seat. "So, tell me, how does one grow up to become a famous artist slash budding paranormal investigator?"

"I guess . . . it's hard to explain. In my mind, I left the art world years ago. I don't remember anything about becoming the artist 'Annie Beyers.'"

"Why do you think you left it? It couldn't have been easy to walk away from talent like that," he said.

"In my other life, you mean?" How do you explain your past to someone, when you aren't sure which past is the one to describe?

He nodded.

"It wasn't easy. I'd imagined something very different for my life. Success came really quickly for me when I was young. It all happened so fast. It was to be quite grand, all of it." He smiled as I blinked my eyes dramatically. "Bougie parties in Cannes and fabulous art shows, and I was going to have it all. The best friends. The best of everything."

"But . . . ?"

"But at the same time, I craved quiet. Craved peacefulness. I wanted two opposite things and couldn't find a way to meld them. But life has a way of choosing the path and making those decisions for you, I guess. There were family issues at play. My father, for one. And my husband, Graham, and I had a hard time getting pregnant before we had Hannah, and after she was born, everything changed. She felt like a pure miracle. I was grateful and didn't want to do anything to mess it up. Art didn't really have a place in my world anymore. I set up a studio in our house when we first bought it, figuring I'd get back into it someday, just as a hobby. But it could never be just that. Art has a way of taking over."

"So, you left it all behind?"

I thought back to the few times I'd started painting again, and the effort it would take to transition from the world inside my studio to grounded life, changing diapers and being fully present for a growing child. "My art took me away from her in a way that unnerved me. Being an artist, you go so far inside your head sometimes the world feels like it's separate from you. I didn't like that feeling anymore. When I was little, my mother was kind and gentle and loving. I have the most beautiful memories of her. Everything was perfect. But then later . . . nothing was ever the same, and I sort of lost her to her art and her illness."

"I ran across some of her work online in a story about you from a while back. It was quite captivating," he said.

I smiled, sadly. "It really was. She was very talented. Until she got sick."

He nodded sympathetically.

"Anyway, it wasn't worth it. I never wanted Hannah to feel the way I had. So, I quit and tried not to think about what might have been." Suddenly self-conscious, I shook my head and made a poor attempt to laugh it off. "Or, at least, that's what I *remember*. Apparently, however, I did return to painting. Obviously."

A service attendant pushed a cart down the aisle, and Jonathan ordered a coffee. "Are you okay with your tea? Would you like anything?" he asked.

I shook my head. "I'm good, thank you."

He stirred a bit of sugar into his black coffee. "I can relate to those feelings a little as a writer," he said, continuing. "Especially fiction. It's hard to pop your head up, once you're really into it. It can cause a lot of trouble, my line of work. Going down the rabbit hole." He took a sip from the steaming cup, and a shadow crossed his features. I realized for the first time he had a similarly weary look about him; a sadness that seemed to mirror mine in some way, beneath the rough facade.

"You write fiction, as well?" I asked.

He nodded. "I do. It's what I'm doing now, actually. Trying to, anyway. We'll see."

He told me a little more about the rest of his work. As we continued our journey, the scene outside the train window had turned to rolling green pastures beneath a big, summer blue sky.

"Mommy, can we go on a train someday, pleeeeez? A big one, like the Polar Express."

"This landscape reminds me a lot of home," I said, absently, a little while later as we traveled through the farms of Somerset. "Our house was set on property like this."

"You and your husband don't live there anymore?"

"No. We live in New York City." I paused. "Or, I do . . . I guess. We're not together anymore." It was the first time I had said it out loud, and it felt like a vise around my chest. I wondered where Graham was and what he was doing at that moment, while I was on a train talking to this man, an ocean away, and my heart ached. Was he thinking of me too?

"It's odd. I can't see you living in a place like that. Rural country," Jonathan said, interrupting my thoughts.

"No?"

"You seem like a city person," he added, gesturing to my appearance. I wore black pencil slacks and a slim black T-shirt, my hair resting below my shoulders in a precise cut. It all sat in contrast to the air-dried hair, breezy dresses, and loose sweaters I'd worn in the past years in the country.

"I guess I'm both. The Country Mouse and the City Mouse," I said with a small laugh. That was always the problem, wasn't it?

"My mum used to read that story to me." His features softened as he said it, and I smiled, imagining him as a child.

"Yeah? Funny, same here."

"My little country mouse!" Mom taps me on the nose as I giggle on her lap. "You'll be a big girl in the pretty city one day." She takes a sip from a pretend cup, pinky in the air.

"I didn't see much in the way of green space when I was growing up. Or anywhere, really. We didn't have money for vacations and such. But one summer when I was around twelve, my parents took us on a weekend trip into the Pocono Mountains. There were lakes and woods and farms. I thought it was heaven on earth."

"Sounds beautiful," he said.

"I'd never seen anything like it. I remembered seeing this farmhouse out in the distance, and that was it. 'Someday,' I said, 'I'll live somewhere like that.' It looked clean and good and hopeful. I never forgot it."

"Sounds like you got it."

"Yeah. I did. For a little while, anyway."

"So," he said, turning back to the subject at hand a few minutes later. "What do you think we're going to find up here in Glastonbury?

Because I don't know about you, but I, for one, will be very disappointed if I don't get to meet my departed great-gran." He pulled a face.

"Honestly? I have no idea," I said, laughing then. "But hey, what do I have to lose?"

"Good point."

A smile played on my lips as Jonathan took a walk to the snack bar, and as the train continued on, my thoughts drifted back. It was funny how certain days in your childhood stand out among the rest so clearly. I could still see my mom pointing dreamily at the houses dotting the countryside.

"Someday, I'd like to live in a place just like that, girls," she says, as Marcie sits beside me. "I'd learn to grow tomatoes and lettuce. Put in a pretty white fence. There'd be no neighbors to bother us, no cars, no noise. I'd plant a hundred lilac bushes. It would be so peaceful." I follow my mother's gaze, staring out the window at all that space and beauty, and wishing so hard that, someday, she might have it all.

"Me too! When I grow up," I tell her, "I'm gonna become a famous artist and buy the prettiest farmhouse in the world, Mom." She looks at me then and smiles as tears fill her eyes.

"It will be beautiful, my Annie. I promise."

I often thought of my mom on those evenings as I sat on the front porch of our Yellow House, the lilacs beside us and the chickens clucking quietly. And sometimes, when the light was right, I'd almost think I saw her in the tall grass. Lovely and watching.

CHAPTER
TWENTY-SIX

"I sort of imagined it would look more like a hobbit's house," I said, staring at Eunice Brown's home from the gravel driveway. The semidetached brick bungalow was approximately three-quarters of a mile from the town center of Glastonbury, a satellite TV dish on the roof, above flowering wisteria vines that climbed the wall beneath it. "Thatched roof, or something. Mushrooms the size of cats growing in the yard."

Jonathan gave me a smirk. "Well, your imagination does seem to still be intact. We're not in a Harry Potter movie. She's got bills to pay and TV to watch, same as everyone else." He looked toward the house again. "But I hear you."

The train from London had taken just over three hours, and the midafternoon sun had clouded over. We walked up the stone sidewalk, past a front garden with loose gravel. Jonathan pointed at a stone sculpture of an angel in the flower bed and raised his brow. I shrugged and rang the bell. But there was nothing but silence from inside.

"Are you sure she's expecting you?" he asked.

I checked my watch. "Piper confirmed with her. We're right on time." I rang the bell again.

"Maybe she's not here. Maybe she had to pop over to another dimension. But you'd think, being a psychic, she'd have seen we were coming and—"

I spun around. "Look. I understand that you think this is all stupid and far beneath you. But could you please not?"

He held his hands up. "Okay. I'm sorry." He zipped his lips with his finger. I shot him a look, and his shoulders dropped. "Good behavior. I promise."

The sidewalk led around the side of the house, and I followed it. In the backyard was a small stone shed with a stone patio and window boxes. Ivy grew up the sides of it, and a sun-and-moon-themed wind chime hung beneath a small awning. I gave Jonathan a sharp look that shut him up just as he was about to say something and knocked on the door.

A woman answered right away, seeming a little scattered. "Hello there, I'm so sorry, I was running behind. I meant to have tea on before you got here, but I'm finishing up a project." There were boxes piled up behind her. "I've been working on getting this shed organized with all of my husband's old research. We're donating it to the university. Pardon the mess. You must be Annie?"

"And you're Eunice?" I asked.

"Indeed. Pleased to meet you." She looked over at Jonathan.

"Oh, sorry," I said. "This is my friend Jonathan. I hope it's okay that I've brought him."

We exchanged a few more pleasantries, and Eunice asked us to follow her back to the house. As we walked, Jonathan and I exchanged a look. Eunice Brown was absolutely nothing like we'd expected. She wore neatly pressed khaki trousers and a loose blouse with a pale flower design. Her silver hair sat on her shoulders, pulled back neatly with a tortoiseshell clip. She led us into a small sitting room, the walls and doorways of which were lined with books that hinted at the esoteric subject matter we were here to discuss. Ghost stories and collections of haunted castles. The mysteries of Stonehenge. A history of pagan rituals. We sank into a small love seat across from a dormant wood-burning stove. A large macramé dream catcher hung on one window. A stack of medicine cards purporting to draw upon the ancient wisdom and tradition of the healing medicine of animals sat on a nearby table, lit with a Tiffany-style lamp. Her home smelled of lavender and amber and old wood. The house was quiet, save for the tick of a cuckoo clock that hung on the wall, marking time as Eunice prepared tea in the adjacent kitchen.

After a few minutes, she set down a tray with an eccentric assortment of colorful mismatched china and joined us in an opposite chair. "So . . . ," she said, "your assistant tells me you've been having some strange experiences, Annie. What can I help you with?"

By way of introduction, I opened my bag and unrolled the canvas painting I'd brought with me from the studio. I pointed at the translucent image of a girl. "I guess the best place to start is here. This is my daughter, Hannah." Eunice took the canvas from me and inspected it closer, her brow furrowed. "Only, apparently, she no longer exists," I said. "Or never did. And I may be losing my mind."

She stared at the canvas for a few more moments. "Extraordinary," she said, mostly to herself. "I enjoy your work quite a bit." She peered up at me over the frames of her black glasses with a faint, bemused smile. "Tell me everything that's happened—*both* versions of your stories, and then we'll talk a bit more." She handed the canvas back and turned toward Jonathan. "Oh, and Mr. Deveraux, I'm sure you are well aware that I am retired, and I assume this will all be off the record?"

He feigned a wince. "You know who I am."

"Indeed I do." She narrowed her eyes, appearing somewhat amused by his presence.

Jonathan nodded. "Agreed. Off the clock. Off the record. Believe me, I don't plan to write about anything like this again anytime soon."

"Fine. Now that we all understand one another, Annie, please continue."

I glanced sideways at Jonathan, regretting a little that I'd invited him. I felt self-conscious about revealing the truth of everything I'd experienced in front of him.

As if sensing my hesitation, he cocked his head with a small smile. "Hey, I'm interested to hear more too."

I nodded and let out a deep breath. "Okay, well . . ." I related the story in as organized a way as I could.

When I finished, Eunice seemed to be thinking it through. "And you said when you saw all the paintings of your daughter in your studio, this one in particular stood out—you noticed something about it. Something that apparently sent you shooting off to London to find Mr. Deveraux, here. What was it? What did you see in the painting?"

I unrolled the canvas again and laid it flat on the table. Jonathan leaned in, his chin on his fist. "Most of the paintings were of Hannah in the fields. But in this one, the back of the house was included. It was spring, and in the window there's a figure of a person. See here?" I pointed. "No face, just a shadow. But the thing is . . . I know who the shadow was. It was me."

"What do you mean?" Eunice asked.

"I remember that day—the one shown in the painting. Except I remember it from the *inside* of the house. I was standing at the kitchen window while Hannah played outside. See, I happen to remember it because I'd just changed her into the dress she's wearing in the picture. She'd spilled jam on her shirt at lunch. I was frustrated because it was a brand-new shirt, and I hadn't wanted her to wear it, but she'd insisted. I'd lost my patience." I looked down. "Seems so stupid now. It was just a shirt." I cleared my throat, wishing I could go back. "Anyway, I was standing at the kitchen sink, rinsing the stain out while she played outside."

"And yet the painting was from the perspective of outside of the house," Eunice said.

"Exactly. I was shocked when I saw it because even though it was just a painting, it felt like whoever had painted it had actually been there. And how, if none of it happened, did the painting come to be, with all of its specific details that match what I remember? I couldn't ignore it anymore. I had to do something." I knew I wouldn't have a chance at moving on until I'd left no stone unturned. I continued filling in the rest of what had been going on—the children's songs, the dreams, the details I shouldn't have known. I was aware of Jonathan watching me, and occasionally darted glances toward him, but he remained quiet.

By the time I finished, Eunice looked at me carefully, with narrowed eyes and a wise smile. "I think we're going to need a lot more tea."

As she puttered around in the kitchen, I picked up a book from the table. *Is Your House Really Haunted? (Maybe Not)* by Eunice Brown. I held it up to Jonathan, and he rolled his eyes. When Eunice returned with a fresh pot, she took a sip from a chipped cup with a bold paisley pattern in primary colors. I set the book back down on the table. "I'm intrigued by the ghostly apparitions you began seeing at your house. Have you always been able to see ghosts?" she asked.

"Um . . . I'm not sure that's what I'd call it. And no. It was just a few times, I guess. And I haven't had any experiences like that since the accident." I glanced toward Jonathan, a little self-consciously.

Eunice cocked her head and gave me a wry smile. "Oh, I don't know, I wouldn't be so sure. I think there's a very good chance you're getting peeks into your other life right now. You may not be seeing them in quite the same way, but I suspect they still exist. Whispering in your ear as you sleep, perhaps. Singing songs, maybe?" She winked.

A shiver ran up my spine. "My dreams?"

She smiled and clapped her hands together. "Perhaps! Tell me more."

"The scenes change here and there, but they always have the same feeling. I can see them, Graham and Hannah, and I call out, but they can't see me or hear me. Or, at least, Graham can't."

"But Hannah can?" Eunice asked.

"Sometimes it seems that way. I'm not sure."

"We all know children are much more capable of seeing things than we are," she said.

"When I wake up, I swear I can smell her—her hair, her skin, or the faint scent of the new carpet in her bedroom at home. I feel like I've been there," I whispered.

She tapped on her book. "You see, many people believe that what we call ghosts aren't really ghosts after all. Rather, they're projections of people who are very much alive in another time and place. Our physical bodies don't travel there, but our essence, energy, consciousness, whatever you want to call it, does. Science has acknowledged that there is a very good possibility that the universe is made of many dimensions and timelines other than our own. Imagine if you cut hundreds of strands of fine thread and lined them up carefully, side by side. One might cross over the other briefly. Perhaps in that moment, we catch a glimpse of the other side, which is what might have been happening at your house, and now in your dreams. And"—she paused—"maybe *they* catch a glimpse of *this* side." I followed her eyes as they glanced toward the canvas at my feet.

"So you're saying my house wasn't haunted by a strange woman. I was seeing . . . myself? From *this* world?" I trailed off, letting this new idea sink in.

"Or maybe even your mother."

I stared at her, unable to reply, remembering the way my mom spoke of a little girl and a farmhouse.

"It's a theory," she said.

I struggled to wrap my brain around it all, and suddenly a thought dawned on me. "So if all this is true . . . if I'm *here*, then what am I doing *now* over there?"

She lifted her shoulders. "No way to know, really. But I can tell you that there's a lot more going on in the space between *here* and *now* than people realize."

I recalled the dream in which Hannah and Graham both talked about missing me and sat bolt upright. "I'm not dead, am I? The accident?"

She smiled. "Not likely, dear."

I exhaled, sinking back into the couch cushions.

She turned toward Jonathan. "Mr. Deveraux, I believe you and I may have more in common than you think. After I began speaking on the matter and my own personal experiences, people picked up on the frivolity of it all—the pop culture dinner conversation topics of movie lines and logos—and sadly, some very poignant political and cultural events. But the readers—both of our sets of readers—they missed the point, didn't they?" Jonathan reluctantly nodded. "All of those trivial things, they aren't important. They just happen to be the examples we can see in mass media. But the true effects can't be proven, can they—because they're often experienced by a small number of people, or maybe even just one? Annie, when did you say you and your husband's memories diverge?"

"The day I apparently had the miscarriage, when I slipped on the icy steps and fell. But I don't remember it at all, as I've said. *I* remember we didn't go out for a walk when the power went out. That we stayed in. There was no slip and fall."

"So that's the fork in the road. Or, at least, the one that seems to be at play right now. There can always be others, of course, forking off in countless directions." Eunice put her hands together, as a professor might do while making an important point in a lecture.

She continued, "Think of all the different ways that life can go in the split-second decisions of a day. Left or right at the road. Run back into the house for your keys or don't. Small decisions that affect the world in ways we only begin to understand. There are entire teams of researchers in labs devoted to understanding multiverse theory. Perhaps in the distant future, science has developed a way to make adjustments to all of these tiny threads. Imagine the capabilities and the ripple effects down to the smallest details in mundane life. It happens to us every day in small things we dismiss—searching your house frantically for a lost pair of glasses that mysteriously appear. Little blips. Turning around and suddenly a cabinet is open when it wasn't before. It can be very subtle. The feeling of something being slightly off. You might have just jumped to another nearly identical timeline in your own life, or even a different time in the past or future. Time and space are rather flexible."

"I don't know. This all sounds like a bunch of sci-fi movie stuff to me," I said.

"Doesn't resonate with you, eh?" she asked, sipping from her cup. She offered a biscuit that looked like it may have seen better days, and I politely declined.

"It does make a bit of sense, though," Jonathan chimed in.

"It does?" I asked, looking over at him, surprised.

"I've talked to the physicists. It's not as far-fetched as it sounds. As much as I dislike saying that."

Eunice smirked at him. "See? And you thought I was a complete loon."

"I didn't—"

She waved a hand. "Not to worry. I've been accused of worse." She turned back to me. I had wilted a bit, feeling like none of this could possibly have anything to do with me and that we'd veered off track. "There are other theories. Ones that I suspect may touch you in a different way, based on what I'm hearing, Annie. Science may have nothing to do with this. It's bigger than that and far more spiritual, if you have an open mind. See, people in my line of work—with the exception of an arrogant few—most of us don't think we're necessarily all that special in our abilities to see what others can't. We simply have the ability to tap into it more readily. And things like this often run in the family—passes down from one generation to another, as it did for me from my grandmother. Other people—*normal* people, some might say—may experience it in other, more subtle or culturally acceptable ways. In dreams, for instance, or déjà vu. Or the feeling you get when you meet someone brand-new and it feels as if you have known them for your entire life."

She glanced at Jonathan, then back to me, and my eyes met his for an extra beat as we both shifted in our seats as she looked on, amused. "Those sorts of things. If there are, indeed, multiple versions of ourselves out there, living different but similar lives, it may manifest as a constant restlessness or inability to find contentment in the life you have. Maybe a little boy grew up dreaming of being a firefighter but was forced to go into his father's furniture business instead. In another life perhaps he *did* get to be a firefighter. And somewhere deep inside, he connects with that reality. He feels it and longs for it. It's like a door cracks open for a fraction of a second and the subconscious gets to peek inside. Emotions may bleed from one world to another."

"But, of course, there's no proof," Jonathan said. "Obviously."

Eunice hesitated, as if about to say something, but changed her mind. "I suppose that could be said. Anyway, there's been some pioneering research in the mental health field on this subject. A doctor by the name of . . ." She looked at Jonathan. "Off the record, Mr. Deveraux?"

He nodded, clearly intrigued. "Uh, yes. Absolutely."

"Dr. Linda Hodgson. She was an esteemed psychiatrist in the field of psychosis. A world-renowned mental health expert."

Her name sounded familiar. I tried to recall where I'd seen it before, the name dancing on the outskirts of my brain, but came up with nothing.

"Before her death, Dr. Hodgson was leading a private research team. It might be of particular interest to you. If you can find it, that is," Eunice said to Jonathan. "It was all a bit hush-hush."

An orange-and-white tabby cat jumped up onto the coffee table between us, and Eunice reached out to run her hand down the cat's back, eliciting a loud purr.

Eunice continued, "The category you place these types of things into . . ." She held out her two hands like a balance. "Science? Spirituality? It's up to you and your personal belief system. But the truth is no one really knows. There's such mystery out there," she added with a gentle smile.

I gazed out the window, at the roses in the garden. I'd always wanted to plant roses outside of the Yellow House but didn't have the confidence that I'd actually be able to grow the intimidating flower. They seemed to grow in England as easily as common impatiens and marigolds do in the States. "But none of this really helps me. Does it," I said more to myself than to Jonathan or Eunice.

Eunice reached over to pat my hand. "If I'm being perfectly honest? Your doctors are most likely right. In my experience, I've come to learn that most things are explainable in pure, logical fact. But if not—if this is one of those rare, very special cases, maybe it's a gift, Annie."

"A gift?" I asked, a little harshly.

"You're getting the opportunity to see what life *could* be like for you. To get your life back on track toward discovering what *truly* makes you happy, here and now. Perhaps there's something to be learned, wisdom to be gleaned. We've all wondered from time to time, the great question of those two magical words . . ." She leaned forward and whispered:

"What if . . . ?"

Her words hovered in the air and then floated away, while the cuckoo clock ticked.

"So if all of this is happening to me—which I still find nearly impossible to believe—which of the memories are real?" I was frustrated and tired.

She shook her head. "Don't you see? Maybe they *both* are."

"But I don't want this," I gestured to the world around me. "I don't want *this* life!"

She leaned in and peered at me over her glasses, once again with a crooked smile. "Are you sure about that? Truly? From what I know, you seem to have a pretty fabulous life. One that others might dream of. You didn't long to be a successful painter? To be invited to a who's who of events? To live a grand life in New York? To travel the world, with your work in famous galleries? Meet new and interesting people? None of that appealed to you whatsoever, at any point in time?"

I hesitated, looking over at Jonathan and back to Eunice's probing gaze. "Well, I mean, yes. But if I had to choose—I'd choose Hannah. I'd choose home. My family. That's where I want to be."

She shook her head and sighed. "That's what they always say."

"What *who* always says?" Jonathan asked.

"The people who have come to speak to me over the years about this sort of thing."

"There have been others like me?" I asked, my eyes growing wide.

"Of course."

"Of course," Jonathan repeated, giving me a look, his skepticism still intact.

"And?" I said excitedly. "What happened to them?"

"I can't say for sure." Eunice began gathering the teacups, then stopped. "I will say this, however: from what I've been able to glean over the years, all the stories seem to have a single moment that is closely linked in both versions of their story. Or a jarring emotional experience that pushes one over the edge, so to speak. I believe that there might be a unifying moment that is nearly identical in two timelines . . . so identical, in fact, that it causes one thread to slip over to the other. For instance, a moment of getting ready for a walk in a winter storm, putting on the same boots, walking down the same hallway . . ."

"Or a car accident, during a summer thunderstorm, driving down a winding rural road . . ."

Eunice raised her shoulders and smiled. "Quite possibly." She hesitated then, mulling something over in her mind. "I am curious, though . . . in your experience, the shift to this life happened after the car accident, right?" I nodded. "What about the time leading up to it? What was going on then? Anything of significance in your other life?" she asked.

I sighed. "I don't know."

"You don't know?" she asked. "I thought your memories from the five years of your daughter's life were intact?"

"They are, mostly. But it gets hazy in the weeks or so before the accident. I've tried but can't remember. My psychiatrist says that this isn't unusual for paramnesia; it's common for there to be a gray area of time, as he puts it. Holes."

"Interesting. And here and now—according to what you know or have been told—around the time of the accident, what was happening?"

"My assistant and my family tell me that I was painting a lot, but was lost in my own head, had become obsessed with my old house. Losing time." I avoided Jonathan's eyes. "Artist thing, I guess," I said, half joking. Eunice stood and leaned down toward me. A large moonstone crystal dangled from a gold chain around her neck.

"I wouldn't be so sure. As I said, life is so mysterious, wouldn't you say?" She patted my shoulder, leaving a scent of lavender in her wake.

As she continued collecting dishes and disappeared into the kitchen, it was clear that our time with her had come to a close, and we thanked her. As we were leaving, however, she called me back. "Annie, dear. I almost forgot. I have a print of yours. Would you mind terribly signing it for me?"

I walked back into the house, while Jonathan walked to the driveway. She held out a small print, which I recognized as a copy of the painting that hung above the sofa at the loft. I signed it awkwardly, and Eunice leaned close. "In your other life, you gained a daughter. But the world lost a meaningful artist. Maybe there is something to be learned. Keep an open mind. It's imperative. Do you understand?"

I nodded, and she continued in a near whisper, "Try to find peace in this life, and the peace may find you in return. In the meantime, should you ever wish to reach me, I'll give you my number. If you ever get back to where you're hoping to, give me a call." She winked.

"Thank you so much. I have your number."

She shook her head. "Not the number you reached me on—that's my business number. I have a different one for you." She rattled it off. I fumbled in my bag for a pen, but she stopped me. "No." She tapped her head. "In here."

"I can't write it down? You want me to remember it?" I asked.

"I'm paranoid and don't much like people disturbing me. Wouldn't want it getting into the wrong hands."

It seemed a little overkill to me, but I agreed. The woman was certainly eccentric. I asked her to repeat it, and she did so, slowly, three more times until she was sure I'd committed it to memory.

We said our goodbyes and I met Jonathan by the road.

"So. That was an experience," he said. He shifted his feet, looking down as if unsure what to say next.

"I'm not sure what to even do with all of that." I looked back toward the house and saw the curtain in the front window close.

"I do," Jonathan said. "We need to find out more about this Dr. Hodgson and her research."

I looked at him in surprise. "We?"

He nodded. "Yeah. We." He had his phone in his hand. "While you were inside, I put a call in to one of my researchers. I asked him to dig up everything he could on this doctor. You never know what we might find, right? Might as well see it through," he said. But his smile hinted at something a little more.

I looked up at him. "Thank you for being here today. For helping me with all of this."

"Like I said, professional hazard."

I chuckled. "Right."

~

By the time we arrived back in London, it was well after dark. I'd dozed off on the train, and when I woke, I was embarrassed to find my head resting on Jonathan's shoulder. The train had been more crowded on the way into London, and we'd been forced to sit side by side. The weather had changed unexpectedly, and in my hasty packing, I hadn't included enough layers. Despite the occasional chill in his personality, Jonathan seemed to emit warmth like there was a woodstove buried beneath the hard exterior. If I was being honest, Eunice's passing but pointed comment earlier in the day resonated. It was odd: as aggravating as he could be when he tried, his company was a preternatural fit. As if we'd known one another for years.

I shifted away, smoothing my hair.

"I got a text while you were asleep," he said. "My guy did some digging and managed to get his hands on some archived footage that Dr. Hodgson left as part of her research."

"Oh wow, how long was I out?" I joked.

He laughed. "Not long. He's very resourceful. You wouldn't believe the kinds of things he manages to dig up. I don't ask a lot of questions about how he does it. I don't think I want to know." He slung his bag over his shoulder, and we walked through the heavy crowds in Paddington, emerging onto the street. I pulled my sleeves down over my hands and curled inward against the chill. "He's sent them all to my place. Hungry?"

CHAPTER
TWENTY-SEVEN

It approached midnight as we sat on a burgundy Indian rug on the floor in front of Jonathan's television. Containers of moo shu pork and vegetable dumplings sat beside boxes of files and videos that Jonathan's researcher had dropped off. Dr. Linda Hodgson was a prominent researcher in the field of neuropsychiatry. We'd been poring over her research and so far hadn't managed to find a single reference to the sorts of things that Eunice Brown had mentioned. Grainy images of psychiatric patients and interviews played from the video on the screen.

"I don't know about you, but I need a break." Jonathan stood, stretching to his full height, just over six feet. "I'm getting a drink." He took off his sweater and tossed it over a chair, leaving him wearing a white T-shirt and jeans. He called from the kitchen, "I'm getting you one too." Before I could say anything, he looked around the corner. "You're having one. You could use it, trust me."

I sighed, rolling my eyes with a laugh. "Okay. Fine. Beer sounds great—something light if you have it." I needed to keep my wits about me.

His apartment was comfortable, with hardwood floors and ornate throw rugs. Framed Saul Bass film posters from Alfred Hitchcock movies were lined up in a series of three above a dark sofa. The center one was from *Vertigo*, and as I looked at the dense orange design of a man drifting off-kilter in the center of swirls, I smirked. I could relate to that.

I walked around the room to let the blood flow through my legs after having sat for too long cross-legged on the floor.

Criss-cross applesauce, Hannah.

A nook separated the living room from the hall, leading back to where I presumed the bedroom was. In it, beneath a tall narrow window, sat a contemporary desk with a laptop computer and piles of magazines, newspapers, and books, including a tattered, dog-eared copy of Chinua Achebe's *Things Fall Apart*. Two stacks of papers that looked like a manuscript sat on one corner of the desk beneath the window, with a heavy rock serving as a paperweight. In the dim glow of the desk lamp, I leaned over to glance at the words just as Jonathan appeared. He leaned his hip on the doorframe and took a sip from his bottle while handing a second to me. It was from a local brewery and felt crisp and smooth as I swallowed, my shoulders instantly relaxing.

He ran a hand through his hair, mussing it, then dropped his hand into his pocket. "You've discovered the great novel, as they say." He chuckled, though he looked somewhat defeated as he followed my gaze to the stack of typed pages.

"What's it about?" I asked, running my finger along the lines of black-and-white Times New Roman beneath his name on the top page. *Jonathan Deveraux.* I liked the way his name sounded in my head.

"Rubbish. That's what. But thank you for asking." He walked over to stand beside me and shuffled a few things on the desk before tapping the top of the manuscript. "I was working on this when everything went down with the article."

"It can't be that bad. Tell me."

He sighed. "It's a novel based on the life of one of the inmates who was in prison where anti-apartheid leaders were also held. The story of a poor, uneducated man learning about literature and philosophy and political theory from some of the most inspiring men in the world, all while together in terribly harsh conditions. And then he goes on to do great things with his life, using what he learned from them in prison."

"It sounds like a wonderful story."

"Thanks. It was nearly finished. My publisher was anticipating a big splashy debut. But then the story that must not be named came out, and suddenly my credibility was shattered. The book deal was shelved, so to speak. And that was that."

On the far corner I noticed a photo of him with a woman, holding hands, and was about to ask about it, but changed my mind.

"Do you still think of publishing it?" I asked instead.

"I don't know. Maybe. Right now I'm finishing up a safer choice— by which I mean nonfiction. An in-depth analysis of politics in the Middle East and North Africa. The great magnum opus will have to wait a little longer, I guess. I need to reestablish my credibility first. Then we'll see."

"So that's what bothered you, isn't it . . . what made you dig in? It was the stuff on the political events."

He nodded. "Pop culture is one thing, but turning meaningful events in history into a viral internet fad? It bothered me and I couldn't shake it. I'd just gotten back to London after living in Africa for three years—covering the ways South Africa had changed. Economic output, trade, migration statistics and trends, health, living conditions. I don't believe in all that conspiracy theory rubbish, but what fascinated me was the group mentality of it and the way that I, myself, an educated person, had been no less suggestible, albeit on a much-less-important topic."

"Pub trivia," I said, smiling. I could tell the subject had deep meaning to him, and it made more sense now. "No wonder you wish you'd never written it. The article, I mean."

He turned his head, looking at me for a long moment with a faint smile. "I'm not so sure anymore. Maybe things do happen for a reason."

I nodded slowly in reply, and the energy in the room seemed to crackle. "Maybe you're right."

A moment later, we heard the voice of Dr. Hodgson speaking from the television, where we'd left a recording to play: "Our belief is that there may be more to certain mental health symptoms: auditory and visual hallucinations, types of psychosis, lost time, dementia even," she said. Jonathan and I both hurried to the living room. Dr. Hodgson was seated at a desk, talking to a male interviewer. Her salt-and-pepper hair was cropped short, and she wore no makeup, with the exception of a faint hint of lipstick. She wore a doctor's lab coat over a button-down blouse. "We're exploring the possibility that perhaps these people may be seeing something that's real. Something the rest of us can't see."

In the back of my mind, though I did not say it aloud, I thought of the ghostlike figure from our house—the spectral woman whom Hannah and I had both seen. The hairs on the back of my neck rose as a shiver went down my spine.

"There are other scenarios that are less compelling, but still important. Look at some of the world's greatest artists, known equally for their madness, sadly, as they are for their art. Take Van Gogh, for instance— who suffered from episodes of sudden panic and lapses of sanity." A quote appeared on the screen in serif type as Hodgson read it off camera:

> "I am unable to describe exactly what is the matter with me; now and then there are horrible fits of anxiety, apparently without cause, or otherwise a feeling of emptiness and fatigue in the head . . . and at times I have attacks of melancholy and of atrocious remorse. There are moments when I am twisted by enthusiasm or madness or prophecy."
> —Vincent van Gogh

Dr. Hodgson continued, "It was during some of these periods that he, and many artists like him, created some of the world's most breathtaking art. What if there is more to it?"

No wonder Eunice had brought up Dr. Hodgson's work.

Van Gogh's paintings flashed across the screen. Included among them was *The Yellow House*, with wide swaths of yellow beneath a brilliant dome of blue sky, reminding me of my own lost home. The painting of a beloved building where the artist had once lived.

Hodgson went on, "Imagine how unsettling or frightening it would be if you had no control over it? It could drive a person to psychosis, especially when it's frequent and they lose all sense of what's real and what's not. A person who had been perfectly happy and functioning begins to descend into a slow spiral."

I was leaning into the screen and felt Jonathan's eyes watching me, no doubt drawing the same comparisons to my mother as I had.

"Annie, sweetie, come dance with me." There's music playing from the radio in the kitchen, and Mom is wearing cutoff denim shorts and a flowery tunic, her hair in a braid down her back. She takes me in her arms, and her hands are dotted with dried paint, as together we bounce to the beat. I look up at her sparkling eyes, high above me. She smells of rose lotion, and for a little while everything seems like it used to be.

"What are you hungry for? Pancakes?" she asks. "French toast?"

I nod eagerly. "Yum!"

"Okay, you got it." She taps me on the nose.

"I have a beautiful granddaughter who looks just like you, do you know that?" Her eyes fill with joyful glee while, at the same time, mine fall.

I nod, wilting. For a moment, I'd let myself hope for a normal day.

"I saw her last evening, and we sang songs together. Oh, I can't wait for you to meet her," she continues. I know she wants me to share in her excitement, but she's gone to that mysterious place in her mind where no one else goes. There's nothing but a sad house and a kitchen where I am standing

in my pajamas with the woman who used to be my mother. I want so badly for her to come back.

The ghosts haunt my world now too. I looked away so Jonathan wouldn't see the uneasiness that had come over me.

"Are you all right?" he asked.

"When my sister and I were little," I said after a moment, swiping at a tear, "our life was wonderful. We never had a lot of money, but it didn't matter. My mom was everything to me."

"Is she where you got your love of art and painting? Your mum?" Jonathan had a knee drawn up and was resting a bottle on it. He paused the TV.

I nodded, smiling. "When it became clear that art was going to be in my future as well, she was my greatest champion. She was radiant and so full of life—like she was privy to a wild kaleidoscope of colors all around her that we couldn't see."

I closed my eyes, remembering all the good things and nudging away the bad. Our house was warm and full of life. There were groceries in the pantry, fresh milk in the refrigerator. There was a natural kind of bohemian lack of order, but it wasn't disorganized and was always clean. "She and my father would hold hands on the sofa in the evenings, and we would pile in at their sides, watching TV. The holidays—they were the best. The whole house decorated in her whimsical homemade things."

"That sounds really nice," Jonathan said, gently. "And your dad?"

"First loves," I said, smiling. "She was the eccentric hippie artist, my father used to love to say. He absolutely adored her. She was talented— even had a gallery showing in the city once, when we were very little. But . . ." I looked up at the television screen, and the scenes held there. "Then things began to change. *She* changed.

"It was small at first." I shrugged a bit, just as I had when I was little, as if to tell myself it was nothing. "Little things, you know?" Piles of her artwork everywhere, the empty fridge, the forgotten meals—signs of a household beginning to fray. "She became erratic. Intensely forgetful. Frenzied. Confused. It wasn't sadness or depression that plagued her—it was this odd combination of confusion and frustration that we couldn't see what she saw. My father sought treatment everywhere he could, but it was expensive. He took on more work trying to keep us afloat and worked himself to the bone. My sister and I tried to take the weight off of him and help my mom as much as we could, but it was hard."

"Mom? We made you something to eat—would you like it?" The curtains are drawn tightly closed, and the bedroom is dark, except for a small spotlight on the canvas in front of her. It smells of paint and thick, stale air. She's making erratic swaths of colors, paint dripping in pools on the floor. Marcie tries her best to clean it up with paper towels. Scatters of crumpled sketches litter the floor. Mom's hair is unwashed, and her clothes hang on her thin frame. She doesn't see us. Eventually, we give up and close the door.

My eyes were filling with tears again, as Jonathan listened quietly. "Sometimes she would come to us, filled with such complete joy, telling us about something extraordinary that she believed happened, but wasn't true," I said. "She'd disappear into herself for long stretches, working on her art. It was extraordinary at first—combining painting with photography—superimposing one over the other to create something half-real and half-imagined. It was stunning. But after a while it turned mostly to nonsense. She started getting some real help a few years before she died, and things got better for a time when I was in college, though."

"You went to school in Paris, right?" he asked.

I nodded. "I went off to France on scholarship, and my sister was doing her thing. It seemed like things were going to be okay. But after a couple years it became worse than ever. She had good spells here and there, though. The weekend before she died was one of those times, and I'm so grateful because I happened to be in town. I had her back just for a little while—the mom I remembered. I hold on to it. There was joy before the end."

"So is that why you left the art world for a time? To get away from it?" he asked.

"It scared me, what happened to her. I didn't want any part of it anymore."

"You didn't miss it at all?" he asked.

"I did. I won't lie. But my dad got sick not long after my mom died, and he was all alone. My sister was off living her life. She just couldn't deal with any of it. Someone had to be there. I came back home. She didn't. And then Hannah was born, so I devoted all my time to her."

"Sure. That makes sense. What about your sister? What's she like?" he asked.

I laughed, swiping another tear. "Do you always get to know people by interrogating them like a journalist?"

"Pretty much. Sorry." His cheeks filled with color, and he ran a hand through his hair.

"It's okay. People used to think we were twins, Marcie and me, but she's about as grounded as they come. The opposite of everything like this. More analytical kind of girl. Solid. She's like you a little, I guess."

He was a good listener, this formerly surly character who had become my friend. "I'm sorry," he said, sincerely. "That you had to go through all of that. It sounds like things weren't always easy. I can relate a bit to that."

"You can?" I laughed, grateful for the change of subject. "Mr. Oxford Educated? I picture you riding down country lanes with your perfect life, on your bicycle, a bottle of wine in your hand."

"Noooo." He laughed, shaking his head vigorously. "Well, maybe the bit about the bike, which was secondhand, by the way, and the wine, which there was a great deal of, but otherwise, it was a much bumpier road than that, trust me. Everything is rarely as it seems. You'd know that better than anyone, I'd imagine."

I smiled a little. "I guess I would."

He had a way of making me feel better, in spite of everything. Like spotting a daisy growing up from a sea of cracked pavement.

CHAPTER TWENTY-EIGHT

We had abandoned the research on the television, both of us tired from the day. We finished collecting the remnants of dinner, and though I'd hesitated at first, I accepted gratefully when he offered another beer. The weather had picked up outside and blew the branches of a nearby tree outside the window. I glanced at Van Gogh's *The Yellow House*, still paused on the screen, wondering if the painter had missed his yellow house as much as I now missed mine. Both houses, alike not only in color, beneath their blue skies, but also in the dreams of love contained in them, forever lost.

When Jonathan returned to the room, he followed my eyes toward the screen. "It's lovely, isn't it?" he said.

"Van Gogh rented it—obsessed over it, really—with the dream that he might finally win the affection and company of Gauguin. He wanted it to be an artist colony, too, but it was really all about Gauguin."

"Really?"

I nodded. "But Gauguin didn't share the feeling and ended up leaving Van Gogh in total despair. Van Gogh spiraled after that and took his own life a few months later. It didn't work out like he'd hoped."

"Jeez. Apparently not."

"Some beautiful art was created within those walls, though. Before the end."

I went to the window, staring down at the street below, watching the wind whip stray leaves through the air.

"The Yellow House." I turned the words over again, echoing my thoughts. "That's what we called our farmhouse too. No relation to Van Gogh or anything. It just worked out that way."

"Up in New York?" he asked.

I nodded. "It had become a haven for me—a symbol of everything clean and good and right in a family." I thought of it perched on its high hill, far out in the country, surrounded by fields and trees and sky. The life I felt coursing through its walls, the whispers it held in its doorways, the heart beating in its kitchen, loved by a family. The kind of place where everything would be perfect for a little girl. A family.

In the months leading up to Hannah's birth, I attended to every single detail with precision, wanting everything to be flawless for her. I went through seven shades of lilac before settling on the one we used to paint her walls. I researched the benefits of organic cotton over traditional fabric. Cloth diapers were lined up in perfect order beside natural soaps and lotions. I smoothed and resmoothed the butterfly-printed sheet on her crib mattress. Tiny prism crystals were hung from the curtain rod on her window, casting a sunlit rainbow to dance across her walls each morning.

I stood at the stove, slow cooking apples, carrots, and squash to be pureed in homemade baby food recipes. I organized her closet daily, hanging dresses side by side. I cut squares and triangles and circles from colored paper to introduce shapes, made drums from pots and pans, and danced with silly faces to make her laugh. I dotted raisins into peanut butter for ants on a celery log. I sat with her in the grass, blowing dandelion seeds for wishes in the air.

Most people would see these as the acts of a loving, devoted mother, and they certainly were. But I knew there was something else to the moments that bordered on obsessiveness. They were an antidote to the fear I had that I would ultimately fail her.

"I spent every day of Hannah's life with this shadow over my shoulders, like at any moment, what happened to my mom could happen to me. It terrified me. I couldn't let anything slip, because I was afraid if I did, it might spiral into something worse."

"But that doesn't sound healthy either. And there's nothing saying that you were going to have the same trouble as your mother. A person needs balance."

"Right. I know. And Graham thought I was being too hard on myself. Doting too much. It was hard on us. He thought I was too isolated after our friends moved away. I loved our house, but Graham thought it had become a kind of gilded cage of our own making." As I said those words, something tickled the back of my mind like a shadow dancing across the screen. No matter how hard I tried, I couldn't quite grasp it, and it drifted away.

I hadn't wanted to say it out loud—not to Dr. Higgins, not to Jonathan, not even to myself—because the guilt still plagued me, but I'd been struggling with periods of intense ennui over the years. Feeling a frustrating, wistful pull toward something bigger, something grander, something out there in the world outside the provincial life I'd created as a wife and mother and the mundane nature of routine in the house. Deep down, I couldn't help wonder if the accident—all this—had been punishment—that it had all been taken away because I couldn't make myself be content, and so it had been ripped from me.

"Are you sure you can trust him?" Jonathan asked.

"Who?" I asked, turning around.

"Graham," he said, taking a seat on the floor. "I've been a little hesitant to ask, but it's reasonable. There isn't any chance he's not being honest, is there? Crazier things have happened."

I took a deep breath and exhaled long and hard. "Believe me, I've been asking that all along. But yes, I can trust him. Or I guess it would be better to say that I can trust that he means well." At the thought of Graham, I felt a rush of affection before it turned into sadness. "He hasn't been entirely truthful, but I don't think it's been malicious. I think we're just . . . done. Whatever has happened, it's not recoverable. And he's been doing the best he can. It must have been very hard for him to be in the midst of moving on, only to have to drop back into a role of caring for me." I joined Jonathan where he sat on the floor.

"You know, there's this British band—The Coral—ever heard of them?" he asked, changing the subject. "Kind of indie rock, trippy." He grabbed his phone, and a few seconds later a song began playing over the speakers. The heaviness in the room retreated into jaunty beats of the music.

"Not really in the know on alt Brit-rock." I shook my head with a grin. "Sorry."

"You're forgiven. But you should look them up; it's interesting."

I raised a brow.

"Seriously! What Dr. Hodgson is saying here made me think of them. James Skelly, the lead singer, has said that some of their music and lyrics came out of some wild drug trips. I read a fascinating interview with him. He believed his hallucinations might actually be glimpses into something real, another dimension that was always present, but only visible when one's brain was in an altered state. It's not the first time something like that has been suggested—it's a fairly common idea."

I knew he was trying to make me feel better, and I was grateful. I narrowed my eyes at him. "You know, you keep talking like this, and I'm going to have to send you a package of crystals and incense as a thank-you for all of this."

He laughed warmly and bowed. "Namaste."

He leaned past me, brushing my shoulder as he reached for the remote to turn the volume down a bit on the stereo. A hint of sandalwood and soap drifted from him, and I watched as he moved. Just then, my phone rang, and Graham's name appeared, and Jonathan saw the screen at the same time I did, catching my eye. Something akin to guilt flashed quickly, and I swallowed it down as I answered.

"Hey," I said into the phone as I walked into the other room.

"Hi. How are you?" Graham's voice was gentle. "I talked to Marcie, but she didn't tell me much. Are you doing okay?" I'd sent him a text letting him know I was leaving town, but I could tell he was worried.

"I'm good, actually," I replied. "Thanks."

"Okay." He grew quiet, and I found myself smiling, imagining his face. "Hey, I know you're doing what you need to do, and I just wanted to say . . ." He paused, and I could tell he was struggling for words. "I understand what you're doing."

"You do?"

"I just mean that I understand that you need to sort things out in your own way. I'm so sorry I was keeping things from you about the paintings, Ann. I shouldn't have. I was just . . . trying to do the right thing. You know?"

"I know you were. I know it's been hard for you too."

"Thanks. And listen." He took a deep breath. "I should probably wait to tell you in person, but I don't want to keep any more secrets from you. I can't stand hurting you anymore. It must be awful enough for you without having to worry that you can't trust the people you love." He stuttered, rephrasing: "The people you care about. So . . ."

I could hear the pain in his voice, and my chest filled with emotion, catching in my throat. I couldn't stand that he was hurting.

"It's okay, Graham. We can talk more about it when I get home."

He hesitated. "Are you sure?"

I closed my eyes, gritting my teeth against the thought of him with another woman. "I am. I'll probably be catching a flight home soon."

"Okay. That's good," he said, quietly. "Where are you now?"

I glanced around the room, at Jonathan's things lining the bookshelves beside me. I ran a fingertip along the titles. A photo of him, much younger, alongside school friends, sat framed in a corner of the shelf. I could hear him in the kitchen. "Just wrapping some things up," I said finally.

"All right, well, get back safe? Charlie misses you," he added.

Do *you* miss me? I wanted to ask. "Will do. Bye, Graham."

We ended the call, and I stood for a long minute, processing the thoughts and feelings swirling in my head like a gently simmering summer storm.

"Everything okay?" Jonathan asked when I returned to the room, feeling as if I were straddling two new worlds.

"Fine, I suppose," I said. "I wish I could go back and make things right. But I don't think I can." I had come to accept that whatever had happened between Graham and me was in the past—in *his* past, anyway—and that if I truly loved him, I needed to let him go. "I'm at peace with it, anyway."

"I'm sure you two did the best you could. Even without everything that's happened, I don't think it's easy—being married to someone who's so devoted to the kind of work that leaves you in some other world and headspace."

"Like an artist, you mean?" I laughed.

"Or a writer." He paused, winking at me. He sat back down on the floor, stretching one long leg out in front of him. "I was engaged a while back."

"You were? What happened?" I asked, plopping down beside him.

"I guess *I* happened. I'm not the easiest person." He laughed a little. "At least that's what Josephine would probably say."

Josephine. I turned the name over in my head, trying to assign it to the photo I'd glimpsed in the other room.

"We were supposed to get married." He held his left hand out in front of him, turning his hand over as he looked at the space where a ring might have been. "But I was already married to my work, I guess. I didn't prioritize right. I didn't see what was right there in front of me. Things would be great, we would be happy, but then I'd get a lead on my next story and go off chasing it, leaving her over and over again. She deserved better than what I gave her." I could hear the regret in his voice.

"Who broke it off?"

"She asked me to choose. Her or the assignment in South Africa. I chose work. And she left. So, I guess we both sort of did. But it was my fault."

I winced. "I'm sorry."

"After a while, I realized what I'd lost and came back to the UK. I begged her to reconsider—promised I'd change—and I did, took a sabbatical from work, everything. I even went to this week-long retreat thing that she'd begged me to go to at one point. A sort of self-help thing for people who, I don't know, need it, I guess."

"You? No way."

He nodded. "I know. Shocking. It was a silent retreat sort of thing." He looked a bit bashful, like he was admitting something he wouldn't normally. "Well, I mean . . . we communicated but not really."

"So . . . like mimes?" I joked. "You went to mime camp to get your girlfriend back?"

He burst into laughter. "Exactly! How did you guess?" He started doing a mime impression that was shockingly spot-on, and I launched into a fit of giggles that wouldn't end. With it, I felt something shift within me, like casting sunlight into darkened corners, healing. Like I could breathe for the first time in a long while.

"So you went to mime camp, and then what happened?" I asked, when we'd both managed to stop laughing and settled down.

He shrugged. "Nothing. I mean, it was good for me, I guess—a week in the mountains, healthy living and all that meditation and yoga and whatever. But it was too late. If I could go back and do things again, I would. But we don't get those chances." His face filled with the pain of regret as he looked off toward the dark window, where rain had begun pelting the glass. He took a long drink from his beer.

"Are you still in touch with her?" I asked.

"Nah, not much. But she's who I was going to see yesterday when you and I were at the pub. Until she texted and canceled. She's moved on, I suppose."

"Ah, well, that explains the mood," I teased, nudging him with my knee.

"Probably not entirely," he joked. "But we'll go with that." His eyes were a pale, languid blue. He mimed a sad face and a tear, making me laugh again. "It is what it is. I've made peace with it, as you said."

You never know what someone is going through, I thought. We had both lost someone we'd loved and were hurting.

We sat in mutual silence for another minute before he turned the volume up on the television, and we returned our attention to Dr. Hodgson. It was her last interview before her death a few months later, and she had come to what she knew was likely the end of her research. "If I could sum it all up—the idea behind it all—it would be this: We may never fully know what lies beyond the horizons of the mind. But perhaps peace may be found in allowing ourselves to embrace the unknown to see what unfolds when we get there."

With those final words hovering in the air, the interview concluded, and the tape went to static. The sudden silence made the room seem smaller, and I looked sideways at Jonathan, leaning against the sofa beside me on the floor. "I just realized—a little while ago, I said all that stuff about Hannah again. I've been trying not to, but I wasn't thinking . . ." I had done my best to be reticent about my "other" life, but in the comfort of his living room, my guard had dropped. "I can't imagine how this must sound. Still going on about a daughter."

He turned his face toward me. "Nah, you're good. It's okay. I don't mind. Oddly, it doesn't sound all that far-fetched when you talk about it." He looked at me with crystalline eyes as he pointed at the screen. "And believe me, you are nothing like what we saw in that video, Annie. Okay?"

"Okay. Thank you for saying that."

Neither of us spoke for a bit. It looked as though he was about to say something else. But at the last minute, he seemed to change his mind, crossing his arms as he spoke. "You know, it's fascinating, really."

"What is?"

"All of this. People from all different angles and philosophies seeming to all meet at the same intersection. Who knows, maybe there is something to it." He shrugged.

I wondered what he had been thinking of saying before that, but let it go. "This, coming from a skeptic like you?" I smiled.

"Even from a skeptic like me." He gazed toward the screen. "It almost makes this stuff . . ."

"Makes this stuff what?"

"I don't know. A little less unbelievable, I guess."

It had been a long day, and my mind swirled with all the information and stories we'd learned. "I know what you mean."

CHAPTER
TWENTY-NINE

As the day is coming to a close and I'm falling asleep, sometimes I'll hear the sound of gravel beneath my feet. It comes to me like a lullaby, repetitive with each footstep, remarkable in its clarity as I long for the place I once called home. They are my footsteps that I hear, the sound of my gait and the moderate, even tempo of my feminine walk as the small stones crunch beneath rubber soles. Immersing myself further into the sound, allowing it to expand, I begin to hear the breeze flowing through the meadow grass that borders the driveway and see the red hues of the setting sun above the woods beyond. I inhale the scent of sweet green.

I pass a small section of four-board fence, one of eight that I once proudly painted, gleaming white on a hot summer day. I'd purchased the paint on a bargain rack, along with two plastic trays and a wide brush, without paying much attention to the proper way to paint a wooden fence. White paint was white paint, I'd thought. Within a year or two of harsh Upstate New York weather, the white had faded and flaked, and now, years later, was chipped and covered in patches of mottled gray that somehow made it seem more authentically rural, and yet sadly unkempt at the same time. It spoke of inexperience. Of city dwellers with soft hands and clean nails. But still, it was my fence. Countless birds had sat there. Red-winged blackbirds. Ravens in sets of ominous threes. The occasional hawk with searching eyes. A small family of chickens. My daughter had climbed those fences. I'd planted wildflowers beneath them. The weeds had flourished. The wildflowers had not. For a few Decembers, I'd hung evergreen wreaths on the sections that fronted the road, the large red bows contrasting with the white snow, offering Season's Greetings to passersby. The fences sat plainly now, decorated only by a FOR SALE *sign that haunts me daily.*

Let's give it five years, we'd said, on the day we purchased the Yellow House with nervous smiles and the excitement that comes with a new adventure and risky life change. By the end, we'd added more to that number than planned, but not nearly as many as we'd hoped. So after six harsh Catskill winters, seven golden summers, one marriage, one beautiful daughter, six chickens, one horse, two failed vegetable gardens, one lost dream, and countless fireflies and rainbows, I'm walking up the gravel driveway to the home on my hayfield island, one last time. Hannah runs in front of me, skipping and bouncing up the driveway, scanning the gravel for the sparkly ones that she treasured.

Our mailbox sits at the bottom of the driveway, near the road, and I'd walked the length of it every day to retrieve the mail over the years. I've just done this for the last time, knowing that the post office would start forwarding our mail the next day. I drop it onto the steps where I'd left the pruning shears.

"Mommy, can I run back to the swing?"

"Okay, but just for a few minutes. It's almost snack time—hungry for anything special to munch on?" I ask.

Her little face curls into thought. "Hmm—carrots annnnnd apples and peanut butter!" She walks down the sidewalk, running a hand along the bushes. She leans over to smell a bloom. "Will there be lilacs in the new apartment?" she asks.

I turn my head so she can't see my face and try to steady my voice against the lump that has instantly formed there. "Maybe not lilacs, sweetie. But I'll bet there's a park nearby with flowers."

She shrugs. "Okay."

"Try to keep your shoes on!" I call, just as she disappears around the corner toward the back of the house. But really, I hope she doesn't. I wasn't sure how many more times she'd be able to run barefoot in meadow grass. She had been sick earlier in the week, and I hoped it wouldn't go to her ears. I wanted her to be able to enjoy these last few hours in our home. She was at an age when childhood memories were efficiently purged by a growing brain, and I knew she would likely not remember anything but a mere hazy feeling of this magical home she'd once lived in. The rest, forgotten.

I reach down to snip a couple of fat blooms from the branches that now towered over my head. I smile proudly at their number, noting that it seemed to have been the grandest year for them yet. But lilac bushes don't belong next to a porch, one learns. They're a wild and unruly breed, and they'd begun to block the views. I didn't mind this, but the new owner might not feel the same. Would likely cut the lilac bushes to the ground. Pull up the roots. Replace them with something more suitable.

"You did a good job," I whisper, touching the leaves and inhaling the fragrance one final time. Lilacs don't grow where we were going.

Graham is texting. His flight from Atlanta has been delayed, and I try not to cry. I miss him and desperately need to feel his arms around me. I tell him it's okay, though. I don't want him to worry. I look up at the approaching storm—the one that has delayed his flight—and think the clouds look like a drifting castle, about to unleash an army of troops. I open the door and step inside my mostly empty house. The moving van had taken some of our belongings and driven them south, while other things were left behind. The move wasn't coming naturally to me. Nor had the necessary purging of two-thirds of our living space and one-third of our belongings, going against the American dream, whereby one must seek to possess and accumulate. This house was the kind of place where people land for good. A final destination home where roots are planted, beloved pets are buried, picnics are held, and grandchildren visit. Most people don't leave Yellow Houses. And most people don't leave things behind.

But sometimes, they do.

We had no buyer. The bank owned it now, and soon I knew the house would sit dark and empty, alone amid an encroaching, overgrown meadow until some opportunistic investor sniffed out the deal, buying it at auction for nothing. "Hello, house," I mutter into an echoing entryway. As I walk through it with tentative steps, filling the space with fresh summer air, the wooden floors creak beneath my feet like stiff bones. The flick of the light switch, a hand rested on the banister, the metallic taste of the well water pouring from the faucet, all caressing me with their familiarity, offering final glimpses of what would become a past life.

WELCOME TO OUR PLACE IN THE COUNTRY. The hopeful wooden sign that had been hung over the kitchen door on the day we'd moved into the Yellow House still remains, a reminder of broken dreams. We'd had our moments, since then, this house and I. The unrelenting cost of maintaining the property, the storms, the wind, the long icy drives to the grocery store, the hour-long drive to the mall, doctors, gentrification; the way that stores and restaurants would close in the winter or any random day in the summer; the way that Hannah had little access to resources of modern-day suburban childhood like ballet classes and karate and soccer and Mandarin—or whatever kids were supposed to be into these days. There were bugs and weeds and breaking parts, and a solitude that had nearly driven me mad. It hadn't been easy, the Yellow House. It was time for a change. I tell myself this to help, but, of course, the choice had not been mine. It had been forced upon me by circumstances. "I tried," I say to the house. "I'm so sorry. I tried."

It was time to go. But at the same time, it seemed wrong not to stay. Yellow Houses don't usually get left behind.

I notice a small purple barrette in one corner of the living room. Crayon marks on the lower wall, evidence of my daughter's attempt to write her name at a much younger age. Upstairs, the king-size bed, deemed too large to fit in the new apartment, sits waiting to be abandoned, left behind. The duvet still has an impression where I'd sat for a few minutes this morning, looking out the window through teary eyes at the farm beyond. A single Dora the Explorer toothbrush sits alongside a sink. A tall pair of brown muck boots and my favorite down parka, items unnecessary in the southern heat where we were heading, sit quietly in their place in the front closet where I'd left them after shoveling snow the past winter. These were our things that would be left behind. I imagined what it might feel like to be a ghost haunting an old residence, stuck in the in-between. We were here. My family had lived in this place. This was my home once.

And then it was not.

The weekend earlier, Graham and I had taken photos of items that we wouldn't be taking with us and posted them on Craigslist, along with a notice for a moving sale, which took place on Sunday afternoon. Some things had sold. Others had not. I wrote descriptions like, "Lovely pine dining set, excellent condition. Seats six. Includes china cabinet and wall mirror." I did not write about the money I'd saved in my midtwenties and the pride I'd felt when I'd purchased the set. Or the birthday parties, the art projects, the pumpkins that had been carved, and the holiday meals that had been served and celebrated on the lemon-polished wooden surface. Or the way I would always be able to remember the unique sound of the vintage-style black metal key opening the lock on the glass doors that held my collection of china and liquors. It was just furniture, I told myself as strangers hauled them away.

They're just things.

Unlike the small room she would have at the apartment, in the Yellow House Hannah's room had been perfect. A monogrammed H was affixed to one lavender wall. In an empty corner, there are impressions in the carpet where a rocking chair once sat next to a window. I stand in its absence, remembering when in the glow of a night-light, I sat with a baby in my arms, staring out at the moonlit fields. French toile and lace curtains. All girl for our first baby girl. Hannah had the best view in the house, we'd often joked. From high above the world, resting her head on the pillows as I read her bedtime stories, one could see out the windows to the farm and the rolling green mountains beyond. She would see concrete from her windows soon, when she looked outside. Just as Marcie and I once had.

211

The basement and attic were full of items covered in ghostly sheets. "Four-poster canopy bed, perfect condition. Includes mattress." Little girls love canopy beds, I thought. I'd always imagined she would use it eventually, transitioning to a teenage bed. But we had no room for storage. It had to be left behind.

"Assorted Christmas decorations." The Yellow House had always looked lovely during the holidays. Stockings adorned the mantel above the fireplace, lights bedazzled the evergreen shrubs, and Christmas trees twinkled in one, two, sometimes three rooms. Among the left-behind items, a carved wooden reindeer sits beneath the attic window, covered in dust and last year's glitter. "Hannah, don't try to ride the reindeer, sweetie. He might break!" I hear myself saying with a laugh, echoing smiles from past Christmas memories. "But I love him!" she replies in a tiny voice, hugging him tightly.

"Christmas reindeer. Much loved. Free to good home."

When I was a child, our mother kept a small, decorative chair in the corner of her bedroom. It was a curious shape, curved with a deep, rounded seat, made entirely of brown wicker that complained when anyone sat in it. I don't know where she got it, only that it had been there since before I was born. I'd crawl into it, sitting cross-legged as I watched her dress for the day. Eventually, as the years passed, the chair came to me, and had sat in my own bedroom corners. When we'd purchased new bedroom furniture a few years earlier, the wicker chair had been sent to the attic. It had meant to be only temporary. But there was no room in the new apartment for sentimental chairs. No one had bought it. I run my hands along the woven wood where it sits. I take a final look at it, abandoned in the corner, clench my teeth, and turn.

Through the dormer window, from high atop my hill, I watch a car pass by and imagine a younger version of myself doing just the same, looking up from the road years earlier.

"How much for the chicken coop?" a man asked on the day of the yard sale. He and his wife had seen the sign on the road and come up to take a look at the offerings. The coop, once quaint and cheerful, sat weathered

and slightly crooked in the weeds at the back of the yard, having broken in a storm a few months earlier. There were no more pets for us—Charlie was buried beneath a tree, having kept me company for nine lovely years that ended at the Yellow House. He had left the rest of us behind, and now we were leaving him.

"The coop? You can just take it. It's not worth much," Graham replied. I recognized a newly hardened edge to his voice. He'd just watched the same people load a small grouping of yard tools into their car. They had been passed down through two generations from his grandfather. Quality tools. Well made. Hard to find these days. There was no yard at the new apartment in Atlanta. And thus, these tools, just things, these heirlooms from another generation, were among the Left Behind, as I'd begun to call them.

For Hannah's first birthday, we bought her a special gift. A rocking cow. Not a rocking horse, but a rocking cow, complete with a big pink bow tied around his neck. We'd smiled at the uniqueness of it and the way it matched the look of the dairy cows that lived on a nearby farm. Rocking Cow was surprisingly well made and was the kind of toy I imagined we would carefully keep and give to our children's children. He had a plush, cushiony back, with black-and-white spotted fur and a comically oversize head placed over two shiny curved slats of wood.

Rocking Cow was made for tiny toddlers. Hannah had outgrown him, we'd said while discussing his fate one day before the move. He took up too much room. There was no storage space, no attic, no basement in the new apartment. Where would we put him? we wondered, but found no answer. And so, Rocking Cow had been among the Left Behind.

The day after the yard sale, with the items that hadn't sold, we pulled up to our county's only place for donating toys and children's goods. On the front door of the building was a sign written in black Sharpie on a piece of cardboard: CLOSED. REOPENS NEXT WEEK. *But we would be gone by next week. Along with boxes of games, a toddler's first dollhouse, and other such items, Rocking Cow sat in the trunk. The skies had just opened up, and rain was pouring down. I saw Graham eye a pile of toys someone else left outside* the front door of the building, beneath a small awning. "We can just leave it out front, I guess?" he asked.

I thought of Rocking Cow, sitting in the rain. "We can't just leave it there. It'll all be ruined."

His shoulders slumped. "I think it'll be ruined no matter what." He'd given voice to what we knew was true. Anything else left behind would end up in the local garbage dump by whoever the bank sent to clean out houses that people couldn't keep. I thought of all the items that were still at the house. Pictured them in a heap along with rotting banana peels, leaking Hefty bags, and circling birds.

"It's not right," I'd said.

He nodded, face drawn. The rain pelted the windows. "So what do you want me to do?" He angled his neck, looking again through the foggy windshield.

"None of this. It's not right." The words caught in my throat and were met with silence. "Just take it all back to the house. We'll figure something out."

The next morning, Rocking Cow, along with assorted other Left Behind items—an ice-cream maker, former wedding gifts, ice skates, baby clothes, a toy stroller for Baby Doll, a real stroller, a box of books and more—were placed on a table by the road along with a sign.

"Moving Sale—FREE"

I noticed a children's board book that I'd read over a hundred times and wondered how it had been forgotten when I packed. I wanted to take it. To squirrel it away. But I wanted to take all of it. So I turned away, and left it behind.

By the end of that day, most everything was gone. Rocking Cow, however, still remained. As night fell, I took him back up to the house and placed him in the empty playroom from which he'd come. He sat beneath a large painted wall mural of a flowering tree in children's pastels, the only hint of the room's former purpose.

I pat his head on my way to the kitchen. The Imagination Movers are playing on the TV, which now sits on the floor where Hannah learned to crawl. I retrieve the apples and carrots from the fridge. The clouds are getting darker, and I'll have to call Hannah inside in another few minutes.

A woman had answered my ad for some playground items. "Oh yeah, I know where you are. The yellow house, right?" she'd said, when I'd tried to give her directions. Around seven o'clock one evening, I heard her pickup drive up the gravel to the house. She had a warm smile and a worn face. With her was a young teenager, whom she introduced as her son. He wore grease-spotted jeans, a stained white undershirt, and work boots below a resigned, absent expression. A large lump of tobacco bulged under his lip, and he spat into the grass every so often as they loaded a Little Tikes climbing gym and sandbox into the truck. "My grandson will just love these," the woman said. Though I hadn't asked, she informed me that the boy she was with, at age sixteen, was the father of the small child who would be the new owner of our things. My face must have registered surprise before I had a chance to filter it. "Not a lot for teenagers to do around here," she joked with a bashful shrug. I smiled and nodded. She placed her hands on her hips and looked around at the property. "Always wondered who lived here. You guys moving?" she'd asked. I replied that we were. We got this question a lot lately. I didn't elaborate. "Boy, real beautiful place to leave."

Yes. Yes it was.

Another car pulled up the driveway after her. A young woman stepped out, keeping a hand on her lower back to balance the bulging pregnant belly. "We saw the sign down by the road. You have a bassinet?" she'd asked. Her eyes lit up when I showed it to her: pristine ivory atop legs adorned with gathered silk fabric. The place where my newborn had slept swaddled beside my bed.

"We've been collecting things for the baby from yard sales. This is . . . wow! Is it really free?" she'd asked. "Yes, definitely. Good luck with everything," I told her. I turned quickly just as the older woman, standing nearby, caught my eyes filling with the tears of bittersweet goodbye to the item I once

believed I'd pass down for generations. An understanding was shared in the brief instant between us and then was gone.

Both families finished loading their items into their vehicles at the same time, and we stood and watched the dust rise into swirling clouds as they drove off toward the road. Hannah had been fortunate, had wanted for nothing. She'd had the best of most things from birth, carefully selected by doting parents. Five years later, as we watched her things go, I wondered about the children who would now enjoy these items and wished them well.

"Sandbox. Smiles included. Bassinet. Please add love, care, and lullabies."

Throughout the week, as the items were sold one by one, Hannah played on her playground in the backyard. Graham had built that playground one piece at a time, bolt by bolt, just the year before. On warm mornings, we'd laugh as Hannah threw off her clothes to run barefoot, naked and free, hair still tousled from sleep, going from the playground to the oak tree swing and back again. The nearest neighbor was nearly a mile away. She could play freely at the Yellow House, alongside Charlie for a while, barking and leaping at the birds that flew by. I hoped the next owners would have children to enjoy it.

The evening after the yard sale, when our house had been picked over, I looked out the window as the sun set on the fields. A small baby deer emerged from the tall grass on wobbling legs, followed by its mother. The two walked around, nibbling at the clover for a few minutes, and then a grand buck joined them. I called to Hannah. "Come look at the deer!" She ignored me, disinterested, and continued dressing a small gathering of princess dolls left for her to play with before the move. Deer were nothing new or exciting to her, having been raised in the Yellow House. "No, really, look!" I said. I knew what it was like to grow up among asphalt, and I knew that it would be many years before she saw such a scene again. I didn't want her to miss it.

Finally, she pressed her nose to the glass, standing on the low, wide windowsill. "It's a family!" she exclaimed.

Together, we watched as the mother, father, and baby deer enjoyed their evening. The buck leaped about, nuzzling the doe, his partner. The baby walked between and around their legs, safe and content in the company of parents. In telling people about a scene such as this, one might think it were overly precious. But in the fields of the Yellow House, there were often scenes like this—a page from a Golden Book come to life, where rabbits and deer nibble side by side: The Deer Family Comes to Play. *Hannah banged a hello at the window, and suddenly the scene froze. Caution prevailed. Off they went.*

House for Sale—Pets Included

In the pink light of summer evenings, we often ate dinner at a small table on the front porch on the weekends, the scene set perfectly by the setting sun on the farm, and the distant green horizon. I'd salvaged the used table in earlier years, sanding and painting it to a country white. It wouldn't fit in the new apartment, so it would remain. Last Sunday, I'd set the table with fresh corn from the local farm and wildflowers from the field. As nighttime descended and the sky filled with stars, we ran about the yard in giggles, catching fireflies in mason jars before setting them free to continue their journey into the flickering fields.

The next morning, I took my place on the porch in a white rocking chair, coffee in hand. I studied the landscape as I had countless times before. A canvas portrait of it sat among the belongings that would be moved to the new apartment, capturing the silos, the mountains, and the fields dotted with goldenrod. But these would be the last times I saw it with my eyes. I tried not to blink. Dew glistened on the grass, and a lone car made its way lazily down the road below. I listened to the quiet that remained. The stillness. And the metronome sounds of the rocking chair in long adagio sweeps.

I'd rocked Hannah and myself every day in that spot. Even in the winter, beneath a warm blanket. But rocking chairs don't belong in small apartments with brick views. The chair belonged with the house; it would be happier there, I decided at that moment. It would stay just where it was.

I wondered who might sit there again someday in my place.

When I finally started crying, I hadn't been able to stop. The coffee grew cold in my hand as I rocked, back and forth, staring out at the farm. I knew Graham was there. I heard him calling my name, shaking my shoulder in an attempt to get me to move—to stand—but it was as if he were someplace outside of the hard shell I had descended into. It was as if the house were crying with me, begging me not to leave it. Soon I would have to say goodbye.

Out of the corner of my eye, I'd seen a figure in the field, hovering in the distance. A woman.

I blinked, and she was gone.

The day passed into night and into morning.

Hannah swings her legs beneath the oak tree. I pour a cup of coffee and inhale the scent as I stand above the kitchen sink, committing the view to memory, holding on to it. A drop of rain hits the window, and I go to the sliding door. "Time to come in, sweetie!"

All around the mulberry tree . . .

She's beside me now, sitting at the table, humming.

. . . the monkey chased the weasel.

CHAPTER THIRTY

I woke with a disoriented start on the sofa where I'd fallen asleep the night before. Jonathan had covered me with a soft brown fleece blanket. I set it aside, sitting up, and looked around his living room at the light coming in through the windows. I could hear him in the kitchen, and I combed my fingers through my hair, trying to orient myself. In front of me sat a steaming cup of coffee and a plate of toast with jam. I looked up sheepishly and tried to smooth my wrinkled shirt as he entered the room.

"Morning," he said, sliding a stack of magazines to the side to make space for the items on the wooden coffee table.

"Good morning," I said, sliding my fingers beneath my lashes in an attempt to clear away yesterday's mascara, which I knew must be giving me raccoon eyes. They felt swollen, and I realized I must have been crying in my sleep. We had been up late into the early morning hours, until I'd finally let him convince me to close my eyes and rest. I'd fallen asleep instantly. I took a sip of the steaming coffee, perfectly brewed, dark with just a hint of sugar.

"Did you sleep okay? That couch is actually pretty comfortable in my experience," he said, taking a seat on a leather wingback chair across from me. "I hate to admit it, but I tend to fall asleep there more often than I should."

I smiled, imagining him asleep behind his glasses with a stack of papers resting on his chest. "I did, thank you. Though I have to admit,

I'm a little embarrassed for falling asleep here. Thank you for letting me stay."

"It was my pleasure. Jet lag—gets you every time."

I swallowed more of the warm coffee and reached over to check my phone, seeing I'd missed two calls.

"Anything important?" Jonathan asked.

"One from Piper and one from Marcie. Probably just calling to check on me. I'll call them back from the hotel." I felt a little awkward. Sleeping on another man's sofa hadn't been part of my plan. But then the word *Connecticut* came to mind, and reminders of where Graham and I stood. The divorce papers sat waiting to be signed on the side table in the loft.

"There are some berries in the kitchen, if you're hungry. Sorry I don't have much else."

"It's fine, really. This is perfect. I should be going in a few minutes." I set the mug down on the table, reaching for a stack of Dr. Hodgson's files that we'd left sitting opened.

"I went through a little more of it after you fell asleep last night," he said. "Mostly more of the same. I'm afraid I didn't find anything else that might be helpful."

I flipped through the pages. Research notes in doctor's scratch. Published articles. A stack of photos showing a patient's artwork next to a team of researchers. I looked at the artwork again as something tickled the corners of my brain, where the sound of Hannah humming still rang from the night before.

All around the mulberry tree.

Suddenly, I sat bolt upright and winced as a flash of light seared in front of my eyes, bursting like confetti.

"Are you all right?" Jonathan asked, leaning forward.

"Oh my God. I remember." I looked over at him. "I remember," I whispered, my eyes welling.

"Remember what?" he asked. "You remember everything Graham's told you? About moving to the city?"

I didn't answer right away. The images and memories were filing in, lining up one by one as I made sense of them. I shook my head. "No. I remember what happened the last week at the house with Hannah. The last months, before the accident. All this time, I could only remember the last couple hours the day of the accident. But the days and weeks before it were blank. My psychiatrist at home has been telling me it could be important—this hole in my memory. And Eunice, even. I've been racking my brain. But I finally remember. Or, at least, I think I do."

Jonathan gave me his full attention. "And?"

I leaned back into the sofa, the sadness heavy in my chest, still palpable from having lived it through my dream the night before. My voice was thick as I spoke, the film replaying. "In my mind, all this time, I've been remembering things at the house as being nearly perfect. But they weren't. Not at all. It was our last day at the house—the day of the accident. We were moving. We'd been struggling financially. The house had always been expensive, but it had gotten out of hand. When we first bought it, it had been a bargain, we'd thought. But all our savings had gone into the constant repairs and the rounds of fertility treatments before Hannah was born, which were a fortune. Graham had gotten offers to go back to working in the city, but we kept saying no. We didn't want to leave. Or *I* didn't, anyway. I wouldn't leave the house. So we tried to make it work, but after the housing market crashed and the mortgage went up, we couldn't keep up."

I had remembered pieces of this all along. But it's the part afterward that I'd somehow forgotten. I hadn't remembered how bad it had gotten. "This spring, we'd fallen behind on our payments. We were trying everything to keep the house, but . . ." I shook my head. "We lost it. The bank foreclosed. The final straw came when Graham's firm closed their upstate office and he lost his job. By then, his offers for work in the city had dried up. He was looking for work, and an old client offered him a job in Atlanta. It was half the money, but we needed to take it. We didn't have a choice."

I stood, walking to the window as I spoke. "I had been trying to get work, too, back in the design field, in the company I'd been working with when I first met Graham. But it had been too many years, and my salary wouldn't have been enough to cover us." The words were pouring out of me in a torrent.

"I became more and more depressed in the weeks leading up to the move. Barely sleeping. Barely eating." I had this vision of myself from a glimpse in a mirror—dark circles beneath my eyes, the sadness seeping through my pores. "The weekend before we were supposed to leave, we had to clear out the house. We were moving to this tiny apartment in Atlanta. It was all we could afford while we got back on our feet." I swallowed hard, barely able to get the words out, the memories flooding in from the dreamlike state in which they'd come while I'd been asleep. "We couldn't take most of our things. We had this awful yard sale, and I remember watching the items go, one by one, and I kind of started unraveling. Graham was worried about me."

I remembered how gentle he was during the last few weeks. How hard he had been working and how exhausted he had become. "In the middle of that week Graham said that he'd woken up to find me standing in the art studio, among a pile of boxes. I hadn't painted in years. I hadn't even remembered getting out of bed." I recalled the look on Graham's face, filled with worry and exhaustion before he enveloped me in a deep hug, both of us sinking to the floor.

I turned, facing Jonathan, who sat on the arm of a chair. "The movers came the next day for the rest of the stuff, and I did what I needed to do. Graham had to go to Atlanta for a quick meeting. That's where he was the day of the accident. He'd been reluctant to leave me. But I swore to him I was okay. It was only supposed to be a day trip. It was our last weekend in the house." My eyes filled with tears. We'd planned one final dinner on the porch at the house, and he'd felt terrible that he would miss it.

I sighed, wiping at my eyes, the memories crystallizing. "No won-der I'd made myself forget. I'd felt so helpless—like my life and every-thing we'd planned had suddenly veered completely off track. I'd once planned a grand life in the city, immersed in a successful career in the art world. And then with Hannah, I'd switched—creating a picturesque life of our dreams in the country. And suddenly *both* were gone, and all I could do was sit back and watch it unravel. I had so many regrets." I looked out the window and shook my head. "I've been remembering it all with such rose-colored glasses. But it seems that no matter what life I'm in, what universe or timeline, I can't get it right."

"Hey," Jonathan said, walking toward me. He cocked his head to one side, his lips curved in a gentle smile. "Nobody gets it right. Not really. We just do the best we can, don't you think?"

I looked up at him. "I suppose."

"Do you feel any better? Knowing a bit more?"

"If that's even what this is. It might just be more of my imagination filling in the blanks, right? I don't know what to think." In fact, I felt worse. I liked the pretty version better. I liked forgetting the ugly parts. "But . . . at least I have one more piece of the puzzle." A puzzle that I would likely never solve. "I suppose it's good that I remembered more about my old life, but it doesn't do me much good here and now in the real world. Strange how much they ended up lining up, though—losing the house, and the life we'd planned, in both worlds. Just in different ways, I guess."

My phone jingled again, drawing me back to the present. Ignoring it, I sighed heavily. The weight of my memories, even those from a different life, would take a while to process.

"Now what?"

I took a deep breath, exhaling slowly. "Now . . . back to reality. I guess it's time for me to get back home. Try to move on." I looked about the room at the piles of research, my attempts to find answers that may never come.

"You're leaving London, then?" I thought I caught a hint of something like disappointment.

"I did what I needed to do." I shrugged. "I have to get back. And honestly, I really miss my dog."

Jonathan smiled. "So what do you think about all of this? Talking to Eunice, the Hodgson research, all of it."

"I was going to ask you the same thing. The investigator. The skeptic. I'm curious. After everything you've seen and heard."

He spoke softly, seeming to consider his words carefully. "I guess there are two options, aren't there? Either you invented the entire thing in the memory-impaired, perhaps slightly brain-damaged, yet incredibly beautiful wonders of an artist's mind. No offense, of course."

I smiled, warmth filling my cheeks.

"Or . . . you are this rare, strange person who somehow managed to switch from one reality to another. A little bit magical either way, if you ask me."

"But either way, the result is the same, isn't it? That's what I've realized. I guess I have to accept this life and move on. To make peace with it. And I think . . ." Tears pricked the corners of my eyes. I could still smell Hannah's apples from my dream, see her legs swinging in the way she so often did, hear her voice humming, the tenderness of Graham's love. "I think I need to accept that whatever I may have had, whatever has happened, it's gone."

"Seems that way."

"So, I'm going to go home. Sort out my life. *This* life. And try to move on. As for the rest of it, I probably will never know. What was that quote, 'Embrace the unknown and—'"

"'See what unfolds when we get there,'" he finished.

"Right. I like that."

"I do too."

"I don't think I'll ever know what happened. But what I have learned—if anything from all this—is that there's a lot of mystery out there. Maybe a little hope."

"Hope?" he asked.

"Hey, maybe they're right? Maybe one day years from now, I'll be walking down a street at a very specific time, in a very specific place, and suddenly I'll turn, and Hannah will be walking beside me." I smiled a little as my eyes welled at the thought.

"And hey, maybe in that world, there will be a stack of successful novels that managed to actually get published instead of collecting dust on my desk," he said.

I nodded, laughing. "You never know. Though I very much think you'll be successful at it, whether in this life, or another somewhere."

"You never know," he echoed.

I helped him tidy the research papers and videos, returning everything to the boxes. Side by side, we placed the coffee cups in the sink.

"Thank you for everything." I stood in the doorway of his apartment, him leaning on one side, and me on the other. Though I didn't say it out loud, I wasn't just thanking him for helping me with the research; I was thanking him for helping me to see that there might be a shimmer of something good on the horizon, even in this version of life. Time stood quietly still, until it had to move forward once again.

"You're quite welcome, Annie. It was truly a pleasure."

～

The following day, my phone sat on the bed as I packed at the hotel before an afternoon flight. "It's sort of nice to think that maybe Mom was something a little special instead of just terribly ill, isn't it?" Marcie said, as I listened to her on speakerphone.

"It is. You'd be surprised, though. It's pretty compelling stuff. After talking to Eunice and looking over all the psychiatric research. It's fascinating."

"But, more importantly, did it help?" she asked.

"Maybe. Yes. I think it did." Though nothing had changed, I felt more in control, having looked at it from every possible angle.

"Well, then, it was worth it." Marcie was always the practical one. "Have you talked to Graham while you've been there?"

"Just once, for a few minutes. I didn't want him to worry. I'll call him again from the airport. I let him know he's welcome to stop by to get the rest of his things," I said.

"So you've accepted that too?" Marcie asked. "I think that's smart."

The way I had oddly sensed the forgiveness and love I'd developed in this life for Marcie, I had innately sensed the decision to let go of Graham. "I have."

"Sooo, is it too soon to ask?" Her tone changed to something more playful. "Might your time with this Jonathan person have had anything to do with this?"

I rolled my eyes. "Absolutely not."

"Uh-huh. If you say so. I looked him up. Or, at least, I asked Piper to send his info to me. Smart, good looking, doesn't seem to think you're a total wacko. I'd say those are three very good points."

"I'm hanging up now."

"All right, all right. Too soon," she said.

"When's your flight get in? Do you want me to pick you up? Want some company?"

"Piper arranged for a car. I'm all set. I think it'll do me well to get home and settle in on my own. But Marcie?"

"Yeah?"

"I love you. Thank you." If there was anything to be grateful for in this lifetime—on this timeline—it was the gift of my sister, once again back in my world. I wouldn't let her go again.

After hanging up the phone and packing up my things, I went downstairs to check out of the hotel. I stood outside beneath the hotel's arched, stone entrance as the morning rain drizzled lightly. After a few minutes, the cab arrived to take me to Heathrow, and just as I was getting in, I heard my name called. I turned to see Jonathan, walking quickly up from the road below.

"I was afraid I wouldn't catch you before you left."

I was surprised to see him. "Jonathan? Hi. What are you—"

"Annie, I was just wondering . . ." He suddenly seemed uncharacteristically lost for words, looking upward at the rain lightly pelting his face.

"Wondering what?"

He laughed then. "I guess . . . well, I guess I was just wondering if you'll be back in London again."

Smiling hadn't come naturally to me since the accident. In fact, it nearly hurt to do so, as if it were a betrayal of everything and everyone I'd loved. But again, thanks to Jonathan, I found the corners of my mouth turning upward. "You barely know me. *I* don't even know me. My past—it's all a blur up until now."

"But isn't it always like that when we meet new people? Our history is all our own perception, anyway. Until we meet and create a new part of the story together."

"Jonathan, I—"

"I don't know any more about your past than you do. But I can say with certainty that I would like to know more about your future." He stood less than a foot from me, and I looked up into his eyes, wondering if maybe he could be right. He took a step closer, and I held my breath, the two versions of me at odds.

"Go back to New York. Take your time," he said, seemingly sensing then exactly what I needed. Time. "And then maybe . . ."

I reached up, brushing my cheek past his, and hugged him. "I'll be back in London," I whispered.

"Okay, then. I'll look forward to it," he said, gazing down at me with warm, soft eyes, nothing like the hardened person who had greeted me on his front step just days earlier. I thought, as I had so many times before, *You never quite know what lies behind a person's facade or what the future holds.*

We said our goodbyes again, beneath the towering turrets of the grand hotel, and he watched me go, on my way back to New York.

CHAPTER
THIRTY-ONE

I polished off the remains of an omelet that I'd made myself for breakfast with the leftover vegetables and three remaining eggs I'd found in the refrigerator. I made notes on a grocery list, planning to go later in the day. A cup of tea beside me, I sat curled on the sofa in the living room, weary from yesterday's flight and still on London time, but unable to sleep. A stack of papers, bills, and mail sat before me, ready to be sorted. They'd been languishing on the entry table for the few weeks since the accident, and I figured I couldn't very well put it off much longer. Charlie's bed sat empty across the room, and I couldn't wait to see him.

One by one I picked up the mail—junk and bills, mostly. I shook my head in disbelief when I saw the amounts of a couple of the bills, and I nearly laughed when I logged in to my checking account to see the amount of money I had. At least I wouldn't have to worry about that anymore.

"We can beg for another extension," Graham says, weary with worry over the bills on the kitchen table. "Maybe they'll give it to us." I place my hand on his and our fingers intertwine. It's well after midnight. "We can at least try," I say. "When's the first payment for school due?" he asks. I tell him it's due the following week, and we both knew there would never be money in the account for it, and we'll have to abandon those plans, as well. He picks up my hand and kisses it, before resting his cheek in my palm. "Don't worry. We'll figure something out."

My smile faded instantly as I remembered the difficulties we'd faced, at the same time knowing with absolute certainty that I would switch places in a heartbeat to have it all back again. I wondered if it would always be like this, or if the comparisons would someday begin to fade.

I forced myself to keep going. Opening get-well cards from people I mostly didn't know, and junk mail. I eventually came to another bill—this one from Dr. Higgins's office. I tossed it into one of the stacks beside me to be paid with the others but did a second glance as the dates caught my eye. I looked at them carefully, lined up one by one, but something didn't add up. The dates on the bill were from visits going back two months *before* the accident. How could that be possible, when I didn't meet him until *after* the accident?

~

I knocked heavily on Dr. Higgins's door for the second time, and finally he answered, surprised to see me. "Annie. Hello. We don't have an appointment . . ."

I marched into his office, relieved that there was no one there. "I need to talk to you."

"Okay, well. I was just on a call, but if you'd like to come—"

I pulled the bill from my purse and held it out to him. "What is this? Why do these dates say that I was here in April and May? I called your billing department. I figured it was an error. But they confirmed that my first appointment with you had been two months *before* my accident. I got your name from the hospital!" But just as I said it, I remembered. Marcie had been the one who had suggested Dr. Higgins, not the hospital. And Graham had been the one to make the first appointment with him. *He teaches at Columbia. He's the best.* I assumed they'd gotten the name from the hospital. It had never occurred to me to question it.

Dr. Higgins glanced at his watch and gestured toward the leather sofa. "Why don't you sit down."

I needed answers. "I don't want to sit. Can you please just explain this to me?"

He gave me a look, and, begrudgingly, I took a seat as he did the same. "Annie, the day you came in here wasn't the first time we had met. I had been treating you for a couple of months prior to the accident. You were becoming depressed and anxious, having trouble. You'd started forgetting things, losing time, as we say."

My hands started to shake. I remembered what Piper and Marcie had described to me—the way I'd been behaving in the weeks prior to the accident. "Tell me more."

"You had vivid dreams that had become disturbing to you," he continued slowly. "About a little girl. I encouraged you to explore them with your art. There was some improvement at first, but in the weeks prior to the accident, there would be episodes in which you had no memory of where you had been or what you had been doing. Given your family history, Graham was understandably concerned, and you were as well. And then the accident happened. As I mentioned, it was best for you to remember things on your own. To you, I was a stranger, and you were a new patient. And so that's where we started."

I tried to process this, but the words wouldn't come out. But then something on the shelf behind him caught my eye. It was a white book that I recognized from the box of research at Jonathan's apartment. I squinted to see the name—*Hodgson*—was written in large type. I realized then why the name had seemed familiar when I'd first heard Eunice mention it. He turned, following my gaze, as I stood. Wheels turning in my head, mechanisms clicking into place as I walked over to it slowly.

"You teach at Columbia," I said, understanding dawning.

As I got closer, several more of Hodgson's books came into view. And then a framed photograph of Dr. Higgins, several years younger, along with a few others, standing alongside Dr. Linda Hodgson. My eyes grew wide. I picked up the frame and turned it toward him.

"You know about her work," I said.

I held out the picture, and he took the frame in his hand. After considering it for a few moments, he sat on the edge of the sofa. "Dr. Hodgson was one of my mentors," he said, finally.

"You were on her research team?" I asked.

He nodded. "One of them. I was very close to the work and studied her theories. We worked together for several years at her institute in Sweden, and then eventually at Columbia."

"So you know, then, what she was working on before she died."

He narrowed his eyes. "What is it you think you know about her work, exactly?"

"I know about the private research she was doing."

He grew somewhat cagey. "That's all very classified. Even I don't have access to some of it. How did you get it?"

"Trust me. I had some very resourceful help," I said.

He raised a brow and seemed both amused and surprised. "I'd say so."

"I want to know. Please. You knew her research firsthand. What do you think?"

He tapped his fingers on his knee, reticent. "All right, I'll talk you through this, but only because I think you won't give up until I do. But Annie, I want to be clear. I'm not advocating this line of thinking for you whatsoever. There's nothing shadowy going on here. Dr. Hodgson was the greatest teacher I ever had. I looked up to her. As I said, she was my mentor. But she went from being considered one of the most brilliant minds in the field of neuropsychiatry to being shunned by the medical community. As much as I admired her, I can't say I fully support all of her theories. But I'll answer your questions. Okay?"

"But surely you couldn't help seeing the parallels in my case." I asked him again: "After hearing everything that I've told you. Everything you've seen me go through. Do you think that maybe there could be something more going on here? That maybe what I was telling you was all in fact . . . true?"

He leaned forward, his elbows on his knees. "In my line of work, I have to act on the best interest of the patient, and given your circumstances, it is most likely just a memory issue. Nothing else. Which, on the record, is what I still believe to be true."

"And off the record?"

He tapped his fingers together. "Off the record? As I said when we first met, the mind is a mystery, as is the universe. And there were some . . ." He hesitated, choosing his words in carefully measured doses. "There were some things about your case that struck me as unusual and perhaps, yes, reminded me of some of the patients Dr. Hodgson was working with, who claimed to have had experiences outside of what science can currently explain."

"Such as?"

"For one thing, the detail you provided was incredibly accurate and charged with emotion, as if you had actually lived it." I thought of Eunice and Dr. Hodgson—two versions of one life, somehow bleeding over into one another.

"But manufacturing whole worlds, Annie, isn't uncommon. Hell, it isn't uncommon in perfectly healthy people, like I mentioned. People create entire worlds, histories, life stories all the time—writers, filmmakers, you understand. But I would be lying if I didn't say that your circumstances lined up in ways that were compelling. Especially in combination with your mother's history."

"Why didn't you tell me more about it? About the theories?"

He shook his head. "Look, Annie, it's most likely that you suffered a major emotional trauma after a lifetime of struggle and loss. Losing your house, while certainly not the worst of what you went through, was probably the tipping point, and you . . ."

"Broke," I interjected.

He shook his head. "I wouldn't say that. You're here, aren't you? Some people do break—I don't need to tell you that. But, Annie, I can tell you this—you're not one of them. You will very likely recover just fine. In time."

"Can I ask you something?"

"Of course," he said.

"What would Dr. Hodgson say?"

"About you?" He gave me a sidelong look, and the corners of his mouth turned upward. "I honestly don't know. But I do believe she would have been very, very interested to meet you. *And* your mother."

But frustratingly, neither of them was here. I stood, walking over again to the row of books by Dr. Hodgson, running my finger along them.

"Have you met anyone else like me?" I asked. "Anyone who's been through something similar?"

"I have, yes. Though nothing quite as significant. Smaller instances. I treated a young girl once with some similar issues."

"What happened to her?"

"She was quite young. I strongly urged her parents to be patient. But they sought more proactive treatment elsewhere, as I understand it."

"And you thought maybe she wasn't imagining things after all?"

He was reluctant, but the expression on his face told me I was correct. "They probably did the responsible thing."

I gave him a look. "For the record."

He tapped the side of his nose, then shrugged. "For the record."

"I see. And I suffered an injury to the head that gave me a case of selective amnesia and cognitive distortion. For the record."

"Most likely? Yes. That is my official diagnosis. But, Annie, if there's one thing I do know, it's that life is mysterious."

There was that word again: *mysterious.*

A moment of understanding passed between us, and I realized how far we had come since the first day I had sat on his leather sofa. Or, at least, the first day I remembered. "And now? What do I do now?" I asked.

"That's up to you. You can either let what you've experienced break you, Annie. Or you can accept that you may never know the answer to your mystery."

"And then?" I asked.

"Choose to go on."

CHAPTER THIRTY-TWO

July in New York is unpredictable—sometimes the heat rises from the sidewalk as the sun pours in shafts down long streets. Other days, everything seems to exist in varying shades of gray beneath a heavy sky. The sounds of the city had become the background noise of my thoughts. When I walked through the front door of the loft after leaving Dr. Higgins's office, I reluctantly admitted to myself that for the first time the place almost felt like home. Or at least familiar, anyway. The space was a quiet refuge, save for the traffic on the narrow rainy streets of SoHo below.

I was upstairs unpacking when I heard the door open. Graham had texted a few minutes earlier to let me know he was on his way up. Charlie made his way toward the steps, tired, and I spared him the trip and met him at the bottom. When he dropped heavily into my waiting lap, his tail thumped wildly on the hardwood floor, his tongue flopping out of his happy mouth in a grin as I scratched his belly.

I looked up at Graham, who stood watching us. I'd had a number of dreams about him over the last few days, remembering him from our time at the Yellow House, and in my head he looked different. Softer. So it was alarming at first to see him—so similar, and yet so changed. His hands were in the pockets of charcoal trousers, fitted slimly beneath a pale-gray shirt. He was neatly shaved, and his body was toned and slender, the body of a man who paid his dues in the early morning hours of a gym. Half of me wanted to go to him and throw my arms around him, but the other half knew he was no longer the same person I loved. And so I stayed where I was.

"You look really good," he said, watching as Charlie and I played.

"Do I? Thanks." I laughed, knowing how untrue it was but happy he thought so anyway. An eight-hour flight and numerous sleepless nights had taken their toll.

"No. Really. You do. Marcie kept me posted a little on what you were up to in London. I hope you don't mind. I was worried, though. How did it go? Did you get to meet that journalist?"

I let Charlie off my lap and nodded, standing. "Yeah, I did. Thanks."

"And?"

How would I ever begin to sum it up? "It was helpful. I'm glad I went."

"You seem . . ." He narrowed his eyes, regarding me closely. "Calmer, I guess. It's good. You look more like yourself."

"Yeah?" *Which version of myself?* "Marcie and Dr. Higgins filled me in too. On your life the past few months. You've been going through more than I realized," I said.

He inhaled sharply, understanding my meaning. I wondered if his new girlfriend was waiting at his new apartment, ready to live their new life, and my chest constricted. "Annie . . . I . . ." His voice splintered.

I placed my hand on his arm, my eyes filling in response to seeing his do the same. "It's okay, Graham."

He stopped short and dropped his shoulders. "I'm so sorry. I didn't know how to tell you. I don't want to hurt you. Or risk making anything worse."

"I know." This man was the love of my life, and yet I was comforting him as I forced myself to let him go.

It's late at night and my hands find him. He meets me immediately with a warm, deep kiss.

"Tell me, how is it, exactly, that we get to be this happy?" he says, smiling against my mouth.

"I don't know. Luck, I guess? Maybe we did something right in a past life?" I reply. It's our first night in our new house, and the air is cold in the bedroom, with the furnace struggling through dropping temperatures outside. But in the world beneath the covers, heat wraps itself around us.

"Life is good, isn't it?" he says.

"Yes." I kiss him again, his mouth taking perfect shape around mine. "It really is."

"I can see it now." He gestures to a wall. "Pictures of our fourteen kids lining the steps . . ."

"Fourteen?" I exclaim, giggling.

"Well, we've been busy."

"Seems so."

"All of their school pictures with hideous blue backgrounds that we'll tell them are the most beautiful photos we've ever seen."

"Well, of course. Because they're ours. Obviously they're beautiful."

"Obviously. And on the weekends we'll take trips to the city."

"They'll have impeccable taste in art and architecture."

"Well, of course. And at night," he whispers, "when they're all asleep, we'll crawl under the covers and . . ." His hand slides down my hip, strong and tender, and I form to his body. "Or . . . maybe I'll just keep you all to myself. Two little old wrinkled gray-haired people, still holding hands every night on the front porch."

I smile. "You're such a romantic, you know that?"

"Complaining?" he asks, kissing my neck.

"Never."

"Is it serious?" I asked, after wiping a tear from my cheek and steadying myself once again. "With . . ." The word catches as I'm unable to say her name.

"I don't know. Maybe. We'll see, I guess." I had a million questions I wanted to ask, but what was the point? I didn't want to think about it. The idea of him with anyone else but me. I wanted to change the subject but wasn't sure what to say next.

We both stood in painful silence—a first for us. Eventually, he looked toward the dining room, where several boxes were piled. "I guess I'm going to get these out of your hair finally. I've got a car on the curb downstairs."

The pain came in rolling waves, retreating and then returning, a sign that the rising tide of this life was beginning to take over, and the old one was disappearing more with each passing moment.

He made several trips to the street until all the boxes, and the remaining traces of him in my life, were gone. He stood at the door, twisting the key from his key ring, before plinking it into the pottery bowl on the entry table with a sound that could have shattered hearts. It was fitting somehow—this final act. We'd bought the bowl from a street vendor on a trip to Mexico back when we'd been dating. I was glad to see it had survived.

"I just want to say thank you for being here after the accident. And that I'm so sorry for everything." My throat tightened, closing around the words I'd so carefully planned. I'd thought about what I wanted to say to him, rehearsed it in my mind on the flight home. But now that he was in front of me, I could barely get them out. I was having to say goodbye to the man I'd married, the man I'd built my whole life with, and I didn't know how to do it.

He shook his head. "You don't have to say thank you, Ann."

"Yes. I do. What you did for me these last few weeks, despite everything we've been through, it meant a lot. I know it couldn't have been easy for you. I wanted to tell you that while I may not remember it all, from what I gather, it sounds like you were right. You did the right thing. It must have been so hard on you—at the house and here—I seemed to be struggling no matter where we were. Blaming you. And

you . . . you were always there, right by my side, loving me through it."
I swiped my eyes quickly, determined to get the words out. "They were
your dreams too."

In my mind, the images continued. Younger versions of ourselves,
surrounded by friends beneath twinkling garden lights at our wedding.
Hammering nails into the side porch of our dream house. Painting in
long strokes. Standing beside ultrasound machines, looking toward the
future. "And I understand why you still have to leave. Why . . . why
we didn't work." I might never remember just how unpleasant things
had ultimately gotten between us, but I knew deep down that there
had been a darkness that we couldn't overcome. One or two mistakes
can be remedied, but more than that and the path veers off somewhere
into a new direction that can't be fixed, no matter how hard we want
to go back.

Graham swallowed hard, and I watched his jaw clench against the
tears that had filled his eyes. He cleared his throat and blinked them
away. "Thank you for saying that. You didn't have to. But thank you,
Ann." He smiled, sadly. "We were really something, weren't we?"

At that, I broke, the conversation tearing me apart.

I nodded. "Yeah. We really were. In another life—I promise—you
and I would've had a beautiful love story." I pictured the three of us,
piled on the sofa together on Friday nights, curled under blankets,
watching movies, Graham leaning over Hannah's head to kiss me.

"You were the love of my life, Annie. You always will be, no matter
what. I want you to be happy." His eyes were full of sadness.

"Are you?" I asked. "Happy? Now, I mean." I needed to know.

He smiled just a little. "Yeah. I'm getting there."

I nodded. "Good."

"Where are you going to go from here?" he asked, eventually.

Every part of me wanted to fight for him. But I needed to see this
through. He needed to know I would be okay.

"Time to move on, I guess. I'll keep up with my appointments with Dr. Higgins. Piper called a little while ago. She managed to get the gallery to delay the new show. She worked her magic and got it moved to December. So I guess I'm going to see what I can come up with." Despite everything, part of me was looking forward to getting back into the studio.

"That's fantastic. I'm so glad to hear this," he said, sincerely.

"I hope it works out." I was nervous I wouldn't have what it would take, but excited to try.

"You're going to do just fine. I know it." There he was, still cheering me on.

A moment passed between us, acknowledging everything that had been said, until finally he put his hand on the doorknob. I braced myself for the inevitable goodbye coming toward me, begging it to stop.

No. It can't end like this.

Just as he opened the door, he turned, looking down at the canvas spread out on the table, the portrait of Hannah running through the fields. "She really is beautiful."

Together we both looked at the image of our daughter. "Yes," I said, knowing how true it was in any lifetime. "She is."

I held my breath, grounding my feet into the floor for strength.

Our eyes met and I held his gaze.

I love you.

He took my hand, interlacing his fingers in mine for one last time, but said nothing. A moment later, he was gone.

No longer able to feel my legs, I dropped to the floor, listening to the traffic below, carrying life on without any sympathy. I looked around the space, considering the objects around me—some from the past I knew, and others from the hazy periphery of my mind's shadows.

From that crumpled place on the floor, I would need to start living again. I would begin painting again. I knew this. I should have never left it to begin with, and I now knew that too. I had money now and wondered if maybe a small cottage might be purchased on a green space of land in the mountains of Upstate New York. Or maybe, just maybe, I thought with a gaze upward, London might be calling. The past, as exquisitely beautiful as it could be, might eventually quiet its siren's call as hope glimmered in the future. Whatever fork in the road had existed in my past, in this life, I would take one step at a time, moving forward.

"What are you gonna be when you grow up, Mommy?" My sweet girl is dressed in a purple princess dress with cowboy boots as we sit cross-legged on the floor in her room. The rain is falling outside on a chilly gray day, but inside we're warm. The fireplace is lit downstairs.

"I already am grown up, silly! I'm a mom! What are YOU going to be when you grow up?"

She scrunches her face, looking upward. "Hmm, a veterinarian, maybe? Or a princess. Or one of those people who play with dolphins. Can people do that when they grow up?"

I scoop her into my arms and pull her into a fit of giggles on my lap. "Of course they can! You have a whole future ahead of you, Hannahbear. You can do anything you want."

As I closed my eyes and recalled the scene, all around me, in every molecule of air, was the fading scent of lilacs.

CHAPTER
THIRTY-THREE

Six Months Later

"I signed off on it this morning, and they absolutely assured me that they would pick it up no later than four p.m. today. That should give you plenty of time." Piper spoke briskly and efficiently, holding her phone in one hand while carrying her laptop in the other. She pointed with her chin toward several papers on the center table in the studio, and after setting her computer down, gestured with an imaginary pen that I should sign them. "We'll be ready as long as you are. Now is there anything at all that you still need? Right. Okay, I'll get that over to you this afternoon, and we'll be set."

There were various documents and authorizations set in front of me. I flipped to the pages that Piper had marked with colorful sticky tags and scrawled my signature. Piper ended her call and scooped up the last page just as I signed it. "Everything good?" I asked. For the last couple of days, my nerves had been dancing like moths.

"You don't need to worry about a thing; it's all set. No pressure, but all things point to it being a smashing success. Your social media accounts are blowing up."

"Right. No pressure," I said with a nervous laugh. "You may have been through this before, but in my mind, I haven't attended a solo show opening of my work since my twenties." The thought of the nerve-racking reception that would take place the following night made me want to go and hide under a pillow.

Piper set a hand on my shoulder briefly before buzzing away. "You'll be fine. It'll be perfect. You're a pro at these things."

The studio seemed strangely empty, most of the contents having been moved in the preceding days to be installed in the gallery, where they would be displayed for the next three months. I gazed up at the swirls of blues and grays on a single large canvas before me—the largest one of all—the spectral hint of a translucent mother and child at play in the snow. It was the last remaining painting in the studio, set to be moved to the gallery this afternoon. I'd had a difficult time parting with it and saved it for last.

Painting came slow to me in the aftermath of the summer, and I had been patient with it. Most nights, even now, I still fell asleep with the sounds of my shoes crunching in the gravel driveway that led to my beloved house as the sun set over the fields. I still heard Hannah's laughs and could clearly see each exquisite detail of her face. Things that had once been mundane had become treasured memories—the feel of my hand on the kitchen water faucet, the exact way to shimmy the stubborn bedroom windows in order to raise them, the sound the hinge made on the back door, the way my body curled around Hannah's in the glow of a night-light. These were my bedtime lullabies.

But the scent of lilacs, ever present those first few weeks after the accident, had departed.

I set no expectations for myself and eliminated any thoughts of deadlines or show openings. I simply put one foot in front of the other, or one brushstroke after the other, as it were. Piper was a constant cheerleader, giving me space to grow and to reacquire my love for the canvas, while gently supporting every anticipated need and nudging me forward. I looked over at her buzzing on the phone once again—thick black tights below a black swing dress and wine-colored lipstick beneath dark-framed glasses—and felt immense affection and gratitude. The snow fell gently behind her through the tall studio windows. "Dreaming of You" by The Coral played over speakers. We were in the mood for celebrating.

I'd been surprised by how quickly it came back—painting. It healed me and propelled me forward. Like so many other things, it was as if my mind and hands remembered a life I could not. The skill was inside me, part of my DNA and part of my history, and it burst forth into the light after having been hidden away. Over the past six months, I'd created the exhibition that would open this weekend. The subject, of course, was always the sweet girl and the once-upon-a-time home that never left my mind. Titled simply:

GHOSTS.

My phone dinged on the center table, and I retrieved it to read the text message:

About to take off. See you in 8.5 hours! PS: don't be nervous, you'll be brilliant x

I smiled, typing my reply to Jonathan.

"When's he get in?" Piper asked, just as I hit "Send."

"How do you know who it is? I could be texting anyone."

"Please." She gave me a wry grin, twirling her finger at me. "There's only one person who can elicit *that* look on your face."

I laughed. "Tonight." In truth, I couldn't wait to see him.

"Well, good. Maybe he'll be able to . . . uh, calm you down before your big night tomorrow," she said with a wink.

I felt a pleasant flutter in my stomach at the thought of seeing him and couldn't help but smile. After saying goodbye in June, Jonathan and I had kept in touch. Tentatively, at first, with the occasional text or email as time passed and I continued to adjust to my new existence. But emails got longer, phone calls began, and when an invitation to a gallery in London came about in the fall, it served as the perfect excuse to return to the city I loved and to the idea of a fresh start with a healing heart. Jonathan and I were taking our time, but today's date had been circled on my calendar as we'd counted down the days until we'd see one another again. In another month, I would be moving to London for good. Not for him but for myself. For my new life. I would be opening a new studio tucked down a narrow street in Clerkenwell. With bittersweet optimism, I welcomed the contrast to the countryside I still longed for, feeling as though the distraction of lights and concrete and the absence of New York would bring a new clarity and awareness to the present and future, ushering in the final stage of grief: acceptance of all that was and would never be again.

Piper set about adding a tag to the canvas and then stood back, looking around the room as if satisfied. She went to her desk, and a moment later I heard the quiet squeak of a bottle being uncorked. "Here," she said, walking across the room with a glass of champagne.

"It's a little early in the day . . ." But I was already taking a sip, letting the bubbling liquid fill my mouth.

"Oh please. You deserve it."

I looked over at her gratefully. "What would I do without you?"

"Hey, back at ya, lady." She returned to her desk and stood up again. "Oh, before I forget, did you get Marcie's message?"

"Oh, I did. Damn. I'll call her back right now. I totally forgot."

"No worries, she stopped by this morning. She's got meetings in town all day, but she just wanted to drop something off for you. I put it over there." She gestured toward a shelf beneath the center table.

"What is it?"

Piper shrugged. Marcie's delivery sat next to Charlie's empty water bowl, which had remained beside his bed as if still waiting for him to walk over and take a drink. I hadn't had the heart to move it yet, although he had been gone for three months already. His leash still hung by the front door of the loft. He'd died curled at the foot of my bed on the first day of autumn. I was forever grateful for the extra time I'd been given with him, but it had been the final connection to the past that Graham and I had once shared, and we'd both taken it hard.

I slid the water bowl to the side and retrieved the packages, one small and one large, tied together with twine. When I opened the first, wrapped in fine ivory paper with a black satin ribbon, it contained a photo of our mother in a gallery, smiling proudly on the day of her first and only exhibit. The photo had once been my father's, but Marcie had had it beautifully reframed. An attached card said: *Congratulations to my talented and lovely sister. I'm so proud of you. Mom will be smiling, right there with you. Love always, Marcie.*

The second was a small shoebox, aged and tattered with a yellowed price sticker. I recognized the brand name of the children's shoes we'd worn often as children and smiled. I opened it to see a second note from Marcie.

A—While we're at it . . . found these recently and remembered that I'd always meant to give them to you. The last time I saw Dad, he gave me a box with a few of Mom's things, and these pictures were at the bottom of it. She was wonderfully talented, just like you. And she would be so proud. Love you.—M

There was a small stack of family photos, mostly from our younger years. Photos my dad had taken of my mom in front of an easel, with a bandanna in her hair and a smile on her face. One in which I stood next to her, paintbrushes in both our hands. I looked to be around nine years old—before she had gotten sick. Her eyes were bright and so were mine. The resemblance between us was remarkable. There was a photo, mostly in silhouette profile, of the two of us, side by side in front of an easel, long dark hair with the light filtering in. My heart ached, longing for those simpler days, recalling her beauty. There were other photos—grainy Polaroids of Marcie and me, playtime in the backyard in a blow-up kiddie pool, summer picnics and holidays—nearly all of them from before Mom had declined, after which most of the family photos and happy memories had declined as well. I picked up a folded flyer from my mom's exhibit—a group show at a small gallery in Greenwich Village. I remembered my father talking about that night with such pride over the years, and the way my mom's eyes would soften with love each time.

Beneath the photos were papers of different shapes and sizes, notes with sketches and outlines that my mom had drawn. I recognized the jagged lines from her later years, when her art became frenetic and nonsensical. Stacks of notes and pages with torn edges. At the very bottom, a large rectangle of soft, weighted sketching paper was folded into tiny squares. The date indicated a time when I would have been around the age of fourteen—difficult years, for sure. I turned it several ways in order to determine which was up and which was down until it became more clear—a black-ink sketch of what looked to be a large tree, diagonal on the paper as if in a fun house.

I traced my fingers over the lines, imagining my mother's hands drawing it, pictured the deep circles that had grown beneath her wild, sad eyes and uncombed hair. But then, as I followed the scattered lines closer, I began to see form take shape in them. A rectangular house, with three dormer windows, crooked in the distance, and the crudely drawn shape of a swing hanging beneath a tree. Swirls of lilac blossoms on twisted branches. I felt the hairs rise on the back of my neck, and my blood ran cold. There was a small smudge of ink on the swing, which I thought at first was a zigzag of lines but then realized were letters. Holding the paper up closer, my eyes widened.

H.B.

I gasped and then suddenly blinked as a memory flashed—a vision of myself as a little girl in my mother's arms, sitting in a chair on her lap as she sang to me.

All around the mulberry tree, the monkey chased the weasel . . . she sings.

I flashed again to another memory—Hannah, hopping through the kitchen on the hardwood floors, humming and singing.

. . . the monkey thought 'twas all in fun . . .

And then to me tucking her in to bed that night, pulling the covers around her.

"My mommy used to sing that song to me too. Where did you hear it?"
I ask her.

"The lady in the backyard taught it to me," she says. "While we danced by the tree."

"A lady, huh? What did she look like?" I ask, entertaining a child's imagination.

"I dunno. She looked like you, kinda. But not you. Will you sing it to me?"

"Well, I didn't see anyone today."

She smiles as if she has a secret.

I dropped the sketch, and it fluttered to the floor in slow motion, my head pounding and dizzy. It couldn't be . . . could it? I thought of my mom, talking nonsense about an imaginary granddaughter all those years ago. "She has hair like Rapunzel's!" she'd say, twirling about like a girl.

I flashed to Eunice's words: "People have been known to go not only from one timeline to another, side by side, but forward and backward. Time and space aren't all that different when it comes to energy and these sorts of things."

She looks like you, but not you.

She taught me a song.

Suddenly, I needed to get to the house. To see it one more time.

"Piper, I have to run. I have to go somewhere."

"Okay, but you have to be back by . . ."

I mumbled a response to her questions and grabbed my keys and the sketch, flying out the door.

Within a half hour, I was at the loft, digging through the back of my closet, where I found a pair of tall farm boots for the snow and my old corduroy winter coat—the only items remaining in my wardrobe from my days back at the house. I imagined I had kept them out of nostalgia, and I could almost feel fresh eggs in the pockets, warm from the nest. The familiarity of the coat was like a soothing family quilt. I looked at my watch, then at the snow falling faster outside. I needed to be back in the city by dark, but if I hurried, I could make the trip in time.

CHAPTER
THIRTY-FOUR

The Palisades Parkway was less busy than usual in the falling snow, and the tree-covered highway was an instant change from the city concrete. I knew it was irrational that my mother's sketch had gripped me so intensely—surely it was my imagination, seeing my own house in it—but I also knew I would find no peace until I went back to the house one more time.

Just under two hours later, I pulled my car into the end of the driveway. I knew from Graham that a pair of retired snowbirds had purchased the house, and so it would be empty at this time of year. I didn't need to worry about them once again, finding me trespassing in their fields. *Just one last time,* I told myself.

There was more snow up in the mountains, and the driveway hadn't been plowed. All around me, everything was quiet in the way that it can be when it's snowing. The only sound was the crunch of my boots as I took each step up the driveway. I stopped midway to take in the vast, wide-open space around me as I stood in the center of a blanket of bluish white on a dark afternoon. It had been so isolating in that place, and I remembered the feeling of solitude from inside the windows where a fireplace once burned. I had both loved and hated it at times; I had learned to acknowledge that without guilt. Nothing was perfect.

Continuing on, I walked to the cut-down remains of the lilac bushes, brushing my fingers across their frosty, broken branches. I wondered if they knew it was me. Finally, I turned the corner around to the back of the house and made my way toward the tree unsteadily, then stopped.

I held the sketch up in front of me, turning it on a diagonal, trying to match it. I took steps backward, giving it more distance. I moved to the left, a few more steps. I turned the paper in my hands just a little more until, like a puzzle piece, it dropped into place. I looked up into the distance at the house and the tree. I looked at the paper, an exact match—down to the precise location of where the swing dangled from a branch, next to which a girl stood with long hair. It was a skewed image, but there was no doubt about it. My mother had somehow seen this place.

"How are you today, Mom?" I ask her while afraid of the answer. I want so much for her to say something normal, something sane. But I can see the glazed, faraway look in her eyes. Sometimes it was nice to talk to my mom, even just to hear her voice.

"Annie, my sweet, it's so lovely! The lilacs are blooming, and she's playing in the fields. We sing together, just like you and I used to do!"

"Who, Mom?" I ask her. "Who's playing in the fields?" She gives me a mischievous grin that looks nearly childlike, and she twirls.

"You'll see."

The old swing dangled lifelessly. I picked it up, holding the aged wood in my hands. Magic and mystery have given me hope that I might see something miraculous there. Something resembling proof. But when I turned it over, there in front of me, I found exactly what I knew I would see—absolutely nothing. No initials. No letters carved by Graham to celebrate Hannah's birth. No *H.B.* Just a plain slat of wood. Hope disappeared, and my shoulders slumped inward.

My heart, which had been pounding furiously, began to slow. I looked up at the tree, into the tall branches that I had loved so much. It had been a fool's journey, coming here. I'd simply seen what I'd wanted to see in my mother's scrawling sketch, imagining letters and some sort of deep, mysterious magic where, of course, there had been none. It was time to let go of this house for good.

The snow fell in tiny flurries, dotting my cheeks as I took a seat on the swing, looking out into the field where the tips of brown meadow grass popped from white. The swing moved beneath my weight as I leaned into its stiff ropes. "This is where I left you, my sweet girl." Not in a car crash on a rainy day, but swinging carefree, hair trailing behind, and bare toes tickling the ground in a field of green before everything changed.

My little girl had played beneath this tree. "Hannah," I whispered, as tears blurred my vision. "Can you hear me? Can you feel me here?" Her heart would beat inside me, alongside mine forever. I knew this. "I have to leave now, sweetheart. But you'll always be right here. I promise. I'll never forget."

I looked up at a dark window, imagining myself inside. I used to love looking out onto my snow-covered field, the stars out and the moon so bright that I could see all the details of the driveway, the yard, the farm, and the empty circles of pressed-down grass where the deer had curled up to sleep on previous nights. Snow chased away the shadows at night. Maybe that was why I loved it—the way it blanketed the dark earth with purity and covered its imperfections. The tiny thrill of wondering how much would fall, and the feel of watching it from rooms warmed by fireplaces. I enjoyed it at night, on whitened sidewalks, in gently falling confetti as time slowed. It used to make me feel alive and thankful and comforted in the moment that everything would be just fine. I loved the crunch of it beneath my boots, the air as pure as air can get and the smell, earthy and sharp. Cold feels less cold when snow falls softly.

Perhaps this was why I painted it so often, loving the enchantment of it. There was no white as lovely as the sparkly white of nighttime snow. Or the rainbow white of sunrise snow. The way the light glistened off it, a sea of diamonds reaching to the edges of a house. There was magic in it. But what I loved most about it was the sound—falling snow on a dark night or a quiet afternoon. The tiny pings of the icier snowflakes bumping up against one another as they fell, hitting tree branches and windows. As if the whole world had stopped to take a quiet breath and then held it. And while I knew that like all things beautiful, its loveliness would eventually fade, replaced by gray, sludgy puddles and the aggravations of icy roads and snow shovels, in those early moments of it all, when it was still untouched, in the perfect expanse of meadow where I once lived, it felt like peaceful perfection.

In a few minutes, I would need to leave, to get back to the city and on with the weekend, but first I would sit for just a little while longer.

"What secrets do you hold, my beautiful house?" I asked, as the wind carried my voice toward the home I longed for, standing grandly in silence.

I inhaled the scent of rural air, the cold clearing my nose and lungs. I hummed a child's song into the breeze.

All around the mulberry tree . . .

. . . and listened to the tiny fragments of snowflake ice hit the ground beneath me in reply.

Time seemed to stand still for a bit, as I swayed gently, back and forth.

I looked upward, watching the snowflakes fall toward me like a kaleidoscope.

Back and forth.

My eyes grew heavy, closing.

Back and forth.

The monkey chased the weasel . . .

It was as if the entire universe had gone still with me.

The noise was faint at first, breaking the silence and causing the hairs on the back of my neck to raise. Then growing louder—the sound of crunching footsteps walking toward me. Startled, my eyes snapped open.

"Oh God, you scared me to death!" I said, my heart pounding out of my chest when I saw him. Graham was walking toward me from the front of the house. I groaned, frustrated as I realized Piper must have told him I was here.

But had I told Piper where I was going?

"You must be freezing," he called. "You've been out here forever!"

"What are you doing here?" I asked, standing.

"Rescuing you, I think," he said, laughing. I hadn't seen him in over a month, and he'd gained a couple of pounds, but it suited him, returned some of the charm to his face.

"How'd you know I was here?" I asked, a little annoyed at the intrusion. "Before you say anything, I was just about to leave and head back. So, you didn't need to come," I quickly added, feeling defensive.

Reluctantly, I let the swing fall from my hand and began walking toward the house.

A light flashed, bright and searing through my head, and I stopped suddenly. A shiver ran through me.

"Whoa, you okay?" Graham ran to me and took my arm, helping me on unsteady feet.

I looked up into his face, at the lines of concern etched there, and did a double take.

Something was off.

I searched his eyes.

"Graham?" I asked again, barely above a whisper. "How did you know I was here?" Then I noticed something else. "And . . ." I swallowed hard. "Where is your car?" Or mine, for that matter. "I . . . I need to get going," I stammered, pulling away from him. "I need to be somewhere tonight and have to finish getting ready for the exhibit."

His face fell, then, and suddenly he looked years older. "Right. Well, I think we need to get you inside."

The light flashed, halting me again, as brilliant gold spread across the horizon, making the ground dance like a sea of glitter.

Around me the snow fell in soft slow motion.

"What do you mean, inside?" My eyes widened. I stood, glued into place and began to tremble.

"Hey, I know you like the snow and all, but you're supposed to be resting, remember? C'mon, I'll make you some tea." He pulled me in tight and kissed the top of my head.

Images of my life—in all its possibilities—danced one after the other through my mind. The painted lavender nursery. The first time I heard Hannah cry and the moment Graham placed her in my arms. The crow of a rooster, calling in the morning as she tosses them scratch. Her hair dangling behind her on a swing. A FOR SALE sign on the driveway. An easel where my hand makes long strokes with a paintbrush. Jonathan's face. The SoHo loft and the divorce papers.

Two lines. Two lifetimes. Two threads. Crossing over.

I turned, taking in the sight of everything, the same as it was just minutes ago, and yet strangely different. From inside the house, I smelled a wood fire as smoke rose from the chimney.

I moved away from Graham, taking slow steps backward.

"Ann," Graham said. "What are you doing? You can't stay out here all day."

Wordlessly, I took one step, then quickly another. I returned to the swing and picked it up. With trembling hands, I felt it at first, the etchings in the wood. Then turned it over . . . .

H.B.

"Oh my God," I whispered, as hot tears dripped onto my cold cheeks. I placed my shaking hand in my pocket to retrieve my mother's sketch, but it had disappeared. And then I heard another sound, like the voice of a small, delicate fairy, together with the crunch of ice crystals beneath small feet, and I froze.

I dropped the swing and spun around, just as Hannah turned the corner into the backyard and walked toward me as if walking out of my dreams. I was afraid to move, to blink.

I held my breath. Until . . .

"Hannah!" The name burst forth in a cry as I dropped to my knees into the cold, wet snow.

She stopped short and cocked her head.

"Sweetie, why don't you head back inside? Mommy and I will be right in," Graham called with the tone of a nervous, protective father.

But she wouldn't move, my girl. She stared at me until, finally, her eyes widened into saucers and a grin emerged. "Mommy!" She took off running toward me and in an instant had barreled into my arms.

I curled my fingers into the softness of her hair, in long strands down her back beneath a thick wool knit cap. Tangible things against my fingertips. I drank in every detail of her as I pulled her into my lap. She curled into a tight ball against my body.

"You're back!" she murmured into my neck. "You know who I am!"

"Whoa, kiddo. Easy does it. And what do you mean, *back*, silly? Your mom's been back for a couple days now," Graham said, gently tugging us apart. "But go easy on her, remember?"

She refused to release her grip. "I knew the real you would come back," she whispered into my ear, refusing to let go.

I looked into her eyes, barely able to speak. "You did?"

She nodded. "I brought you lilacs." Hannah leaned in close, as if telling the most delicious secret. "And I sang to you. Could you hear me?"

All around the mulberry tree . . .

She hummed the tune.

The breath was knocked from me before I laughed through thick tears, nodding as I pulled her in close, never wanting to let go. "I heard you, sweetheart."

Beside her, Graham knelt down. "Ann, look at me." He gently took my chin in his hand, carefully watching my face, looking from one eye to the other. "Your memory? Has it . . . has it come back?" he asked.

I looked up at him, taking in the remarkable love on his face, in his eyes. I reached my hand up and placed it on the side of his cheek, his touch warming me instantly. "I'm not sure what's happening," I told him, though pieces began slowly fitting together. New memories flashed, side by side with others. Waking up in a hospital. Returning home on unsteady feet with Hannah and Graham by my side. "But I think so." I saw the relief wash over him, as he encircled me in his arms, the three of us together beneath the oak tree, where the snowflakes fell.

When we walked to the house, warm air wafted from the doorway like a miracle, inviting me forward, until I stepped into the foyer. My house. *My house.* Tears streamed down my face. An entry table sat at the bottom of the steps, lined with pictures of us on various vacations. The pottery bowl sat on the corner, holding keys. Graham's coat hung on a hook. A clock ticked nearby. The floor creaked beneath my feet as if to greet me as I took small steps filled with nervous wonderment.

Hello, house.

Nothing had ever felt so beautiful.

I missed you.

Everything was a little hazy at first, time feeling like a disjointed thing, skipping about as I gazed in wonder at everything I'd missed so much. Graham brought me to the sofa, near to the fireplace, and soon set a cup of tea in my trembling hands.

"What happened to me?" I asked.

He laughed, running a hand through his hair. His eyes looked older and tired, but full of warmth. "That is a very big question. The short answer? A lot." Hannah had removed her coat and curled in beside me. She looked up at me and gave me a smile wise beyond her years. "Do you remember having an accident?" he asked.

When I nodded, he continued, filling in the details of the last six months. I learned more about the accident. Hannah had escaped with a broken arm but was otherwise okay. I, on the other hand, suffered major injuries and was in a coma for over five months. Graham had stayed with me nearly round-the-clock until, eventually, I was moved to a facility meant for longer-term care. Just shy of six months after the accident, I had slowly begun to wake up.

"You were okay physically," Graham explained, "but other things—your memory and personality—were off. Different somehow."

"You didn't know who I was, Mom," Hannah said with a little laugh.

"I didn't?" I took her chin in my hand. "Sweetie, I'm so sorry."

She shook her head. "It's okay; I didn't mind. I knew you'd come back." She leaned into me again.

Graham smiled at her, but I could see the toll it had taken on him. "And boy, you didn't much care for me." He laughed a little and looked down. "Sometimes you'd wake up and ask to go back to a loft in the city. You were pretty confused." He sighed heavily. "A few days ago, the doctors let me bring you home. You still didn't remember things, but oddly, you seemed happy to be back home, here at the house. Really happy, actually. Like it was the best place on earth. You walked around every room, like you'd been gone for years. Smiling at every detail. The doctors said we'd have to wait it out, and that hopefully your memory would eventually return. And I guess they were right, because here we are." His eyes grew teary and he took my hand.

"But wait. What *about* the house?" I asked a moment later, wondering why all the furniture was back. "We were moving, before the accident."

"Ah. Well, we have your sister to thank for that. I know you might find this hard to believe, so brace yourself." He chuckled. "But Marcie . . . well, honestly, I don't know what we would've done without her. Right, kiddo?" Graham winked at Hannah and she nodded.

"She and Hunter stayed here with Hannah after the accident, so I could be with you at the hospital. The move to Atlanta was no longer a possibility, obviously. Marcie and Tim covered the mortgage to buy us some time and save the house so we could stay. At least for a little while, until we can figure something else out. Ann—your sister— she's been amazing. You wouldn't believe it."

My eyes welled with tears as images of Marcie flashed in my head— the way she cared for me in the loft, the conversations we'd had and the friendship we'd regained. "Yes. I would believe it."

The clock ticked on the mantel, moving time forward in its linear path. *It's late. I have to get back to the city. I have to get to the airport and the exhibit . . .* I shook my head, trying to make sense of the two realities still blending together in my mind. *No. I don't. There's no one at the airport, and there is no exhibit.*

"Ann? You okay? I know it's a lot," Graham asked.

I swallowed hard, feeling the tug inside me toward this other world. But looking from him and then to Hannah, I nodded. "Everything is perfect."

It's as if two threads were lined up, perfectly side by side, until they crossed over. I recalled my conversation with Eunice:

I believe that there might be a unifying moment that is nearly identical in two timelines . . . for instance, a moment of getting ready for a walk in a winter storm, putting on the same boots, walking down the same hallway . . . or a car accident, during a summer thunderstorm, driving down a winding rural road . . .

. . . or perhaps the moment of sitting on a swing behind a beloved house, at the exact, identical moment of snow fluttering around me.

. . . so identical, in fact, that it causes one thread to slip over to the other.

I stood, walking over to the window, and gazed out at the swing gently swaying beneath the tree. In another world, I'd have left by now—would be driving back to the city to meet someone at the airport, returning to a stunning loft in the city, preparing for a grand exhibit opening of my finest work. Was it real? This other world? Or had I made it all up like a dream while asleep for all those months? I felt a pull to go back, to see it again . . . but then Hannah joined me by the window and curled around my leg, looking up at me with gentle eyes, filling me with pure, contented joy. I knelt down and pulled her into me, holding on as if never wanting to let go again.

"Want to see something?" Graham asked, and I turned. "You might find it pretty incredible. Should we show her?" He looked down at Hannah and the two grinned. "Follow me."

Hannah took my hand and, behind Graham, led me up the stairs to the door to the studio. "When we brought you home, you came straight to this room and started painting again. The doctors said it was okay as long as you didn't tire yourself out. It's pretty much all you've been doing, except for taking a few breaks to go sit outside on the swing. I was pretty worried, but they said to give it a little time. Guess he was right." He leaned forward. And then by some incredible miracle, my husband kissed me.

"Ready, Mom?" Hannah asked, squeezing between us as we laughed.

"I don't know," I said breathlessly. "I think so!"

They opened the door and I walked in.

I hadn't been prepared for what I saw there.

"You've been working on it. Pretty amazing, isn't it?" Graham said.

I had seen it before. Not here, but there, in another world, in my studio. Or maybe just in my mind. It wasn't complete and was in its early stages. Yet I knew every detail of what it would someday be. Set before me on a large easel was a single painting, an exact replica of the featured piece from the exhibit that would've taken place in another ghostly lifetime. A portrait of the beloved house in which I now stood, a grand oak tree in the swirling snow, and the miraculous daughter who held my hand beside me.

CHAPTER
THIRTY-FIVE

One Year Later

Conversations were buzzing, along with the clink of glasses and jazz. I'd been standing for hours and was relieved by my last-minute decision to forgo the black heels and opt for the red flats instead—a pop of color with my slim black slacks and black cashmere sweater. Graham was engrossed in conversation with Marcie's husband, Tim, about his latest project, which happened to be a few streets over from the gallery in which we were standing on a Friday night in the West Village. Graham's newly opened firm was still developing its legs, but the future was very promising.

The walls were lined with paintings in various sizes, all sharing the same otherworldly theme. Quotes in black sans serif font spanned the entire length of one wall:

> *MY INTENTION IS TO CAPTURE THE LONGING FOR LOST PLACES*
> *AND THE WHISPERS OF ROADS NOT CHOSEN.*
> *—ANNIE BEYERS*

Seeing one's name in 174-point font could be a bit humbling even on the best of days, and I hoped I could live up to the expectation. Remarkably, however, a few moments earlier, my agent had pulled me aside to tell me that nearly every painting had been sold. The exhibit had been entitled *Hiraeth*, calling upon the wistful and beautiful Welsh word that described the bittersweet longing for lost places and persons—those either real or having never existed at all.

Marcie handed me a glass of champagne and leaned in close. "See that woman behind me—the one with hair that looks like a bird?" I peered over her shoulder. "The one in blue. Don't look!" she said in my ear.

"I think it looks more like a tidal wave. But don't laugh." I hushed her. "She's a critic, and she could crush my career in two sentences."

Marcie grimaced. "Really? No! She just cornered me."

I nodded. "Truly."

"Ugh. Brutal world you live in."

"Oh, I don't know; it's not so bad." I smiled, my heart swelling as I looked around. "What'd she do that was so awful, anyway?"

"She talked my ear off. She's putting her Central Park condo on the market and wants me to stage it."

"That's great!" I replied.

"She showed me pictures on her phone. It looks like something from *Beetlejuice*. No. Just . . . no."

We erupted into silent giggles, just as Hannah and Hunter came bouncing over, two cousins, thick as thieves. Graham scooped Hannah up and onto his hip. "What are you two up to? No good, I'm guessing," he teased the kids, tapping Hannah on the nose as Hunter tugged on Marcie's dress, asking if they could have yet another Shirley Temple.

"You look sleepy, pumpkin." I ran a finger down the side of Hannah's soft cheek and cupped her chin.

"I'm not!" she chirped, but then followed it up with a wide yawn.

"Aunt Marcie's going to take you home in a little while."

"No!" she pleaded. But when Marcie told her that she and Hunter could have a sleepover, she was all smiles once again. Graham moved beside me, placing his hand on the small of my back.

"How are you doing, beautiful?" he asked, kissing me.

"I'm perfect. I couldn't ask for a single thing," I said, my heart filled to the brim.

"Are you guys headed back upstate in the morning or staying in the city all weekend?" Tim asked.

"We haven't decided yet. We'll probably head up tomorrow afternoon, though. There's a family sledding day at Hannah's school on Sunday, so we'll want to get back for that," Graham answered. "Otherwise come up if you guys want."

The others continued to talk as people came up to greet me, offering congratulatory handshakes and commenting on the success of the show. I looked around the room at the people I loved and the life I'd created. On a daily basis, I still pinched myself.

In the days that followed my return on that snowy day, life carried on.

When Graham's old business partner Kevin called to offer him a chance to work with him on a project in the city, instead of saying no, I encouraged him to take it. That job turned into another, and into another, ensuring financial stability and the eventual opening of a brand-new firm. The roof was fixed, the boiler replaced. Fences were rebuilt and pipes were mended. The house became everything we wanted it to be, safe and secure. Hannah played in the fields.

I was no longer afraid—I was grateful. Because I had turned out like my mother after all—in all the most wonderful ways. Instead of shunning the art and imagination that ran through my veins and in my DNA, I welcomed it and shared it alongside my daughter, just as my mother had once shared it with me. Together, we spent afternoons dotting canvases and papers in blues and reds and yellows and oranges, turquoise and purples and all colors of the rainbow. At first, it was just for fun. But then it blossomed into the career that I'd always wanted. I'd seen it with my own eyes—how successful I could be—and I didn't waste a single moment doubting myself. I didn't need to choose between dreams, I discovered. We were the three musketeers—city mice who played in the city, and country mice who nested in a beautiful yellow farmhouse.

Still, I couldn't help but wonder in the quiet moments early on. Had any of it been real?

Then, a few weeks after my "return" to life, as I'd come to think of it, I'd been writing out a grocery list when suddenly, from nowhere, a series of numbers popped into my mind like a pop of confetti. Curious, I jotted them down, realizing with a start that it was the phone number Eunice had given me. Nervously, I'd dialed the number and, to my utter shock, was surprised when she answered.

"Hello? I'm looking for Eunice Brown, please?" I stated it like a question, never believing what would come next.

"Yes. Who's this?"

I recognized her voice instantly. "Oh my God, Eunice! This is Annie Beyers!"

She hesitated a moment. "Where did you get this number?"

"Well . . . I think you gave it to me. I don't suppose you remember? We met at your house. You were kind enough to meet with me and . . . a friend. You gave me your number and told me to call you if I ever found what I was looking for." *Right?*

"I see. And tell me, Mrs. Beyers, what is it you have found?" I could picture her clearly, looking over at me above reading glasses, her tabby cat resting alongside. I wondered if she knew more than she was letting on.

"I'm not sure yet. But if it's what I think . . ." I laughed then, close to giggling in wonder. "I think it was all real! I got it all back, Eunice," I said, tearfully. "My life. I don't understand it. But I got back to where I'd come from." There was silence on the line, and for a moment I thought we'd been disconnected. "Eunice? Are you still there?"

"May I ask you an odd question?" she said, finally. "When we met, did I serve you tea?"

"Tea? Well, yes, you did."

"Hmm." She paused. "And do you recall the pattern on the china?" she asked.

What a bizarre question. The answer came to mind instantly. "There wasn't a pattern, really. Every piece was different. Kind of a mismatched set."

"Mrs. Beyers . . . you and I have never met," she said, eventually. "Not here, anyway. In this world."

"I don't understand. I just called you. You gave me your number. I wasn't sure I would reach you, but I did." I thought she, of all people, would have understood.

"As you might imagine, Mrs. Beyers, in my line of work, things can get a bit . . . blurry. But you're not the first person who has called this number, suggesting something similar. Every piece of my china pattern is crimson and white, by the way. It was passed down to me from my grandmother. And yet every single person who has called with a story like yours reports the same odd details—that I served them tea in an eclectic colorful pattern of mismatched china and gave them this number. Sounds a bit eccentric, even for me, but perhaps charming. Why don't you tell me more."

I relayed the entire story to her, while she patiently listened. As the conversation began to close, I asked her a question that had been nagging at me every day since I'd returned.

"Eunice," I started, unsure if I wanted to know the answer. "What about the *other* me? Is she happy? I'm happy here, but what has it cost the other version of me? After trading places." The oddness of referring to myself as two separate people was compounded by the guilt that in another world I might be struggling.

"Don't you see, dear? You didn't trade places, as you put it. There is only *one* you. You are her, and she is you. One Annie, living in two dimensions. But while the rest of us experience just one life, you had the rare precious gift of experiencing two versions of what could potentially be many that are out there. Just as you remember everything you've experienced, it is likely the same in that other world."

"But doesn't she—I—long for Hannah?"

"Things have most likely returned to the natural state in which they belong, with the idea of Hannah existing in a place of imagination—a hope for what *could* be rather than what was."

I imagined the peace that might have come to me that snowy day as I returned to the city as the "other" version of myself, while saying good-bye to the house. "So I'm okay then? *There*, I mean?" I quietly asked.

"Are you okay here and now?"

I smiled. "Very much. Yes."

"And how did you feel that last day in the other world, as you call it? Was there hope for a happy future?"

I thought about this. "I think things were on their way."

"It seems to me as though, perhaps, you've had the opportunity to fix some things in not one, but both lives. At least until this point. What happens in the future, or in any of the other universes that may be out there in this extraordinary and mysterious life, is anyone's guess."

I knew she was right. Not only had I been given the miraculous ability to see what life could have been like had other choices been made, but I had gotten the chance to learn from it. To appreciate life more. I lived every day celebrating the beauty of living in each simple, precious moment.

Eunice Brown would be the one and only person I would ever tell. Anyone else would say that it had all been a trick of the mind. An injured brain's imagination or a daydream on a swing during a snowfall. But Eunice would always be there to remind me that, sometimes, we have to accept that life is full of mysteries, and we may never know all the answers.

After my return, I never saw the ghosts of myself walking the fields. It made me happy. It made me think that in my other life, in that other version of my days, I had found peace and happiness there, just as Eunice had said. I did, however, once catch a glimpse from the corner of my eye of a woman who looked like me, but not me, as Hannah once put it. My beautiful mother visiting from her painful existence, strolling a lovely field to gaze at her granddaughter as she played beside the lilacs. I wanted to go to her, to tell her I understood. But then I blinked, and all that was left were the branches and the wind in a golden sunset.

Eunice had said that the catalyst for leaping could likely be intense wistfulness—the vague feeling of yearning for a different life, the intense regret of missed opportunities and mistaken choices. For my mother, I wondered if perhaps it had been a combination of both. I wondered what she'd once dreamed of so strongly that it had taken her across the far reaches of space and time, away from the house where we lived. Whatever she dreamed of, I hoped she'd found it, if only for a little while.

"Soooo, how are you feeling about everything? Happy with the way it's going?" Marcie's voice drew me out of my reverie. She handed me a fresh glass of champagne. "I'm no expert, I'll admit, but this looks a hell of a lot like a success to me."

"It does, doesn't it?" I said, clinking my glass against hers.

"I wish Mom and Dad could be here to see you. They'd be thrilled, you know. Really proud of you."

"Thanks, Marce." I leaned against her shoulder. We were both looking at a wall near the entrance to the gallery, where a framed photo of our mother, taken at her own exhibit, hung neatly. Alongside it was her framed sketch of the Yellow House and Hannah's swing, found after digging through many old boxes. Below them was printed:

DEDICATED TO MY MOTHER, WHO WAS MAGICAL.
—*ANNIE BEYERS*

"Hey, by the way, where'd you disappear to this afternoon?" Marcie asked.

A cool wave of air drifted in, as more people entered. "Just an errand. Something I needed to do," I replied.

"Everyone was wondering if you'd chickened out," she teased.

"Nope. Just had to run out," I said, as a smile played on my lips. We all have our secrets.

Earlier that afternoon, the driver had stopped at a red light on the corner of Eighty-Second and Columbus. "You can let me out here," I'd said, noticing the traffic jammed on the busy thoroughfare. With Central Park to my left, I walked down the sidewalk. The heat from the sun just barely warmed my shoulders in the winter cold. In contrast to the buildings that surrounded it, Book Culture's window displays welcomed visitors into its cozy interior. A chalkboard easel sat on the sidewalk, listing that weekend's events. I saw his name and smiled, as butterflies danced in my stomach. I'd arrived just in time, with a few minutes to spare before he would leave.

When I had looked him up, just after returning to the Yellow House, I'd found that Jonathan was still living in South Africa. It would be another few months before he returned to London. Google searches and an online subscription to *The Guardian* allowed me the chance to follow his career and read the stories he produced. There was no mention of him ever having written a story on parallel lives and time slips in this world. His career followed a steady trajectory, and he'd recently published a nonfiction history book.

I entered the store and followed the signs to the "Politics and History" section near the back.

Jonathan sat at a table with a stack of books before him. I hovered near a tall shelf and watched him for a few moments, heart pounding.

He wore a charcoal-gray cotton shirt beneath a black sweater, pulled up at the sleeves in the exact way I knew he liked to wear them. I could still picture him so clearly in my head—the turn of his wrist as he straightened them just so. His pale beard was cropped close, and the corners of his eyes creased just a little as he spoke politely with an older gentleman, who held a book in his hand. I waited for the man to leave and saw Jonathan glance at his watch.

Slowly, I approached the table. "Hi," I said, a little nervously. He looked up at me with the blue eyes I knew, and I stopped breathing for a moment.

His face was blank, but pleasant. "Hello."

With trembling hands, I pulled a book from my bag. A black-and-white photo of him leaning on a large rock in the desert graced the back cover. The book detailed the state of politics and culture in South Africa, titled *Freedom Quest: Post-Apartheid*.

He wasn't overly friendly, which made me almost laugh. *Aloof as always, my dear.*

"So, would you like me to sign this or . . . ," he said, finally. I realized I'd been staring, hoping for some tiny hint of recognition that I knew would never come.

In my mind's eye, I pictured him outside his front door, annoyed on the day we first met. My head resting on his shoulder on the train. The way he'd cradled my face in his hands the one, single time we had kissed on a fall day in London, standing by the roses in Islington Green. I smiled, wondering if in another place in space and time, perhaps we were together there right now. What it must have looked like as I'd greeted him at the airport on the snowy night before the exhibit and the way things might have unfolded from that point onward.

What I might be doing in another life. On a day like this.

"Yes, thank you. My name is . . ." My voice hitched for a moment as I tried to manage the range of emotions swirling together from two separate lives. "My name is Annie. Annie Beyers."

"Nice to meet you, Annie. May I?" He held his hand out, and I placed the book in it, his fingers brushing mine just briefly. He signed it quickly with a black marker.

"It's good," I managed to say. "Your book."

"Oh." He chuckled. "Thanks. You and that other guy who just left may be one of the only few who bought it, but I appreciate you coming." He sounded self-effacing, but he was really just being modest. His book had been nominated for the prestigious Baillie Gifford Prize and had garnered excellent reviews. Still, I felt his wish for something different. I wanted to reach out to him. I wanted to place my hand on his, to pull him inward and say:

I know you.

I wish you so much happiness.

Even though it will not be with me.

"You're a good writer, you know. What you do, the things you report—it's important. It matters," I said, instead.

He gave me a skeptical look. "Thanks."

He returned the book to me, and I opened it to the front, where he had quickly signed his name, tracing the drying ink of his signature with my finger. Then I turned the page.

This book is dedicated to my beloved wife, Josephine.

I took a deep breath, grateful for the knowledge of his happiness in this world. His face no longer wore the haunted look I'd noticed when we'd first met.

"Thanks again. It was nice meeting you," he said, after a few final moments. He checked his watch again, and I couldn't help but laugh inwardly. Always eager to leave, this one. I placed the book back into my bag.

"Yes. You too," I replied, hearing the tightness in my own voice as I struggled to retain normal composure in such an abnormal circumstance.

He was already standing, packing up his things to leave the store. I watched him toss his satchel over his shoulder diagonally and smiled. I knew his motions well—the way he moved.

Finally, I made myself take a few steps, walking away. But just as I was about to leave, I turned. "Jonathan."

"Yes?"

"You should write the novel."

He slowed, his eyes meeting mine and narrowing in question. "Novel?"

"It'll be incredible."

He gave me a quizzical look, regarding me more closely as if noticing me for the first time. "Do I know you?"

I gave him a wide, heartfelt smile and felt my chest tighten as I shook my head. "Maybe in another life."

I held his eyes for one more moment, blinked away the tears that had formed there, and then I walked out the door.

Every life has choices. Do we take the job or don't we? Do we buy the house or not? Do we break off the engagement or go through with the wedding? Do we go through the yellow light or wait? Our path— the people we love, the life we lead—is forever altered by each decision large and small.

When I allowed myself a final glance through the window, I saw him still standing in the same place, watching me walk away.

Some choices are easier than others. The key is to be at peace in the moment. To celebrate the here and now. No life is perfect, I've learned. But if you're lucky, it can come pretty close.

~

I returned my attention to my family, to the people I loved, and to the gallery, which to my amazement was still filled with guests. It was getting late—the exhibit would be closing soon.

"Ms. Beyers?" I turned to see a young woman with long red hair, and I nearly jumped. It took everything in me not to throw my arms around her.

"Hi there," I said, trying to appear nonchalant, while bubbling inside.

"My name is Piper. Piper Anderson," she said. "I'm so sorry to bother you, but I am a huge fan of your work. I just started looking for . . . well, I know it's a little weird to ask, but is there any chance at all you happen to be looking for an assistant?"

Hannah dodged between us and we laughed. I scooped her into my hip, never wanting to let her go. "This is my daughter," I said. "Hannah, this is Piper."

Piper leaned in, smiling. "Oh! Hello there!"

From one face to another, I watched them all. Happy and safe as life moved forward anew, each day from now on, a mystery ready to unfold, in this world and in others. Behind them, high on a wall as if watching, hung a large painting of a yellow house, where two ghostly figures, a mother and daughter, walked in the field.

ACKNOWLEDGMENTS

In its essence, this book is a love letter to a time and place, and I'm deeply grateful to a number of people for helping me bring it to life. First and foremost, thank you to Beth Miller, my kind and tireless agent, for believing in my work and continuing to make me a better writer. And to my wonderful editor, Alicia Clancy, who saw something special in this story and helped it to shine, my most heartfelt thanks.

It takes a really good group of people to send a book out into the world, and I'd like to thank Writers House and the talented team at Lake Union for helping to do just that. I'm also grateful for another gifted editor, Anne Brewer, for her thoughtful insights and suggestions earlier on.

I've always had a fascination with the fluidity of time and space, the idea of moving forward and backward, and of what could be going on "in another life." When I was little, I started writing letters to my future and past selves, certain I would get a reply. Maybe, in a way, this is one of them.

When diving into the research on this subject, I looked straight to Brian Greene, who is as close as there is to a rock star in the world of theoretical physics and string theory. His enthralling way of explaining a very complex subject still dazzles me, and his books *The Hidden Reality* and *The Fabric of the Cosmos* frequently served as a touchstone while I wrote, simultaneously grounding me in reality while letting my head float to the clouds. Life, like Annie's story, is a combination of both.

Many thanks to others as well, including the Imagination Movers, for providing the perfect soundtrack to a modern-day little girl's childhood life at home, and to Rich Collins, in particular.

To Aldo Raffa, an incredibly gifted psychic intuitive, for raising the curtain and helping me to gain a better understanding of paranormal phenomena and insight into the world beyond what we see. There's a little bit of magic in every moment one spends with him.

Those friends who not only helped with early pages but also inspired me over the years to write more and to write better, and others who have kept me company, cheering me on along the journey of this book in particular—you already know how much I completely and totally adore you, so I won't echo it here! Just know that I'm so grateful you've been in my world.

And Christa Tyler, my beloved best friend, forever partner in crime, and trusted first reader. I'm not sure what I would do without you—in this life or any other.

Thank you to my mother, Diana Gronholm, for a lifetime of love and support and for passing on the appreciation of stories that imagine the way things might have been; my father, Ron Fulks, who would've loved this; and my grandparents, Orlando and Mary Prete, whose home in the country shaped my childhood and showed me how healing big summer skies, fresh air, and green fields could be. Without them, who knows how the story would have gone.

To my family and most dearly Matt, whose unwavering patience and encouragement gave me the time I needed to continue putting words on pages. And finally, to Morgan and Ella—this is a story about a mother's love; no matter how old you grow or how far you go, I'll always see you as two happy little girls playing in the tall grass of a yellow house.

TOPICS & QUESTIONS FOR DISCUSSION

1. One of the themes of the book is the idea that memory is often unreliable. Dr. Higgins explains to Annie that our memories are highly suggestible and that we fill in missing details with imagination (chapter 10). Do you think he's right?

2. Annie assigns meaning and a kind of spirit to the items that she's lost or left behind in the Yellow House, grieving them one by one. "It was as if the house were crying with me, begging me not to leave it" (chapter 29). Do you believe that objects and homes have emotional value or energetic essence beyond the practical and tangible? Talk about an item from your life that you've lost and how it affected you.

3. Annie feels pulled between the facts presented to her versus what she feels in her heart and gut is true. Have you had an experience when your instincts led you in one direction without fact or reason?

4.   The structure of the novel lies in exploring two worlds for Annie—one in her memories from the Yellow House, and the other in the present settings of New York and London. Do you feel the author was successful in moving the reader between these two worlds? What kinds of imagery were used to create the feelings in one world versus the other?

5.   The story explores how fate can lead us down different paths in life. "There is a very good possibility that the universe is made of many dimensions and timelines other than our own," Eunice explains. Do you believe this? Has there been a defining fork in the road that altered your path and if so, explore what you might be doing right now "on a day like this" in another life.

6.   Annie's mother suffered from a mental illness that deeply impacted Annie's childhood experience. How did it affect Annie's confidence in herself and the way she navigated her situation?

7.   Eunice helps Annie further understand the possibilities of her situation, citing things like déjà vu, time travel, and paranormal activity that can provide insights into a world beyond the one in which we live. What is your opinion on this? Have you ever visited a psychic or had a brush with the paranormal?

8.   Jonathan says to Annie, "Our history is all our own perception, anyway. Until we meet and create a new part of the story together." Do you agree with his suggestion

that the details of our past aren't all that relevant when meeting someone new?

9. If you could magically return to a home or place from earlier in your life and find it just as it was, where would you go?

10. The story is told from Annie's unreliable point of view, which even she has trouble trusting as fact. How did her questionable perception of reality and events affect the story? Did you believe in Hannah's existence? Which of the characters did you trust the most?

11. A breaking point for Annie occurred when they were losing their beloved house to foreclosure as a result of the financial and housing crash of 2008 that affected countless families across the U.S. in a similar way. Discuss the cultural significance from this time.

12. Did you think Graham and Marcie were justified in hiding some facts from Annie, or do you think they should have been forthcoming from the start?

13. In an attempt to escape her fear of inheriting her mother's illness and repeating the events of her own childhood, Annie is consumed with being a "perfect mother" making everything as "perfect" as possible for her daughter's life; and Marcie makes a career creating perfect, flawless photos as an online influencer. Do you think the idealized standards of motherhood portrayed on social media affects today's parents in a positive or negative way? How?

14. We see two versions of Graham—one from their life at the Yellow House and another from their current circumstances. What were some of the differences in his personality? Did you sympathize with his experience?

15. Annie is often torn between her love of the country and her love of the city. What about you? If you could choose one of Annie's homes to live in, which would you choose?

ABOUT THE AUTHOR

Photo © 2021 Alyssa Kay

Kelley McNeil worked in the entertainment industry promoting concert tours and theatrical events for more than a decade before turning her attention to writing. She loves telling stories with a good pen and good music on hand, often with her two daughters bopping along nearby. She's a native of Pittsburgh, but you can find Kelley living in South Florida most of the time and in London the rest of the time. For more information, visit www.kelleymcneil.com.